"Nina, honey, I have to talk to you about your baby."

Memories flooded back—a scrunched face, tiny fingers, a warmth against her breast. For a few minutes she'd known pure joy…then the nurse had taken her baby away and Nina had signed the adoption papers with tears blurring her vision. When she was sure her voice wouldn't shake she said, "What about her?"

"She's living forty miles south of Vancouver in Beach Grove," Dora said softly.

"H-how do you know?"

"Her mother called me. Apparently the girl has run away and is looking for her biological parents."

"Why did—?" She stopped. "I don't even know her name."

"Amy," Dora replied.

"Amy," Nina repeated. In her heart she'd always thought of her as Sweetpea. "Why did she run away?"

"She found out accidentally that she was adopted."

"How did she find out?"

"She gave birth to a child of her own, a little girl," Dora said. "She had complications and—"

"Wait a minute—Amy had a baby?" Nina whirled to face her mother. "I'm a *grandmother?*"

Dear Reader,

When I was growing up I lived a couple of miles from where Reid's fictional house is set, high on the hill with a view of Boundary Bay and Mount Baker. I have so many fond memories of the beach, it seemed a natural place to set *Beach Baby*.

As a little girl I roamed happily over sandbars and shallows with my sisters and brother as we hunted for crabs and sand dollars. My mother taught us to swim in the sun-warmed waters and we built forts out of driftwood on the beach. As we grew older we rode our horses across the tidal flats.

When my own children were young I took them to the same beach and relived a happy childhood through their eyes. Now when I visit my hometown I walk along the dike and dream of the good old days.

If the idyllic summer setting of *Beach Baby* was an exercise in nostalgia, writing about parenting a mischievous toddler was a reminder of the busy, distracted life of a young mother. In *Beach Baby* Nina has the added challenge of dealing with an ex-fiancé, two teenagers and a whole host of extended and blended family.

I had a lot of fun writing this book, and I hope you enjoy reading it. I love to hear from readers. Please write to me at P.O. Box 234, Point Roberts, WA 98281-0234, or visit me at www.joankilby.com.

Sincerely,

Joan Kilby

BEACH BABY
Joan Kilby

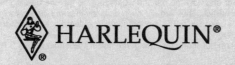

HARLEQUIN®

TORONTO • NEW YORK • LONDON
AMSTERDAM • PARIS • SYDNEY • HAMBURG
STOCKHOLM • ATHENS • TOKYO • MILAN • MADRID
PRAGUE • WARSAW • BUDAPEST • AUCKLAND

ISBN-13: 978-0-373-71364-6
ISBN-10:   0-373-71364-9

BEACH BABY

Copyright © 2006 by Joan Kilby.

This edition published by arrangement with Harlequin Books S.A.

www.eHarlequin.com

Printed in U.S.A.

ABOUT THE AUTHOR

When Joan Kilby isn't working on her next romance novel she can often be found sipping a latte at a sidewalk café and indulging in her favorite pastime of people watching. Originally from Vancouver, Canada, she now lives in Australia with her husband and three children. She enjoys cooking as a creative outlet and gets some of her best story ideas while watching her Jack Russell terrier chase waves at the beach.

Books by Joan Kilby

HARLEQUIN SUPERROMANCE

*The Wilde Men

Don't miss any of our special offers. Write to us at the following address for information on our newest releases.

Harlequin Reader Service
U.S.: 3010 Walden Ave., P.O. Box 1325, Buffalo, NY 14269
Canadian: P.O. Box 609, Fort Erie, Ont. L2A 5X3

To Becky, Gael and Johnny for many
happy childhood memories at the beach.

CHAPTER ONE

Midnight, Paris. Luke Mann lurked in a darkened doorway listening for muted footsteps. Tucked inside his leather bomber jacket were documents that could bring down a Middle Eastern government. A dash across the cobbled street and he would be inside the safe house, his mission accomplished. Spurred on by visions of a peaceful retirement in a sun-drenched Tuscan villa, Luke stepped out of the shadows.

An Uzi submachine gun rent the stillness. Rat-a-tat-tat—

REID ROBERTSON STARED at the computer screen. Now what? Why was he killing off Luke just as he was about to retire? Come to think of it, why was Luke retiring when he was only forty-five? Maybe Luke was merely wounded. Maybe the guy with the Uzi would miss. Maybe there was no Uzi. Maybe *Reid* wanted that villa in Tuscany.

From Tara's upstairs bedroom came the reedy scrape of a bow traveling up and down a minor scale.

Distracted, Reid dragged both hands through his hair. He shouldn't complain; at least she was practicing. He gazed past the computer monitor, out the window of his beach house. Tidal flats shimmered under the hot August sun, yanking Reid's mind further away from dark alleys.

Sales on his ten previous spy thrillers were respectable but Reid wanted this book to break out, maybe even make the *New York Times* bestseller list. If he didn't fold under the pressure of the deadline his agent had talked him into so the book would be out in time for Christmas, the new Luke Mann story could lift Reid into the major leagues.

The doorbell rang. Reid groaned at the interruption. Daisy, his golden retriever, raised her muzzle off his bare toes and lumbered to her feet to follow him out of his office and down the hallway.

Reid opened the door. If this was another Boy Scout selling raffle tickets—

"Amy!"

His *other* daughter, the one he couldn't acknowledge but who occupied a special place in his heart as his first born, stood on the doorstep. He hadn't seen her for three years and suddenly, or so it seemed, the braces had come off, her skin had cleared and she was all grown up. In her arms she held a little girl about a year old with curly red hair and curious blue eyes.

"Hey, Reid. How're you doing?" Amy licked her lips nervously as she shifted the child to her other hip. Her naturally blond hair swung almost to her waist and she wore a low-slung long cotton skirt and a batik top that left her taut midriff bare. "I was in the neighborhood and thought I'd drop in."

In the neighborhood? Amy lived clear across the country in Halifax. Although come to think of it, Reid hadn't heard from her in over a year, even though he regularly sent cards and letters—in the guise of a favorite "uncle," that is.

"Come in." He stepped back, noticing now that her hair needed washing and her clothes looked as though she'd slept in them. With a glance at the toddler, he added, "Who's this?"

"My daughter, Beebee," Amy said.

Reid did his best to hide his shock. The last time he'd talked to Amy she'd been excited about getting the lead role in her high-school play. Now she was a mom and this was no dress rehearsal. But she was too young!

Despite his misgivings he was drawn irresistibly to stroke the child's downy cheek. "Hi there, sweetheart."

Amy tightened her grip with an anxious glance at her daughter. "She makes strange."

Maybe, yet at Reid's touch the little girl's face crinkled into a dimpled smile. She chuckled softly as she gazed up at him from beneath curly dark brown lashes. Reid smiled back. "You're a little charmer, aren't you?"

"Well, what do you know?" Amy said with a wondering grin. "She likes you."

"Of course she does." And Reid couldn't help being tickled at finding himself a grandfather to such a cutie. "When did she come along?"

"Nearly twelve months ago." Amy's smile faded as she assessed Reid. "Didn't Jim and Elaine tell you?"

Jim and Elaine? Since when had she stopped calling her parents Mom and Dad?

"Elaine didn't send her usual chatty letter with the Christmas card this year." He'd wondered about that but assumed she'd been too busy. Reid knew what that was like. Since Carol had passed away he often didn't get around to cards until it was so late he was embarrassed to send them. He picked up Amy's duffel bag. "Come in."

Amy glanced around the foyer at the brilliant white walls, dark chocolate floorboards and tall vase of blue and purple hydrangeas next to a slim mahogany table. "You have a nice place."

"Thanks." Carol had had good taste; he, on the other hand, lived inside his head and barely noticed his surroundings. "Do your parents know where you are?"

Amy tossed her head. "If you mean Jim and Elaine, they're not my parents."

Jim and Elaine not her parents? Had they finally told her she was adopted? Reid had warned them that someday Amy would discover the truth. It looked as if that day had come at last.

The nervous energy that had carried Amy this far suddenly seemed to evaporate. "Do you think I could sit down?" she said. "I walked from the bus stop at the shopping center and Beebee's getting too big to carry."

"You should have called me. I'd have picked you up." Reid led the way past the formal living room he rarely used to the family room adjoining the kitchen. A wall of windows overlooked the bay and French doors led onto a small lawn separated from the beach by a retaining wall. "I'll get you both a cold drink. Then you'd better start at the beginning and tell me everything."

Tara appeared at the top of the stairs, her violin hanging loosely at her side. At fifteen, she was tall and graceful with a pale oval face and long chestnut-brown hair. "Who's here?"

"You remember Amy, the daughter of our friends in Halifax?" Reid said. "And this is her little girl, Beebee."

"Hi, Tara." Amy smiled warmly. "Long time no see."

"Hi." Tara's gaze flicked to Beebee, surprise and curiosity evident in the slight lift of her dark eyebrows. Well she might wonder—Amy was barely nineteen.

"Go ahead and finish practicing," Reid told Tara. "Amy needs to recuperate from her trip."

Reid brought a pitcher of orange juice and a plate of muffins into the sun-filled room facing the beach and set them on the glass coffee table in front of the wicker couch. He waited while Amy and Beebee drank thirstily, then asked, "Was it Beebee's arrival that caused the rift between you and the Hockings?"

"They blew their stack when I got pregnant," Amy admitted. "Then during the birth I had complications requiring a blood transfusion. Neither of them were a match. That's when I found out I wasn't their biological daughter." She sat forward on the couch, her fingers curled tightly into her palms. "I confronted them and they admitted I was adopted."

Reid would never forget the day Nina gave Amy up in a private adoption. He'd been heartbroken. And furious with Nina for giving away their child without his knowledge or consent. Later, after they'd said ir-retrievable words that had broken them apart forever, he'd also been furious at himself for not being with her sooner, when she'd needed him.

"It's true," Amy said, taking his silence for disbe-lief. "All those years they let me believe I was their child."

"You're still their daughter," he said. "They raised you as their own, loved and cared for you."

"My whole life has been a lie. I'm not sure I'll ever forgive them." Amy picked up her muffin then set it down again, untasted. "It wasn't just that they'd lied, although that was bad enough. When I got pregnant they tried to pressure me to marry Ian—Beebee's father. They said they were too old to raise her and I was too young to do it on my own." Her voice tightened and became fierce. "I'm *not* too young to be a mother."

In Reid's eyes she was still a little girl, but he re-membered being nineteen, headstrong and so certain he was as mature as any adult. "No," he said, quietly. "You're not too young."

"I knew *you'd* understand." Amy blotted her eyes with the back of her hand. "You've known me all my life. Did *you* know I was adopted?"

Reid hesitated. The Hockings had allowed him contact with his daughter on the condition that he never tell Amy he was her biological father or that she was adopted. Even now they must not have told her the whole truth or she would never have come to him.

Luckily for him, Beebee chose that moment to wriggle off her mother's lap and drop to the floor. Within seconds the toddler was pushing at the French doors.

"Come back, Beebs." Amy ran after her daughter and swung her into her arms. "She's a miniature Houdini. She can open practically any door," Amy said almost proudly. "You have to watch her all the time."

"She's certainly fast on her feet," Reid said, seizing the opportunity to steer the subject away from himself. "How old did you say she was?"

"Eleven months and one week," Amy told him. "She was walking at nine months and saying her first words at ten."

"What about Ian?" Reid asked, trying to recall what Elaine had told him about Amy's unassuming young boyfriend. "Is he in the picture?"

"No," Amy said decisively. She sat back down with Beebee on her lap and curled her arms protectively around her child. "We were living together up until I got on the bus to come out here. Now I don't want anything more to do with him. He's a *murderer*."

Reid's eyebrows rose and he bit his lip to suppress a smile at Amy's melodramatic emphasis. "Don't tell me Ian's turned to crime," he joked.

Amy closed her eyes on a long shudder. "He got a job in a meat-packing plant."

"A meat-packing plant? You mean, as in food?" Perhaps it wasn't the high-flying career a father might wish for in a son-in-law but it was honest work. "Is *that* why you broke up with him and moved across the country?"

"You act like it's nothing! They slaughter animals and wrap their body parts in plastic."

Reid thought of the defrosted chicken thighs sitting in his fridge, ready to be cooked for dinner. "I'm sure he only wanted to support you and Beebee."

"Well, yes, but he's a vegetarian just like I am," Amy cried. "So what if the job pays well? Where are his principles?"

"Jobs are tight and you two probably need the money," Reid argued.

"I was working part-time at the grocery store. He could have looked around for something better." Amy dug a purple stuffed rhinoceros out of her duffel bag to distract Beebee, who was again eyeing the doors longingly. "Oh, you don't understand."

"No, I don't." Reid couldn't help feeling sorry for Ian whose main crime seemed to be a sense of responsibility and a desire to take care of his family. There had to be more to their break up than simply Ian's choice of work. "What are you going to do?"

"I've come to Vancouver to work in the movie industry," Amy said, brightening. "I'm going to be an actress. It's what I've always wanted ever since I was a little girl."

"Amy, be sensible," he said, filled with dismay.

"Don't you start in on me. You're not my father."

Reid bit his tongue. Now that Amy knew she was adopted, was the promise he'd made to the Hockings still binding? He'd never agreed with their decision not to tell her even though Elaine had strong reasons but he'd better not say anything until he spoke to them. "Toronto has a film industry," he pointed out. "Why didn't you go there? It's not as far to travel."

"I don't know anyone in Toronto," Amy said. "I wanted to get as far away as possible from Jim and Elaine. And Ian. Besides, *you're* here." Amy's eyes grew large as she kneaded her fingers into the soft fabric of her skirt. "Could Beebee and I stay with you awhile? Just until I get a job. We won't be any trouble, I promise. I'll help with housework and stuff."

Reid had wanted to be a father to Amy ever since the too-brief moment when he'd seen her puckered newborn face and felt her tiny hand curl around his finger. His heart leaped at the thought of her and Beebee living in his house. But he had a book deadline—how would he ever finish with the two of them around? And what about Tara? Although Carol had known Amy was his daughter, Tara didn't. How would she take to having Amy and her young child, virtual strangers to Tara, sharing their home, interrupting their quiet lives?

"You should call Jim and Elaine, let them know where you are and that you're safe," he said, stalling. "They must be worried to death."

"If I do that, can I stay?"

She looked so desperate Reid wondered if she'd used her last dime to pay for the bus ticket out west. "Of course," he relented. "You're welcome in my house for as long as you want."

"Thank you, Reid. This is going to be so cool." Amy jumped up and hugged him. "There's another reason I came out west."

"What's that?" he asked.

"Elaine told me I was born in Vancouver and given to them in a private adoption," Amy replied. "She wouldn't tell me who my biological parents are but I'm going to find them. I'm going to find my mother and father."

God help him, Reid thought. He ought to tell her the truth right now. That he, who'd followed her progress from hand puppets to art-house productions, was the father she was seeking. He ached to tell her. But she wouldn't see the truth his way. She would run from him, too, if she found out he'd also lied to her all her life. Where would she and Beebee go with no money and no friends or family to stay with? On the street, in a shelter?

Later, he'd tell her, when she'd settled in, when she wasn't so fragile and hurt. He just hoped he found the right time before she discovered who he was.

And before she found Nina.

"NINA, HONEY, THERE'S something I have to tell you." Dora Kennerly wiped her sudsy hands on a tea towel and sat opposite Nina at the kitchen table. Her tired hazel eyes appeared anxious but a hopeful smile played about her lips.

"Good news?" Nina took off her suit jacket, having gone from her air-conditioned BMW to the sweltering heat of her parents' tiny bungalow on Vancouver's east side. Today the temperature had climbed into the nineties—almost unheard of in Vancouver.

"I think so." Dora wore a cheap cotton housedress and thin leather sandals, and dyed her graying auburn hair herself yet she had a serenity and an optimism that decades of low income couldn't extinguish. "I mean yes, it's wonderful news."

Nina produced her weekly gift of a box of her mother's favorite chocolates and handed it across the table. "Have one of these to celebrate."

Dora peeled the cellophane off and lifted the lid. Eyes closed, she breathed in the rich chocolate aroma then gave Nina a beatific smile. "You spoil me."

"You deserve it," Nina said. Her mother and father had a hard life with few luxuries. They wouldn't accept Nina's offers of trips or clothes or a new car, so she gave them small treats like Belgian chocolates and Cuban cigars, specialty teas and subscriptions to magazines. Without asking, she'd had their old water heater replaced and paid to have the house painted. They'd made sacrifices to give her an education and she wanted to repay them now that she was able to.

Dora chose a chocolate and popped it whole into her mouth, then pushed the box across the table.

Reluctantly, Nina waved it away. "I'm on a diet."

"You're already thin," Dora scolded, her voice thick with chocolate. "I don't know when you eat. While other people are having dinner, you're in the studio. Would you like me to heat up some cabbage rolls?"

"No, thanks," Nina said. "You know I can't stomach food before I go on air." She picked up a drugstore flyer to fan her face, lifting wisps of blond hair away from her damp skin and made a mental note to have an air conditioner delivered. "You were about to tell me something important."

Dora reached across the table to take Nina's hands in her cool dry fingers. "It's about your baby. Can you believe it's been nineteen years?" She shook her head. "Time goes so fast."

Nina tugged away and rose to go to the cupboard for a glass. Memories flooded back—a scrunched face, tiny fingers, a weightless warmth against her breast. For a few minutes she'd known pure joy…then the nurse had taken her baby away and Nina had signed the adoption papers with tears blurring her vision. Now she ran the water till it was cool, then filled the tumbler and drank. When she was sure her voice wouldn't shake she said, "What about her?"

"She's living forty miles south of Vancouver in Beach Grove," Dora said softly.

Nina lost her grip and the glass dropped into the sink with a clatter. The adoptive parents had moved across the country to Halifax. For years afterward Nina had ached for her lost child the way an amputee aches for his severed limb. Through sheer effort of will she'd put the whole painful episode behind her. Now her child was nearby and Nina's heart quickened as if her daughter were in the next room. "H-how do you know?"

"Her mother, Elaine Hocking, called me," Dora said. "Apparently the girl has run away and is looking for her biological parents."

Elaine and Jim Hocking, the wealthy older couple Dora had cleaned house for who couldn't have a child of their own. Nina sat down with a thump. She used to fantasize that this day would come but had never dared to truly hope.

"I know this is a shock," Dora said. "This wasn't supposed to happen. The Hockings never wanted their daughter to know she was adopted."

"I never understood that," Nina said. "Why not?"

"Apparently Elaine Hocking was herself adopted into a family who had tried for years unsuccessfully to have a child," Dora explained. "No sooner had they got Elaine than the woman became pregnant. Elaine says she was treated diffrerently from the biological child and never felt as loved or as special. She didn't want her adopted daughter to feel in the slightest way second rate so they let her believe she was theirs in every way possible."

"I should never have given my baby up," Nina said. "I should have tried to keep her somehow." But at the time she'd felt she'd had no choice.

The summer after she'd finished high school, she'd

worked at a golf course in the same beach community
where her daughter was now. That's where she'd met
Reid Robertson, the father of her child and the love of
her life. When the summer was over, he'd left his lifeguard job and gone back to Yale with a pledge of love
and a promise to return. But when Nina had found
herself pregnant, Reid's mother had stepped into the
picture.

Serena, smoothly coiffed and impeccably groomed,
had craftily treated Nina as an equal collaborator in her
determination to do what was best for Reid. Nina had
been swayed by her arguments, too young and inex-
perienced, too in awe of the Robertsons' wealth and
social standing, to realize how controlling Serena was.

Maybe if Reid had been closer to home and he and
Nina could have talked face-to-face, things might have
turned out differently. He called her every week but that
wasn't enough to counteract Serena's intimidating personality. Over a formal luncheon for two at the Robertsons' mansion in Shaughnessy, Serena calmly, rationally,
kindly, explained how Nina was ruining her son's life.

"He says he's going to quit university and find a job
to support you and the baby," Serena said. "Naturally,
I only want what's best for you both but such a course
of action would be a terrible waste of his potential,
don't you agree?"

"Yes, of course." Nina watched Serena to see which
fork and knife she used on the radicchio salad served
by a uniformed maid. "He loves Yale. I don't want
him to give it up."

"Just imagine the scenario that would follow," Serena went on. "He'd end up in some dreadful job for minimum wage, in a fast-food joint or washing cars. Probably he'd have to work two jobs just to make ends meet without a spare moment to write his stories. Within a year or two he'd resent you and the baby. Oh, he wouldn't say anything, not Reid, but *you* would know how he felt deep inside. You would feel *responsible*." Serena drank from a crystal water goblet then delicately blotted her mouth with a linen napkin. "I'd hate to think what that would do to your relationship."

Nina knew all about Reid's dream of becoming a writer, how much it meant to him and how tenaciously he was pursuing it. It was his unshakable belief in himself, his utter certainty about what he wanted to do with his life that she most admired about him.

"The last thing I want is for Reid to give up on becoming a writer," Nina said. She smiled her thanks to the maid who'd silently removed her salad and replaced it with salmon. "But does he need to go to university to do that? And if he did quit to get a job, would it have to be such a poor one? Couldn't he work for Mr. Robertson and write on the side?"

Exactly what kind of work Reid might do for his father, Nina had only a vague idea. The Robertson family had made their money several generations ago in the mining industry and now were diversified into many areas including property development and light manufacturing.

"Those two men!" Serena shook her head with an

exasperated sigh and a conspiratorial smile that suggested she and Nina were allies. "These days they're like a couple of bull moose butting antlers in the forest. Reid is determined to be independent. Reginald point-blank refuses to give Reid a job if he quits university to get married. Not that Reid expects or even *wants* to work for his father but he would do it for the baby. *If* his father would agree, which he won't. Nor will Reginald give Reid any money to continue university if he marries. So you see, my dear, Reid is damned if he does and damned if he doesn't."

"I'll go away," Nina blurted. "I'll have the baby on my own. When Reid's finished studying we can be together."

Even as she said it, she wondered how she would manage. Her father had lost his job as a longshoreman and his unemployment benefits had run out. Leo's pride prevented him from applying for welfare and Nina had inherited the same stubborn conviction that a person should support herself. The family couldn't live on what her mother made cleaning houses; they'd been counting on Nina finding a job and bringing in income. That was *before* she got pregnant.

"My dear, you know Reid," Serena said, her smooth, confiding tone honeyed with a mother's indulgent smile. "With his strong sense of responsibility— quite remarkable in someone so young—he would never allow you to do that."

What she said was true, Nina realized. Reid would put her and the baby first, even if it was to his disadvantage.

"Please don't think it's *you* Reginald and I object to," Serena went on. "Or your family. It's just that you and Reid are so young. You've got your whole lives ahead of you. But if you and he marry and have a baby…" She trailed away, having already painted Nina a bleak picture of the future.

Serena was right. It would be a disaster for Reid. The last thing she wanted was to hold him back, or worse, have him hate and resent her. And she didn't think she could raise her baby without him. Nina put down her knife and fork, too sick at heart to eat any more of the exquisite food.

"But what can I do?" Nina said. "It's too late for me to have an abortion. And I wouldn't want to, anyway." She was only four months along but already she had a fierce love for her little sweetpea.

With a sympathetic smile, Serena reached across the table and placed a manicured hand atop Nina's. "There's a lovely couple in our sailing club, Jim and Elaine Hocking. They're a little older and can't have children of their own. Your mother knows them—she cleans their house. Jim and Elaine would give your baby a warm, loving home with every advantage."

Surrounded by fine china and old silver, with the scent of roses wafting through the open window on the warm breeze, Nina began to cry. She thought about her situation and knew she wanted the best for her baby. And she knew, too, that that was something she couldn't give.

Still feeling a gentle pressure on her fingers, Nina

swallowed. Then she heard her name spoken, bringing her back to the present. It was Dora who was squeezing her hand.

"With all my heart I wish your father and I had been able to talk you out of giving up your baby," Dora said. "If only you'd accepted Reid's proposal—"

"Marrying Reid wasn't an option." Agitated, Nina paced the small space between table and stove. "All he ever dreamed of was being a writer. If we'd married he'd have ended up flipping burgers and wondering which he hated more, his job or me. Cutting him loose was the best thing I ever did. For all of us."

When Reid had come home from Yale for the birth and found out she'd given up their baby for adoption, they'd had a raging fight. Before her eyes, she saw his love for her shrivel and fade, like a wisp of black smoke. She'd felt angry then, too, and betrayed. After giving up their baby for his sake and for the sake of their future together, she'd lost his love anyway. Her sacrifice had been for nothing. Now all she had left were regrets.

Forget Reid. Forget his quirky smile and intelligent eyes, the way he made her laugh, the way he'd made her shiver and burn when his hands moved over her skin.

Forget Reid? Nina sighed. She'd never managed that.

"Why did—?" she began then stopped. "I don't even know her name."

"Amy," Dora replied.

"Amy," Nina repeated. In her heart she'd always thought of her as *sweetpea*. That is, when she allowed herself to think of her at all. "Why did she run away?"

"She found out accidentally that she wasn't Elaine and Jim's biological child and was angry at them for not telling her she was adopted."

"How did she find out?"

Dora hesitated. "She gave birth to a child of her own, a little girl," Dora said. "She had complications and—"

"Wait a minute—*Amy had a baby?*" Nina whirled to face Dora. "I'm a *grandmother?*"

"And I'm a great grandmother." Dora blinked as if she could hardly believe it, either. "The child is nearly a year old. She's called Bea or something. I didn't quite catch it."

"I'm thirty-seven," Nina said. "Which means Amy would have been only—" quickly she did the mental calculations "—eighteen when she had her baby." Nina leaned her head against her hands. Like mother, like daughter. She tried to imagine Amy as an adult, but the face was a blank. Stabbed by that terrible sense of loss all over again, Nina asked, "Did she give her baby up for adoption, too?"

"No, she left home to live with the baby's father then she quarreled with him and came out west." Dora bit her bottom lip. "She asked Elaine for your contact details and Elaine called me wanting to know if she should give Amy your name and address. I hadn't heard from Elaine since they moved back east. It's a good thing you've never managed to convince your dad and me to move to a fancy apartment or she might not have found us."

Nina looked up. "Did you give her my phone number?"

"I wouldn't do that without consulting you," Dora said. "But I did manage to wangle Amy's local address out of Elaine."

Her daughter was no longer a hazy memory consigned to the past but a real person confronting her in the here and now, maybe asking hard questions like *Why didn't Nina find a way to keep her?* Despite having sworn off chocolate, Nina fumbled in the box and popped a rich dark piece in her mouth.

The back door opened and Leo Kennerly came in from the yard. "Nina, I didn't know you were here."

Leo worked as a handyman and gardener these days. His blond hair was graying but his blue eyes were still sharp; his work shirt was worn but his shoulders were still broad. He took a can of beer from the fridge and popped the tab.

Nina rose to greet him with a kiss on his cheek. "Mom was telling me about Amy."

Leo took a long drink of his beer then pressed the cold can against his sweaty neck. "I'd think twice before you interfere in the girl's life. She's not your responsibility."

"I don't want to interfere," Nina said. "She wants to meet me and I'd like to meet her."

"This isn't about obligation, Leo," Dora said. "It's about connecting with your own flesh and blood."

"Amy's upset with the Hockings for lying to her," Leo said. "How do you know she's not angry with Nina for giving her up as a baby?"

"You've got a point," Nina conceded. "Amy might feel I abandoned her." What if *Amy* rejected *her?* She didn't know if she could bear it.

"If Amy was angry she wouldn't come looking for you, Nina," Dora countered. "She deserves to know her biological family. Jim and Elaine never should have kept that from her."

"The Hockings are her real parents," Leo said. "With Nina the link is only genetic, bits of DNA she has in common with Amy."

"You don't mean that," Dora protested. "Family is family."

Leo put his arm around Nina's shoulders and pulled her close. "I just don't want Nina to get hurt."

"And *I* want her to know the joy of having a daughter." Dora's face softened into a smile. "And a granddaughter."

Nina broke free of her father's embrace and raised her hands to halt the exchange. "Dad, I know you want the best for me but if I can do anything for my daughter at all, even if it's only to satisfy her curiosity, then I want to make up for the lost years. Mom, do you have her address?"

Dora rose and went to the notepad beside the phone and tore off a slip of paper. "Here it is."

Nina raised her eyebrows when she saw the street name in the upmarket beachside community where she'd met Reid so many years ago. "Is she renting? How can she afford that area?"

"I, uh, believe she's staying with a friend of Jim and Elaine's," Dora said. Leo choked on his beer.

"Are you all right, Dad?" Nina asked.

"He's fine." Dora thumped him on the back and threw him a warning glare.

Nina wondered briefly what that was all about but she didn't have time to find out. She stuffed the paper into her purse and glanced at her watch. "I'm going to be late for my show."

"Call me as soon as you've made contact." Dora put her arm around her daughter's waist and walked her to the door. "I can't wait to meet them."

Nina paused on the steps and turned to her mother. "Do you think she'll like me?"

"Of course she will. Everything's going to be okay," Dora said, hugging her. "Call me soon, okay?"

When Nina had gone, Dora went back to the kitchen and sat in front of her chocolate box, pretending to study the guide on the lid.

"As if you don't know what's beneath every swirl and squiggle," Leo said. He straddled a chair and lifted her chin, forcing her to look at him. "Why didn't you tell Nina that Amy's staying with Reid Robertson?"

Dora shrugged, averting her gaze. "She didn't ask."

"*Dora.*" Leo shook his head. "That's as bad as a lie."

"Oh, Leo." Dora laid a loving work-roughened hand

on his leathery cheek. "Nina will find it hard enough to face her daughter. You know perfectly well she'd never go out there if she knew she might run into Reid."

CHAPTER TWO

LUKE MANN WAS LYING wounded in an abandoned warehouse next door to the safe house, the envelope undelivered. Reid hadn't the foggiest notion how the agent was going to get out alive. Ever since Amy and Beebee had arrived a week ago, neither he nor Luke had made much progress.

Reid's gaze kept drifting from the monitor to the window overlooking the beach and the broad curving bay. The tide had receded a mile or more; children waded in pools between sandbars, and shorebirds with long narrow beaks prodded the sand for worms and mud shrimp.

Beebee's strawberry curls popped up from behind a log. The little girl's chubby limbs beneath her pink sundress were bare and already turning brown after a week in the sun. She toddled a few steps before crouching to pick up a shell embedded in the coarse gray sand.

Reid smiled when she sat down abruptly to examine her treasure. Beebee was adorable—until she was frightened or thwarted, then look out. The kid had a pair of lungs an opera diva would envy.

A moment later Reid was frowning, scanning the beach. Where the heck was Amy? It wouldn't be the first time Beebee had gotten out of the house and wandered off by herself. Keeping a watchful eye on the little girl, Reid moved to the side window from where he could see another angle of the beach. Still no sign of Amy.

Beebee stood and continued her meandering progress down the sandy beach. Muttering under his breath, Reid thrust his bare feet into sandals and went through the family room and out the open French doors to cross the lawn. As he dropped over the retaining wall onto the sand, Daisy overtook him and galloped ahead.

Reid caught up to the toddler in a few strides. "Beebee!"

A sunny smile lit her round face. "Weed!"

Dropping to a crouch, Reid nudged Daisy and her slurping tongue aside and brushed off the grains of sand stuck to Beebee's cheek. "Where's Mommy?"

"Me find shell," Beebee said happily, thrusting the broken cockle under his nose.

"Very nice," he said. "Let's go show your mom." Getting to his feet, he took her hand and started leading her back to the house.

Beebee followed, chatting away. He lifted her over the low concrete wall and carried her through the house, calling to Amy. He came to the ground-floor bedroom she shared with Beebee and pushed open the door. Amy was pacing between the crib and the bed, speaking to someone on the telephone.

"So I have an appointment this morning?" she said, her eyes alight with excitement. "Cool! Thanks again." Amy hung up and turned to Reid.

"Look who I found wandering down the beach," he said.

"Beebee, you naughty girl," Amy scolded gently and tried to take her daughter.

"Me find shell," Beebee informed her, showing no inclination to leave Reid's arms.

Reid readjusted his hold on the sun-warmed little girl and she snuggled into his side. "I'll put a hook on the French doors," he told Amy. "In the meantime, you should keep a better eye on Beebee. She could have been lost or drowned."

"I put her in her playpen in the living room. She must have climbed out." Amy twined one long golden lock around her finger. "Can you do me a big favor?"

"Maybe," Reid said warily, thinking he could guess what was coming after overhearing her phone conversation.

"Can you look after Beebee for a couple of hours?" Amy asked. "I have a job interview."

"How long will you be?" His publisher's deadline was looming and he was way behind on his weekly page quota.

"A couple of hours, three at most," Amy said. "Please, Reid, just this once. An L.A. production company is filming a movie in Vancouver and they're looking for extras. They pay a hundred dollars a day and guarantee at least ten days work. You know I could use the money."

Beebee was wriggling in his arms so Reid set her on the floor. She toddled off to put her shell among her growing collection on the windowsill.

"Okay, go ahead." He transferred his gaze to Beebee. "Looks like it's you and me, squirt." She glanced up at him with a trusting toothy grin that would have softened the hardest heart. God knows, it reduced his to a puddle.

Amy bestowed Reid with a brilliant smile. "*Thank you.* You're seriously cool for an old dude."

"Amy," he began. "There's something we need to talk about." He'd spoken to Elaine on the phone yesterday and she'd given him the go-ahead to tell Amy who he was but between his book, Beebee and helping Amy with job applications, he hadn't found a quiet moment to talk.

"Can it wait until I get back?" she said. "I'm already late." Without waiting for an answer, she bent to hug Beebee. "Be a good girl for Reid and don't run away again. I'll see you both in a little while. Wish me luck."

"Sure," Reid said, ashamed of his relief at the temporary reprieve. "Break a leg."

Lunchtime came. Reid piled phone books on a kitchen chair and sat Beebee down with a peanut-butter sandwich and a glass of milk. She ate out the insides, smearing her face with peanut butter and leaving the crusts. Daisy wagged her tail hopefully, never taking her eyes off the dangling strips of bread.

Tara glided into the kitchen looking tired and disgruntled in spite of her immaculately pressed mint-green T-shirt and beige shorts. She rummaged in the fridge for an orange and grumbled to Reid, "The kid woke me up at six this morning."

"Tawa!" With a grin, Beebee offered the tattered remnants of her sandwich to the older girl.

Despite herself, an answering smile tugged at the corners of Tara's mouth but she frowned and replied brusquely, "Beebee eat." Rolling her eyes at her father she added, "She's got me talking like a two-year-old." Tara peeled her orange over the sink, fastidiously placing each scrap of peel into the garbage as it came off. "There are toys and laundry all over the living-room floor. That was Mom's favorite room."

"We never use it since she passed away," Reid said quietly. "Maybe it's time someone did." He handed Beebee her milk. She slurped it, dribbling most of it down her chin. Reid wiped her face with a cloth and said to Tara, "I remember when you were this age. You were so neat you hated having a mess on your face or hands."

"I still do." Tara pulled apart the juicy segments with her fingertips and shook the drips off before popping one into her mouth. "Why did Amy come here, anyway?" Tara demanded. "How long are they going to stay?"

Reid hesitated. Tara deserved to know the truth, too, but telling her before he talked to Amy didn't seem right.

"I don't know how long they'll be here," Reid said at last. "Amy's looking for work and that takes time. She's a little mixed up right now. I wish you'd be more friendly. You used to look up to her when we lived in Halifax."

"Yeah, well, I was just a kid back then. Anyway, it's not like I knew her that well. Most of the time when you went to see the Hockings, you went on your own."

"My family knew them when they lived in Vancouver," Reid explained. "Your mom didn't have the same connection." Or interest, he added silently.

"Whatever," Tara said. "I'm going to the community center with Libby after lunch to see what they've got for summer art courses. Can you drive us?"

"I would but I have to look after Beebee and we haven't got a car seat for her."

"Yesterday you couldn't take me to the mall because you had to help Amy with her résumé," Tara complained.

"The mall isn't far," Reid pointed out. "Amy walked from there carrying Beebee *and* a duffel bag."

Tara blew out an explosive breath. "You think Amy's so great! She's got her stuff all over the bathroom, she won't eat anything we eat and now she's got you babysitting. Everything's changed since she arrived." Tara glared at him. "She's taken over our house."

She's taken over you. Tara couldn't have said it more clearly if she'd spoken the words. Reid was seeing another side to his quiet sweet-natured daughter. He shouldn't be surprised she was jealous of the time he spent with Amy and Beebee; she'd had him all to herself for three years since Carol had died.

"Her parents are old friends and *I've* known Amy since she was a baby. Putting her up for a couple of weeks until she sorts herself out doesn't seem too much to ask."

Tara rinsed off her hands and dried them. "She'd better be home in time for us to go to my violin recital tonight. You can't bring that baby."

"I know," Reid assured her. "I'm sure Amy'll be home any minute."

After lunch Reid tucked Beebee into bed for a nap and went back to work. At first he kept an ear out for Amy but as time passed and she didn't return, he got deeper and deeper into his story.

"Where my mommy?" Beebee suddenly spoke at his elbow.

Reid started. Still engrossed in his narrative, he answered distractedly, "She'll be home soon."

Beebee tugged on his sleeve and Reid dragged his gaze away from the monitor to see her staring at him with bright blue unblinking eyes. "Want Mommy."

Out in the bay, water covered the sandbars and wind surfers skimmed the white-flecked waves. He glanced at his watch. Four o'clock. The tide was in but Amy wasn't.

By six o'clock Tara was in a flap. Her recital was at seven and they needed twenty minutes to drive to the hall. After tears and angry words, she called a friend for a ride and stomped out the door without Reid.

After dinner, Reid sat on the couch with Beebee on his lap and switched on Nina's current-affairs show.

Tonight she was interviewing a man who'd narrowly missed being hit by a chunk of meteorite that had fallen through his roof while he'd been eating breakfast.

"That's your grandma," he whispered into Bee-bee's ear.

Nina had done something different to her hair. The chin-length blond strands had been tweaked into a wayward whimsical style. The sparkle in her eye, her vivacious laughter had her guest hanging on her every word. And the way that red suit clung to her figure—she and Amy could have been sisters. Reid had to admit, Nina still had it.

Sometimes he thought about calling her and getting together for a drink, for old times' sake. Then he remembered how the old times had ended and realized that wouldn't be such a good idea. Anyway, she was probably happily married, with a family.

Amy would be thrilled to find out her biological mother was in the entertainment business. For Amy's sake, he prayed that Nina would be as thrilled to hear from her daughter. Elaine had told him she'd given his address to Nina's mother. He'd waited for Nina to call but so far nothing. Maybe she wasn't interested in meeting their daughter. Or maybe his presence put her off. Regardless, he had to tell Amy the truth tonight. Surely he could find the words to make her realize how much he cared, how the lie had been forced upon him….

He glanced at his watch. Seven o'clock and Amy still wasn't home. He was starting to get seriously worried. Two or three hours, she'd said. Here it was ten hours and counting. Where was she? Why didn't she call?

Reid switched off the TV. What if Amy'd had an accident or been abducted? She could be injured or in trouble. His writer's imagination combined with a father's sensibilities had no trouble conjuring scenarios of death, dismemberment and disaster.

Reid dragged a hand through his hair and racked his brain trying to remember if she'd written down the number or address of where she was going. If it was anywhere, he decided, it'd be in the spare bedroom she and Beebee were occupying.

NINA PULLED INTO THE DRIVEWAY of the house where Amy was staying just before 8:00 p.m. The evening air was sultry with a whiff of salt and the two-story white house glowed in the twilight.

Nina checked her reflection in the rearview mirror. She'd removed the heavy studio makeup after her show and now her skin looked pale and somehow fragile. There were faint shadows under her blue eyes and she'd chewed all the color off her lips. Whipping out her lipstick, she reapplied a pale pink gloss and quickly ran her fingers through her hair. She was as ready as she'd ever be.

Her high heels sank into the white gravel driveway and she quickly moved to the concrete path leading to the front door. Who lived here? she wondered. Someone with a few bucks, if the late-model SUV in the carport was anything to go by. The beat-up wooden sailing dinghy with a broken mast and peeling paint next to the SUV seemed out of place.

Her stomach gave a faint rumble, reminding her that after she'd finished work she'd driven straight here without changing her clothes or stopping for dinner. Too late now. She buzzed the doorbell and pressed her palms against her linen skirt. Through the frosted-glass strip beside the door, she could see a light on in a back room but the front of the house was dark. She should have called first instead of just turning up. Amy might be out. She might be busy. She might—

The front door opened to reveal a man in a sleeveless T-shirt and shorts. His rumpled dark hair was cut close at the sides and laugh lines framed his mouth and eyes.

"Reid?" She froze to the spot. Even after all these years, she would have known him anywhere.

"Nina?" He went still. "What are you doing here?"

"Me?" she croaked. "What are *you* doing here?"

"I live here," he said.

Low blood sugar combined with shock caused Nina's knees to buckle and black spots swam before her eyes. Reid sprang forward and gripped her elbow. "You'd better come inside and sit down."

He led her through the foyer and into a formal living room strewn with toys, unfolded laundry and movie magazines. Nina sank gratefully onto a soft couch. Reid placed the back of his warm hand against her clammy forehead. It could have been a gesture of tenderness and concern but his voice was brusque. "Are you all right?"

"I'm fine," she lied, feeling anything but. She'd come here to meet her daughter and found Reid instead. She could hardly believe it was him standing before her. She'd known he was back in Vancouver ever since he'd been interviewed in the local media. She knew he'd been married and had another daughter, that his wife had died a few years ago.

He looked the same, though a little older, of course. His features had lost the softness of youth and were stronger, more defined. Like an optical illusion, one second he was her closest friend and lover, then she blinked and he was a stranger. In spite of everything, she looked hungrily for the humorous twist to his mouth, the twinkle in his dark eyes. But he wasn't smiling; he was scowling at her. Time alone couldn't extinguish the rancor they'd parted with.

"Where's…" Nina swallowed hard at the fresh ordeal of speaking their daughter's name. "…Amy? My mother said she's looking for her biological parents. I guess she found you first."

Reid cast her an odd glance. "Uh, yeah."

"I had no idea this was your house," Nina said. "Or I would never have…I mean, I would have called first." This was so awkward; she, who lived to talk, had no idea what to say to him. Nina glanced around. "So, where is she?"

"She's…out."

"When do you expect her back?"

"She's missing, actually," Reid admitted. "I'm getting worried."

"Missing!" Nina sat up straighter. "How…where? When was the last time you saw her?"

"She left this morning around 9:00 a.m.," Reid said. "She was going into Vancouver to audition for a walk-on part in a movie." He moved a teddy bear out of the way so he could sit beside Nina. "She was very excited about it."

Out of habit, Nina pulled a notepad and pen out of her purse and jotted down the time and place, glad of something concrete to focus on during this surreal experience. "So she's an actress?"

"She's performed in high-school productions. As far as I know, this is the first professional job she's gone for." He ran a hand through his hair. "She wouldn't leave Beebee this long unless something happened."

"Is Beebee—" Nina began then thought she heard a childish giggle and stopped. "What was that?"

Reid tilted his head. "I don't hear anything."

"Never mind. Neither do I, now. Beebee is an odd name. Is she our—?" Nina tapped the pen against the paper. This was too weird. "Is Beebee Amy's little girl?"

"Yes." Reid lifted his head, still listening. "I put her in her crib but she keeps getting out. I'd better check on her."

Before he could move, a tiny girl with flaming curls and yellow sleepers wriggled out from behind the couch, giggling madly, and ran into the hallway and toward the front door. Over the top of the low divider separating the living room from the foyer Nina could see a small determined hand trying to turn the knob.

"Beebee!" Reid cried. "What do you think you're doing?"

"Oh, she's so sweet!" Nina exclaimed, forgetting everything else in the joy of seeing her grandchild. "She's got my mother's hair."

"Don't be fooled by that angelic face," Reid said. "She's an escape artist." He lunged across the room, tripped on a stuffed elephant and fell sideways into a pile of towels. "Oof! Don't let her get away."

Beebee gave the doorknob a final twist and the door swung open. Nina heard a last gleeful chuckle and then the little imp pattered down the steps and disappeared into the night.

"Damn! I forgot to turn the dead bolt after I let you in." Reid struggled to right himself amid the tangled laundry. "You can't take your eyes off that child for a minute."

"Then why did you?" Nina picked her way across the room through toys and clothes. "If you're supposed to be looking after her, you're not doing a very good job."

"Just...get...her!" Reid swore as a pair of toddler's overalls wrapped themselves around his ankles and brought him to his knees.

Nina paused in the doorway to scan the yard. Beebee was running down the driveway as fast as her little legs could carry her. Nina took off after her, her high heels wobbling dangerously in the loose gravel. "Beebee! Come back here, darling. Come to—" She broke off, the word *grandma* sticking in her throat. "Come to Nina."

The headlights of a car approached, on a collision course with Beebee barreling straight for the road. Nina shouted, "Beebee, stop this instant!"

Beebee slid to a halt and spun to face Nina, her mouth a startled O. Her surprise at this stranger speaking so harshly swiftly turned to mutiny. She drew in a lungful of air then emitted an ear-piercing shriek. The passing station wagon turned a corner but Beebee's high-pitched noise went on and on, like a car alarm that wouldn't turn off. A couple walking their miniature poodle down the street frowned at Nina and whispered to each other.

"It's a game we play," Nina called to the couple, laughing. "I'm her…her older female relative." She marched over to Beebee and picked up the child who was still screaming and as stiff as a board. "Beebee, stop," she pleaded in an urgent undertone. "I'm not going to hurt you."

"Ow, yeow, yikes." Arms flailing, Reid hopped over the sharp gravel in bare feet. He reached for Beebee. "Come here, honey."

"Weed!" Beebee kicked off from Nina's stomach, launching herself out of Nina's arms to dive into Reid's waiting embrace. She threw Nina an angry, suspicious glare then buried her face in Reid's shirt.

"Oomph." Nina doubled over. "What is wrong with that little banshee?"

"You scared her."

"*I* scared *her?*"

"She makes strange at first," Reid said. "Beebee, this is Nina. She's…" He glanced at Nina and she shook her head. "A friend of your mommy's."

"Where my mommy?" Beebee asked plaintively.

"She's coming." Reid stroked her damp curls off her forehead. In his arms, she heaved a deep sigh. "Let's go inside and put you to bed." He walked back to the house on the grass and pointed out the first star glinting in an indigo sky. "Make a wish, Beebee."

"Mommy," Beebee said and stuck her thumb in her mouth.

"She'll be home soon."

Nina held the door open for him to go through. "Ou-yay ouldn't-shay ake-may omises-pray ou-yay an't-cay eep-kay."

Reid set Beebee on the floor. "Go get your dolly. It's bedtime." Then he looked at Nina as though she were demented. "What on earth are you saying?"

"Ou-yay ouldn't-shay—"

"She's forgotten all about her *om-may*. She's not even paying attention to us anymore," he added, nodding at the toddler.

Beebee was busy piling clean laundry onto Daisy's back and giggling when it fell off. Dog and child distributed clothing around the room—a sock behind the couch, a T-shirt next to the window.

Nina, too frazzled to sit still, followed behind, picking up the clothing as she went. "We should call the police."

"Too soon." Reid locked the door and bolted it, then slid the chain across. "She has to be gone twenty-four hours before they'll file a missing-persons report."

Nina dumped her armload of clothing onto the couch and began to fold the individual items, finding the mindless activity soothing. "Is there no way to contact her? An address or a phone number?"

"I've searched her room. She didn't leave anything written down that I could see," Reid replied.

"How long has Amy been here?" Nina looked around at the clothing and toys. "They seem very settled in."

"A few days…maybe a week."

Maybe a week? Reid had always been a little absentminded, lost in his own world, but even for him, the answer was vague.

Before she could probe further, the front door rattled as someone tried to enter. A second later the bell rang. Reid strode across the room, unlocked and flung open the door. Beebee tried to shoot through the gap only for Reid to grab her by the scruff of her pajamas and haul her unceremoniously into his arms.

A young woman with waist-length blond hair hurried inside. Nina felt the butterflies in her stomach buffet her rib cage. At last. Her daughter. Frozen to the spot, Nina watched her in amazement. She was beautiful. She was *real*.

"Amy!" Reid exclaimed with relief. "Where have you been? What happened to you?"

Amy lifted Beebee out of Reid's arms and hugged

her to herself. "Mommy's here." She glanced at Reid over Beebee's shoulder. "The bus I was on collided with a dump truck in the tunnel. They just sideswiped each other but it caused a pileup that took hours to sort out."

"I heard about the accident on the radio coming out here so I went around by the bridge," Nina said. "Are you all right?"

Amy glanced at her with a puzzled frown. "Not a scratch on me. Ambulances took us all to Emergency to get checked out."

"Why didn't you call?" Reid demanded. "I know you don't have a cell phone but you could have borrowed one."

"I didn't have your number with me. Crazy, huh? I never thought I would need it." Amy stroked Beebee's back while the little girl played with her hoop earrings. "There was a public phone booth in Emergency but no phone book. I guess I could have dialed directory assistance but I didn't think of it at the time. I'm sorry if you were worried."

"How did you get home?" Reid asked.

"They brought out another bus." Amy peered around Beebee to study Nina curiously. "You look familiar. Are you by any chance…?"

Related? Did she see the resemblance? Nina wondered breathlessly. *She* could, in the eyes and the shape of the mouth. "I'm…" she began, but her breath had lodged in her chest, preventing her from speaking.

"You are!" Amy said. "You're Nina Kennerly from

the TV show *Chat with Nina*. Reid watches you every night." Amy turned to Reid. "You didn't tell me you knew Nina Kennerly. Are you two friends?"

Reid threw Nina an unreadable glance. "Something like that." He touched Amy's arm. "Maybe you should get Beebee settled. She's had a lot of excitement tonight."

"I'll put her to bed," Amy said and carried her child down the hall to their bedroom.

"I didn't know what I should say when she asked me who you were," Reid said quietly. "What are you going to tell her?"

Nina began picking up toys and piling them into a toy box in the corner. "The truth, of course. That's why I came out here tonight."

Amy returned and flopped into a chair, blowing out a sigh that fluttered her wispy bangs. "Whew! What a day. But I got the part as an extra."

"That's great," Reid said.

"How exciting," Nina added warmly. "What role do you play?"

"I'm a tourist." Amy glanced at her, at the toys in her hand, and wrinkled her brow. "Excuse me, I know you're Nina Kennerly but are you, like, Reid's girlfriend or something?" When neither Nina or Reid replied, she said, "Am I being nosy? Just tell me to mind my own business."

Nina sat on the arm of the couch, looked at Reid, then back to Amy. Her throat suddenly felt very dry. All the speeches she'd mentally composed to break the news gently fled her brain and she blurted, "I'm your biological mother."

No one moved in the frozen silence. Time itself might have been suspended were it not for the quiet ticking of a mantel clock. Amy stared. Nina gazed steadfastly back, her heart pounding in her throat. She usually had so much to say she couldn't get it all out but, at the moment, her wits and her voice failed her.

Finally, Amy blinked and swallowed. "My mother?" she said in a choked voice. "The woman who gave birth to me?"

Nina bit her lip and nodded. Was Amy pleased? Disappointed? It was hard to tell.

"I don't understand," Amy said. "How did you find me?"

"Elaine called my mother to tell her you were in town looking for me and gave her Reid's address."

Amy's gaze flicked to Reid. A faint frown crossed her features as if there were a connection here she didn't understand and couldn't work out.

"I know Elaine Hocking is your real mother," Nina went on in a rush. "I know I can't ever take her place and I wouldn't want to but if I could in some small way be part of your life, part of Beebee's life—" she drew a breath "—I would be so happy."

Amy went completely still for another agonizing minute. Then tears leaked from her eyes and she rose from her chair to start forward only to falter, as if unsure.

"Oh, my dear." Nina's eyes flooded as she pulled her daughter into an awkward embrace. "Oh, my dear sweetpea."

Amy drew back, blinking with surprise. "Sweetpea?"

Nina felt heat bloom in her cheeks. "It's a pet name I had for you. I didn't know your real name, you see. I shouldn't have burst out with it. I must sound silly and sentimental."

Amy shook her head, wiping her eyes with the heel of her hand. "It's cool."

Nina let out a long breath, easing but not releasing her pent-up anxiety. It still didn't seem possible that this young woman should be her daughter. *Her daughter.*

Amy turned to Reid with an amazed smile. She'd recovered her composure and was coming alive with excitement. "Can you believe this? Nina Kennerly's my mother! Ever since I found out the Hockings weren't my biological parents I've been going crazy wondering who I am, where I came from." She swung back to Nina. "And now *you* can tell me who my father is."

Taken aback, Nina threw Reid a swift glance. "Surely you know."

"I told you, Jim and Elaine wouldn't give me any information." Amy clasped her hands in front of her. "Please, I want to know all about him. Was he good-looking and smart? Was he kind?"

"He was all those things and more." Nina frowned

at Reid, silently demanding to know what the hell was going on. She'd assumed Amy knew who he was, but apparently not.

"He sounds wonderful," Amy said.

"I was very much in love with him," Nina said, suddenly wistful. "For a while we talked about getting married."

"That's so romantic," Amy said. "What went wrong?"

"I…we had a terrible fight. We were both so young, and I knew I couldn't provide for you on my own. His parents arranged for a private adoption." Nina glanced at Reid again, eyebrows raised. He gazed back at her with a stony expression.

"Do you know where my father lives now?" Amy said. "Do you think he'll want to see me?"

"Well," Nina began, looking from Amy to Reid. *What was going on here?*

"I know he will." Reid cleared his throat. When he spoke again it wasn't with his customary assurance. "Amy, I don't know how to tell you this. I've wanted to say something for years. I should have told you this past week—"

"What is it?" Amy broke in impatiently. "What do you know about my father?"

"*I* am your biological father."

Amy turned to him, shocked back into speechlessness. Her excitement turned to disbelief. Finally, she spluttered with nervous laughter. "What! You can't be."

Reid stepped forward, a hand tentatively extended. "Please don't be upset."

She pulled away from him, her face crumpling. "I've known you all my life. You're a friend of my parents. Of Jim and Elaine. You're *Uncle* Reid."

"No," he said soberly. "I'm your father."

"I've been here a week," Amy cried. "You knew I was looking for my birth parents but you never said anything."

"I couldn't at first. I promised the Hockings—"

"You're just like them." Angry tears spilled over as she backed away. "You lied to me, too. I don't *want* you to be my father. Do you hear me? *You're not my father.*"

CHAPTER THREE

REID FELT THE WAY HE imagined Luke must have felt when he'd been shot in the gut—too much in shock to feel pain, but he was bleeding inside. "Amy, let me explain—"

Before he could finish, Nina directed a sharply spoken question to Amy. "What do you mean, *you've known him all your life?* Didn't you just get to Vancouver recently?"

"Yes, but Reid is a friend of my adoptive parents," Amy explained. "He was *Uncle* Reid when I was little. He came over at Christmas and Easter. He gave me birthday presents and once he even came on vacation with us. He taught me to swim."

"Jim and Elaine weren't big on water sports," Reid mumbled.

Nina turned to him. "You've been in Vancouver for what, three years?"

Reid nodded. They'd moved back after Carol had died. Leaving Amy had been a wrench, but he'd wanted Tara to know his parents better now that it was just the two of them.

"Three years," she repeated, dismayed. "Yet you never once called me and said, hey, Nina, would you like to see a picture of your daughter?" She paused. "I presume you have photos?"

Again Reid nodded. Whole albums. "Why would I call when it was *you* who—" He broke off, aware of Amy listening intently to their exchange.

They heard a car pull into the driveway and all heads turned toward the door. Then he heard the car door slam and Tara calling good-night.

She entered the living room a moment later, her face lit with excitement. "Dad, you'll never guess. I got a special commendation for my étude—" She broke off abruptly, her gaze flitting from Reid to Nina to Amy and back to Nina. "What's going on?"

Reid rose to his feet. "Nina, this is my daughter, Tara. Tara, this is Nina."

"From the TV show?" Tara's face turned wary and Reid knew why—it had never been a secret that Nina had been the woman in Reid's life before Carol. With strained politeness, Tara added, "It's nice to meet you."

"Nina is Amy's biological mother," Reid added. He might as well get the explanations over with at once.

Tara's smile froze and she clutched her violin case to her chest. Reid could almost see the wheels turning in her mind. Nina was Amy's mother. Nina was also Reid's old girlfriend. Therefore—

Reid cleared his throat. "Amy's *my* daughter, too. And your half sister."

Tara's mouth opened and shut again but no words

came out. Her gaze returned to Amy, who was accepting a tissue from Nina. "Is this true?"

"Apparently." Amy blew her nose noisily. "I'm not happy about it. He's lied to me all my life."

"That makes two of us." Tara turned back to Reid, her eyes filled with accusations.

"Now wait just a minute," Reid said and started with Amy. "The only way the Hockings allowed me to see you was if I agreed not to reveal our true relationship. If I told anyone else, including you—" he looked at Tara "—or you—" he added to Nina "—I risked losing access."

"You led a double life," Tara said. "Going from Mom and I to…" On the verge of tears, she pointed at Amy. "To *her*."

Reid shook his head. "It's not the way you make it sound."

"When you give a child up for adoption, you *give them up*," Tara insisted. "You're not supposed to hang on and try to be part of their life."

"*I* didn't give Amy up," Reid countered. "*Nina* did."

"So you still blame the whole thing on me," Nina said angrily. "I might have known."

Amy moved to stand closer to Nina. "At least she was honest about her actions."

"I wasn't blaming you," Reid said to Nina, getting more and more exasperated.

"Sure sounded like it to me!" Nina said. "Your mother—"

"Oh stop fighting! I wish you'd all just go away!" Tara ran out of the room and pounded up the stairs.

Silence fell. Reid rubbed the bridge of his nose, conscious of a tension headache coming on.

"It's obvious I'm not welcome here," Amy said quietly and rose. "I'll pack my things."

"Where are you going to go at this late hour?" Reid said, alarmed at the thought of her leaving.

"You can stay with me," Nina offered. "I'd love to have you."

"No!" Reid exclaimed. Nina and Amy turned to him, startled. "It's late and Beebee's asleep. Anyway, we don't have a car seat."

"That's true," Amy said, sitting down again. "I wouldn't like to risk driving all the way into Vancouver without her properly secure." She wrapped her arms around her knees, looking lost.

"You can continue to stay here," Reid assured. "I'll talk to Tara. This has been a shock to her."

"And me!" Amy said.

Reid glanced helplessly from Amy to Nina, who quickly looked away. There'd been so much left unsaid when he and Nina had parted nineteen years ago and tonight's emotionally charged revelations had only widened the gulf between them. He'd touched a nerve with his remark about Nina giving Amy up. All he'd meant was that *he'd* never wanted to.

"Well, I'd better go." Nina picked up her purse and moved to the front door.

Amy followed and Reid trailed behind. "Will I see you again?" Amy asked Nina.

Nina paused at the bottom of the steps. "Of course.

Since you don't have a car, it's probably easier if I come back here. Unless Reid has any objection?"

Her challenge hung in the air. He couldn't keep her away if he wanted to and they both knew it. The last thing he wanted was a tug-of-war over Amy.

"I have no objection," Reid said. "Come for lunch tomorrow if you like."

He left Nina and Amy to say good-night to each other, then went upstairs and knocked on Tara's door.

"Go away." Her voice sounded strained, as if she'd been crying.

Ignoring her edict, Reid entered. "We need to talk."

Tara was lying on her bed, curled on her side, reading a Manga book. Reid sat beside her and stroked her back. "I'm sorry, honey. I was going to tell you as soon as I'd told Amy."

"There you go, putting *her* first again." Tara still hadn't looked at him, making a pretense of being absorbed in the illustrated story.

Reid pressed his lips together, reminding himself that no matter how mature Tara seemed at times, she was still only fifteen and bound to feel betrayed. "Just because Amy's my daughter, too, doesn't mean I love you less."

Tara shrugged and turned a page. "Whatever."

Nothing could have been more calculated to push Reid's hot button than that insolent claim to indifference. "Will you put that away and talk to me!"

Tara closed her Manga book and tossed it onto her bedside table. Then she scooted up to lean her back against the headboard. "You should have talked to me *before* you allowed Amy into our house. What would *Mom* have said if she knew you had a secret daughter?"

"Your mother knew about Amy," Reid said. "She was the only person I told. She accepted that Amy was a part of my life."

"Did she? Or did she just not have a choice?" Tara said. "Now that Mom's gone, I suppose you'll go back to your first family."

"Nina and Amy were never my family," Reid said. "You and your mother were. You still are." He held out his arms. "Come on, honey. Give your dad a hug."

Tara blinked red-rimmed eyes but she made no move to go into his arms. "I'm tired. I want to go to sleep now."

She'd never refused him a hug before and the significance of it cut him to the bone. Reid rose stiffly, feeling as if he'd aged twenty years in one day. Had he gone from having two daughters to none?

Downstairs all was quiet. Amy had gone to bed and there was no light underneath her door. Reid went into the living room to turn out the table lamp. His hand paused on the switch. Nina's leather-bound notebook and gold pen lay on the side table where she'd forgotten them.

Suddenly he recalled the light perfume she wore and the unconsciously seductive sway of her hips. Attraction and antagonism churned in his gut. If he'd thought Amy and Beebee disruptive to his quiet lifestyle, their presence was nothing compared to the havoc Nina could wreak on his peace of mind.

Reid picked up the notebook and pen and placed them on the mantelpiece where Beebee couldn't get them. For good or ill, Nina was back in his life.

AMY HEARD THE DOORBELL the next morning and, with a nervous glance in the hall mirror, hurried to open the door. Nina, in white capri pants, a sleeveless turquoise top and glittery sandals, looked casually glamorous. Amy still couldn't get over the fact that Nina was her *mother.*

"I'm so glad you came!" Amy greeted her with a warm smile and leaned forward to exchange tentative kisses on the cheek. She lowered her voice and added, "It's like a morgue around here this morning."

"Are you all right?" Nina asked, frowning slightly and searching Amy's face. "You look tired."

"I didn't get much sleep last night," Amy admitted. She felt Beebee's small hands clutching her calves as her daughter peeked around Amy's long cotton skirt at the newcomer.

"Neither did I," Nina said. "I guess we all had a lot to think about." She bent forward to smile at Beebee, "Hello, sweetheart."

Beebee shrank back behind Amy's legs.

"She makes strange," Amy apologized and lifted Beebee up. "Come on, Beebs, say hello to Nina."

"Don't force her," Nina said. "We'll make friends in time."

"Come in." Amy led the way through to the back of the house. From the second floor came the sound of a violin concerto. "That's Tara," she explained to Nina as they passed the stairs. "She's awfully good, although I get the feeling she doesn't practice as much as Reid would like." Glancing at the closed door leading off the family room, Amy added, "Reid's working. I think he's behind on his book."

With explanations over, there was an awkward pause. All the way across the country on the bus, Amy had imagined a dramatic meeting with her mother, her fantasies alternating between tearful recrimination and joyful reunion. What she hadn't expected was this uncomfortable distance between them, this not knowing how to talk to each other. There was so much she wanted to know, facts and dates, whys and hows. More than anything she wanted reassurance that, despite being given away, she'd been loved. She realized now with a wince at her naiveté that was something she could never ask for.

As the silence stretched, Nina moved to the windows. "What a lovely view of the mountains."

"Do you want to go for a walk on the dike?" Amy suggested. Movement and action might break the ice.

"That sounds good." Nina seized on the idea with obvious relief. She watched Amy smooth sunscreen on Beebee's cheeks and nose, and strap her into the stroller. "Is it too far for her to walk by herself?"

"I always end up running after her on the way out and carrying her on the way back," Amy explained.

"This is better, then," Nina said. "We'll be able to talk."

Amy smiled tentatively. "That's right."

Nina removed a digital camera from her red leather purse and left the purse behind on the kitchen table. She helped Amy carry Beebee's stroller down the steps and they walked along the street to the pedestrian gate at the entrance to the dike, a raised gravel road that sloped away to the beach on one side and the marshland on the other.

The dike ran around a point between Reid's beach and the next beach, holding back flood tides from the marsh and pastureland. Rabbits hopped through the long grass, birds sang from the hedges and ducks paddled down the deep, wide channels that criss-crossed the low-lying fields.

Amy pushed the stroller over the bumpy track. No cars were allowed on the dike but there were people walking their dogs or jogging, plus the occasional kids on bikes. They'd gone a few hundred yards when Nina slipped her camera off her wrist.

"Hold it there, Amy, so I can take a photo of you and Beebee to show my parents. Beebee looks a lot like my mother, your grandmother. Her name is Dora. She had red hair, too, which turned auburn as she got older."

"I never had grandparents that I remember," Amy said. "Both Mom's and Dad's—I mean *Elaine's and Jim's* parents passed away when I was very young." Amy adjusted Beebee's sunhat so her face was visible then crouched beside the stroller so Nina could take their photo. "That's why I came out west, to find my real family."

No sooner did she say that than she felt guilty. Despite her anger toward her mom and dad, she loved them and knew they were good parents. But what hurt her so badly—besides the lies—was that they couldn't understand her curiosity about her biological parents. They seemed to think she was only doing it to get back at them. Nina's silence as she lowered her camera and checked the photo she'd just taken made Amy feel ashamed. Would she get on her case the way Reid had?

"I'm glad you came to look for me," Nina said at last. "I've wondered about you over the years. What you looked like, your personality, if you were happy."

"We look similar, don't we?" Amy said shyly, searching Nina's face and finding no disapproval, only a near mirror-image of herself. "Like mother and daughter. We have the same heart-shaped face, the same dark blue eyes."

"For me it's like looking in a mirror and seeing myself twenty years younger." Nina held out a slender manicured hand adorned with an opal ring set in gold. "We even have the same fingers. See how narrow they taper and how the index finger bends in slightly?"

Amy nodded, stretching a tanned arm tinkling with silver bangles next to Nina's. Her skin was softer, smoother, but other than that they could almost have been twins. It was as though she'd found the piece of herself that had been missing all these years. Maybe. It was too soon to take anything for granted.

"I want to take you to meet your grandparents," Nina said. "They're dying to get to know you and Beebee."

"I'd love that. Tell me about them," Amy begged. "I want to know everything."

As they walked along the dike, Nina related details of her family history, about growing up in the small house in Vancouver's east side, about her father almost losing his hand in an industrial accident, her mother's gentle humor and her father's pride. Amy listened eagerly, asking questions as rapidly as Nina could answer them. Their constraint vanished as their conversation wove a pattern of half-finished sentences and intuitive leaps of understanding punctuated by frequent bursts of laughter.

The only thing they didn't talk about was Amy's birth. Nina seemed to shy away from the subject every time she came close. And she wouldn't say anything more about her early relationship with Reid either. The burning issue in Amy's mind was why Nina and Reid had given her up for adoption. The question was on the tip of her tongue more than once, but she was afraid her hurt and resentment would come out in her voice. Afraid that the truth might ruin the growing connection between her and Nina. And yet, wasn't that the main reason she'd traveled four thousand miles across the country? To find out the truth?

"Let's see, what else can I tell you?" Nina said. "We're all very healthy, with no hereditary diseases in the family. You're lucky that way. You have good genes on both sides." She paused and asked cautiously, "Have you met Reid's parents?"

"Reginald and Serena came out for dinner last Sunday. They're very reserved and formal and they positively dripped money. They were nice to me and they fussed over Beebee but it didn't occur to me they were her great grandparents." Amy's voice held a wobble. "Reid didn't say a word about my relationship to them. I still can't believe he lied to me. He was always so supportive, always encouraged me to follow my dreams. I *trusted* him."

"He loves you," Nina said, stepping aside so a gray-haired woman could power-walk past. "He's proved that beyond a doubt."

Amy brushed her hair out of her eyes and slowed to turn her gaze on Nina. "Does love justify the lies?"

"He made a promise to the Hockings," Nina said. "He thought he was doing the right thing."

"I don't understand why you're defending him," Amy said. "I've been here over a week. He knew from the first day that I was looking for my biological mother yet he didn't tell me who you were. *Why?*"

Nina shook her head. "I can't answer that. Maybe he thought I would give him away. Have you tried talking this out with Reid?"

"I'm too angry to talk to him," Amy said. "He went straight to work after breakfast and hasn't come out of his office all morning."

A jogger ran by in a burst of pounding feet and spraying gravel. When he'd passed, Nina changed the subject. "What about Beebee's father?" she said. "What does he think about you coming out here?"

Head down, Amy shrugged unhappily. "I didn't tell Ian I was leaving, much less where I was going."

"Why not?" Nina asked. "What happened to make you run away from him?"

"We fought over his job at the meat-packing plant," Amy said, avoiding Nina's gaze. "We're both vegetarians."

"Don't you think he has a right to know where his daughter is?" Nina asked, gently, and Amy felt a hot burst of shame. "Is there another reason you left?" Nina added. "You can tell me. If you want to talk about it."

Amy hesitated; she'd been longing to confide in someone. Her mom and dad didn't understand and she couldn't talk to Reid. "Elaine and Jim want us to get married and Ian agrees," she blurted out. "I just don't know if I love him enough to settle down with him."

"I see," Nina said. "Does he love you?"

"He says he does," Amy said. "But we're so young. I've seen the statistics on teenage marriages."

"You have a child," Nina said. "You could try to make it work for Beebee's sake."

"That's what Jim and Elaine say." Amy lifted her hands off the stroller's handles in frustration. "But Ian's never actually proposed. I've never accepted. The decision to be together was forced on us when Beebee arrived," Amy said, then added hastily, "not that I regret having her."

"I know what you mean. It's complicated," Nina agreed. "I'm not sure I'm qualified to give advice. All I know is, you need to be very certain about the choices you make now because they'll affect you, Beebee and Ian for the rest of your life."

"That's what worries me," Amy said, feeling the familiar weight of uncertainty over the future pressing on her. "Right now I need some time out. I need to feel I can make it on my own if I have to. I need to find out who I am before I can become some-one's wife."

They came to a halt at the end of the dike. The trail sloped off in several directions through the grassy wetland. A park with barbecues, swings and a baseball diamond lay on the far side, next to a parking lot. To their left, a large gray bird wading through the shallows flapped away, its long legs trailing behind.

Beebee pointed a chubby fist. "Bird."

"This is where we usually turn back." Amy paused to gaze at Mount Baker floating above the distant horizon on the far side of the bay. The mountains were an unexpected bonus to this side of the country and she never tired of them.

"Did you ever consider giving up Beebee for adop-tion?" Nina asked.

Surprised at the question. Amy replied more fiercely than she intended. *"Never."*

Nina flinched. "I admire you for that," she said. "My own situation was…unstable when I was preg-nant with you. I'm glad you had the security of having a well-off family and a steady boyfriend."

"I don't want anyone's help," Amy insisted. "I told you, I want to be able to support myself."

"I understand that, more than you might think. But

even when you ran away, you had Reid to turn to," Nina pointed out. "What would you have done if he hadn't taken you in?"

Amy didn't like to contemplate that or to be reminded of her obligations to Reid. She frowned and bent over the stroller to check on Beebee. "I would have survived."

They started back in silence. Amy struggled with the stroller over the rough path, even as she struggled with her conflicting emotions. Suddenly the day seemed ruined, herself on the verge of tears. Then she felt a touch on her shoulder and turned to find Nina watching her with anxious eyes.

"There are decisions I regret, mistakes I've made," Nina said. "Since you turned up, I've felt incredibly lucky, as though I've been given a second chance. I'm in no position to pass judgment on you. But you're my daughter. I'd just like to get to know you."

Amy glanced away then back again, blinking to clear the moisture in her eyes. How had she ever thought this would be easy? "Well, that's what I came west for."

"Let me push for a while," Nina said, taking over the stroller. "Tell me, what type of music do you like? What kind of books? I want to know everything about you. We have so much to catch up on," she continued before Amy could reply. "We'll go to Stanley Park and take the ferry to Vancouver Island. Oh, the aquarium is wonderful. Beebee will love the killer whales. I'll take you on a tour of the television studio."

"That would be fantastic." Amy's heart lightened and so did her step. "I couldn't believe it when I found out my mother was a TV star."

Bound to a chair, Luke struggled against the ropes cutting into his wrists. His ankles were tied, too, bending his knees at an unnatural angle that cut off his circulation. Before him paced the General, his chest festooned with colorful medals against his dark green uniform. Luke heard sounds coming from behind him and knew the General's henchmen were preparing their instruments of torture.

"Where are the documents?" The General spoke flawless English with just a trace of an accent.

"I don't have them." Before the soldiers had stormed the warehouse, he'd shoved the manila envelope beneath a loose floorboard.

"I don't believe you. You want to destroy us." The General gave the nod and a man in a dark suit slowly stubbed his burning cigarette out on Luke's arm, sending the acrid smell of his own singed flesh up his nostrils.

Sweat poured down Luke's back. Or was it blood from the gunshot wound that had reopened when they'd dragged him from the warehouse to the basement of this burnt-out church? "I'm only trying do what's right. I'm protecting innocent people."

REID LEANED BACK IN HIS chair and put his bare feet up on his desk while he read over the passage. What a load of crap, he thought, shaking his head in disgust. Luke Mann didn't try to defend his actions like some guilty politician. Never apologize, never explain, that was his motto. With a few keystrokes, Reid deleted what he'd spent all morning laboring over.

Tara was mad at him. Amy said she'd never forgive him and Nina suddenly occupied the moral high ground. Was it any wonder he couldn't write? Thank God Beebee still regarded him with affection.

On a wide, high shelf to his left sat framed photos of Tara and Carol, a scented candle Carol had claimed would encourage creativity, except that he never remembered to light it, and a carved wooden box where he kept his treasures. He opened it now, pushed aside the baseball card his grandfather had given him, a bald eagle feather, a moon snail shell, a set of poker dice and, in a separate compartment of its own, a child's gold bracelet set with tiny pink stones.

The bracelet had been Amy's, his gift to her on her eighth birthday. It had come back to him in a box of clothes and toys Amy had outgrown, which Elaine had passed on to Tara. Reid had intercepted the bracelet for sentimental reasons, keeping it as a reminder of Amy's childhood when he'd moved back out west. Then he'd gotten Tara her own bracelet.

Reid lifted the thin gold links out of the box and felt the fine weight flow over his fingers. Over the years he'd thought about giving it back to Amy but it was a child's bracelet; probably it meant more to him than it did to her. Carefully he returned it to its compartment.

Through his shut office door he could hear Amy and Nina out in the family room, the soft cadence of their voices punctuated frequently by laughter. He'd followed their progress on the dike with his bird-watching binoculars until they'd rounded the bend and he couldn't make out their figures any longer. Now they were back, getting along like a house on fire.

Another gale of laughter brought him to his feet with his hand on the doorknob. To what? Ask them to keep it down or to join them? How did Nina do it? Neither of his daughters were talking to him or to each other but, as soon as Nina had arrived, suddenly the house was filled with conversation and laughter. He'd forgotten how much she liked to talk.

He pressed an ear to the closed door. What was so funny? He should be glad that Nina was getting along well with Amy, except that it stung, coinciding as it did with his abrupt fall from grace. He forced himself back to the computer. He absolutely *had* to write ten pages today if it killed him.

Upstairs Tara was drawing her bow across the violin strings as loudly as she could, as if trying to drown out Amy and Nina. Another burst of laughter from the family room was followed by a piercing screech of the violin's top string.

That was it. He couldn't work in here. Reid grabbed his laptop and slid his feet into his sandals. As he came out of his office Nina and Amy stopped yakking to look at him.

Reid put on his sunglasses and a baseball cap and headed for the French doors. "I'm going to write on the beach," he said to no one in particular and left without a backward glance.

Nina had been almost as aware of Reid's unseen presence behind the shut office door as she was of Amy and Beebee, right in front of her. "He was always quiet," she said to Amy, "but he didn't use to be this antisocial."

"He gets grumpy when his book isn't going well," Amy said. "Some days he hardly speaks to anyone. He just mutters to himself about some guy called Luke."

"That's the hero of his novels," Nina said.

"I've tried reading his books," Amy added. "I can't get into spy thrillers."

"They're not usually my cup of tea, either." Yet she'd read all of them. Nina got up and went to the window to watch Reid stalk down the beach to sit cross-legged in the sand against a log with his laptop across his knees. "That doesn't look very comfortable."

Amy came to stand beside her. "He told me once he couldn't work outside because of the seagulls."

"They can be noisy," Nina agreed.

"It's their beady eyes," Amy corrected her. "They fly in and circle around, coming closer and closer, hoping for food, I guess. They stare at him until he can't think."

"Gulls aren't the only distractions around here,"

Nina murmured, lifting her eyes to the ceiling where Tara's bow toiled up and down a scale.

"Mommy." Beebee patted Amy's bare leg beneath her denim cut-off shorts. "I hungry. Want nummies."

"Okay, sweetie." Amy hoisted the little girl into her arms. She cast a last glance out the window in Reid's direction. "I'll put something together for lunch."

Nina gazed thoughtfully at the solitary figure hunched over his laptop. What was it about Reid? He'd never been the life of the party yet he had a way of drawing people to him even when he seemed oblivious. Amy was mad at him yet she clearly missed having his attention and his company.

In the kitchen, Amy had her head in the refrigerator and was rustling through the vegetable crisper. "We've got plenty of salad stuff."

"Dad likes meat," Tara said, coming into the room. She had a faint frown on her pale oval face. Her baggy T-shirt and shorts swamped her boyish frame. "And so do I."

"Well, *I* won't touch meat," Amy said flatly, shutting the fridge door with a bump of her hip. "If anyone wants to eat it, they'll have to get it themselves."

"No problem," Tara rejoined.

Nina suppressed a smile. Looking at the two girls side by side, no one would have guessed they were half sisters. Except that they displayed the classic signs of sibling rivalry.

Poor Reid. He would have his hands full with these two.

CHAPTER FOUR

TARA TOOK AMY'S PLACE at the fridge and pulled out a plate of cold leftover chicken. This was followed by sliced ham, salami and a package of raw ground beef.

"You're going to put all that on the table?" Amy said in disbelief.

"Why not?" Tara replied defiantly. Noticing Beebee looking at her, she bent down to offer the child a piece of salami. "Want some real food, kid?"

Beebee stuffed the salami in her mouth and held out her hand for more. Tara readily supplied her with another piece.

"Beebee!" Amy said. "You don't like meat."

"Yes me do," Beebee mumbled around her mouthful as she nodded vigorously. "More."

Oh, dear, Nina thought as Amy glared at Tara, who was smiling smugly. World War Three was going to break out any minute. "I'll take Beebee down to the beach and let you two girls sort out lunch."

Amy gave her a grateful smile. "She loves the beach but just don't take her—Ack! What are you doing!" This last was directed at Tara who was about to dump the raw hamburger meat into Amy's salad bowl. "I'm using that."

"I need it, too!" Tara made a grab for the bowl.

"We'll just get out of the way." Nina took Beebee's hand and led her outside. She dropped off the low retaining wall onto the sand and swung Beebee down. The sand was blazing hot on her bare feet and she hurried across to the band of barnacle-covered rocks at the edge of the water. Gathering Beebee into her arms, she hopped wincing into the shallows, sighing with relief as her feet settled into the soft sand where sunwarmed water lapped around her ankles.

"Here we are, Beebee." Nina started to lower the tot into the water. Without warning, Beebee started kicking and struggling, her face turning red as she shrieked in alarm. "What's the matter?" Nina asked, still trying to set her down. Maybe the tiny crabs that scuttled away at their approach had scared her.

Embarrassed by the stares she was getting from other beachgoers, Nina picked Beebee up and waded out until the water was up to her calves. Children loved the water, or so she'd been told. This ought to be deep enough. Again she lowered the baby into the sea, hoping Beebee would relax in the warm water swirling around her.

Instead Beebee screamed and clung to her with a death grip, her face convulsed in terror and her tiny fists clenched into white knuckles. Nina pulled her up again and helplessly patted her back. "Beebee, honey, what is it?"

Suddenly there was a splashing behind her and Beebee was straining with her whole body, reaching out. Nina turned and Reid was there, taking Beebee from her. *Again.* What was it with her and this child? She had to be the worst grandmother alive.

"Are you trying to drown her?" Reid shouted, jiggling Beebee up and down.

"I was trying to calm her," Nina replied.

"Didn't Amy tell you? Beebee's *afraid* of the water," Reid said. "When she was ten months old she slipped right under the bathwater and ever since she's been terrified of getting wet."

"Amy started to tell me something," Nina remembered now. "But she didn't finish." Sheltered in Reid's arms, Beebee eased off crying as if by magic. "How do you *do* that?"

"I'm her grandfather. She likes me." He stroked Beebee's cheek with the back of a forefinger. "You need to get to know children gradually, let them come to you. You can't just pick a kid up and take off. Especially not this one."

Nina held out her hand to Beebee. The child glared balefully at her and pressed closer to Reid.

"Anyway, it's only fair that at least Beebee likes me." Reid started walking back to the beach. "Now that you've alienated Amy's affections, and Tara's mad at me, too."

"You alienated Amy all by yourself when you lied to her," Nina pointed out, brushing at the grains of sand clinging to the wet hem of her capri pants.

"It wasn't my choice," Reid said. "If you were in my position would you have risked being cut off from Amy?"

Nina had to admit she probably wouldn't. "I wish you'd told me about her. If not when she was younger then later, after you'd moved back to the West Coast."

Reid put Beebee down on the soft dry sand of a bar and handed her an empty clam shell to dig with. She immediately sat down and started to bury his feet. "I didn't know if you were married. Maybe you had a husband and other children. The sudden appearance of Amy could have been awkward."

"There's no husband. No other children," she admitted.

Reid hesitated then asked, "Boyfriend?"

"Not at present," she conceded stiffly. "I'm too busy with friends and parties and tennis and charity work—" She broke off, aware she sounded defensive and afraid she'd give away the truth—that the busier she kept herself the less she noticed what was missing from her life.

"I'm surprised some guy never snapped you up," Reid said.

Nina started to make a flippant reply then stopped. What was the point in evading the question? "I dated a lot through my twenties but I was so busy building my career I didn't notice the time passing. When I was thirty I met Bill, a news anchor at a rival TV station. I thought he might be the one. We lived together for a couple of years before we broke up."

"What happened?" Reid asked.

"We couldn't agree on whether to have kids or not. After that we just sort of drifted apart." Nina shrugged. "It was probably just as well we didn't marry. He wasn't my type." She smiled a little sadly. If she was really honest, Bill's main fault was that he wasn't Reid. "Anyway, that's all water under the bridge." Nina stooped to take Beebee's hand. "Come on, Beebee. Time for lunch."

"Nummies." Still clutching her clam shell, Beebee followed Nina to the edge of the sandbar then balked, refusing to walk into the water.

"Shall I carry you?" Nina asked and received a gracious nod. Hoisting the child into her arms, Nina waded to the edge of the barnacles.

"There's a path cleared through the rocks over here," Reid said, making his way up the beach by a sandy trail.

"Now he tells me," Nina murmured to Beebee and changed direction.

Reid retrieved his laptop and towel and they went back to the house, pausing on the lawn to brush the sand off their feet. Reid rubbed meticulously between Beebee's toes, getting every last grain of sand out. "There you go," he said, releasing her. "Let's see what your mom and Tara have cooked up."

Beebee ran ahead, pushing through the French doors. Reid stood back and allowed Nina to enter first. She took one look at the lunch and gasped. "Oh, my God."

Enough food for ten people was laid out on the dining table separating the family room and the kitchen. Amy stood at one end, presiding over salads, cheese, boiled eggs and tuna. Tara stood watch over the other end, with numerous plates of cold sliced meats and one of cooked hamburgers.

"Is this a test?" Nina murmured to Reid.

"No matter what we do, we'll fail," he replied.

"Then we'd better brazen it out." Nina advanced, saying merrily, "What a feast!" She hesitated a moment before choosing to sit at Amy's end. "I don't know where to start. I'll have to have some of everything."

Reid strapped Beebee into her high chair then took a seat next to Tara. Nina noticed he quietly motioned for Daisy to sit at his feet under the table and couldn't help wishing she had a dog to help to finish her plate.

"Some of the salads were left over from yesterday," Amy explained. "But they're still good."

"I'm sure they are," Nina said, helping herself.

"Would you like a hamburger?" Tara passed the plate.

"Thank you." Nina smiled at her. "They look delicious."

Beebee stretched out her hand for a hamburger and Nina glanced at Amy. Amy shook her head.

"It won't hurt her," Reid said. "A growing child needs iron and protein."

"She gets all the nutrients she needs," Amy insisted and put a hard-boiled egg on Beebee's plate. Beebee glanced at the egg with disdain then imperiously swept it onto the floor. Daisy pounced and the egg was gone in one gobble.

"When do you start work on the movie, Amy?" Nina said, pretending that hadn't just happened.

"Filming starts on Monday." Amy filled her plate with salad. "I have to be there at 6:00 a.m. so I'll have to leave by 5:00 to catch the bus."

Reid tackled a plate piled high with a sample of everything on the table. "What are you going to do with Beebee while you're on the set?"

"I…I was going to talk to you about that." Amy toyed with a lettuce leaf on the end of her fork. She seemed to be having a hard time looking him in the eye. "I'll put her in day care but I might need someone to take her there since I have to leave so early."

"Who would that someone be, do you suppose?" he asked rhetorically. "Since you don't want anything more to do with *me*."

"I don't know," she said miserably.

He let her stew for another minute. Nina tried unsuccessfully to catch his eye and was about to kick him under the table when he added in a kinder tone, "Amy, I'll gladly do anything for you and Beebee. But don't you think Beebee would find a whole day in child care awfully long?" Reid looked to his other daughter. "Maybe Tara could babysit?"

"No way!" Tara immediately protested. "I want to take a Manga course at the community center. It starts next week, too."

"Manga?" Reid repeated, frowning. "Not another activity. I'm not happy with the way you've let your violin practice slide."

"But Manga's so cool," Tara said. "I love the art-work."

"I have vacation time coming up," Nina broke in. "I'd be willing to look after Beebee at my place." Willing? She'd kill for the chance to spend time with her granddaughter. She offered Beebee a piece of cheese, which the little girl accepted with an angelic smile then deliberately dropped to the floor. Below the table, Daisy's jaws shut with an audible clack.

"Do you know anything about looking after a small child?" Reid asked doubtfully. "It's not as easy as you might think."

"I'm perfectly capable of looking after a toddler for a few weeks," Nina said, bristling. "How hard can it be, especially since Beebee's my own flesh and blood?" Already she could see herself bonding with Beebee, becoming a surrogate mother to the little girl, discovering the joy of parenting she hadn't had with Amy.

"That's awfully nice of you to offer," Amy said, then added bravely, "I'd pay you of course."

"Nonsense. It would be my pleasure," Nina assured her.

"You can't take Beebee to live in the city, away from familiar surroundings," Reid said firmly. "She's had enough changes in the past month. Where would she run around? How could she play at the beach?"

"She doesn't even like the water," Nina argued. "And if she did, I'm only a block from English Bay. There are parks and beaches galore within walking distance."

"Is your apartment baby-proof?" Reid demanded.

"Well, no." Anything but, Nina mentally added, thinking of the expensive glass ornaments and numerous objects that could hurt or be damaged by an inquisitive and energetic toddler. She could pack them away but Reid did have a point; there wasn't much room for Beebee to run around in the second-floor apartment she rented in a house on Pacific Drive. The owners lived on the main floor and had exclusive use of the backyard. Plus they were elderly and might not fancy having a baby around. Nina cringed inwardly at the thought of Beebee and her piercing scream. "I suppose I could commute between here and Vancouver."

"Or we could trade places," Amy suggested excitedly. "You move into my room here and I'll stay in your apartment. It would save us both a lot of time."

"I don't know how Reid would feel about that," Nina said, glancing at him.

"If it means Beebee remains here then it's fine," he replied.

Nina was silent. Could she really bring herself to stay in Reid's house after all the heartache they'd caused each other? She was afraid, she realized suddenly. Afraid of the glimmer of attraction she still felt for him. In spite of everything, she idealized Reid, viewing their love affair through the filter of a young girl's memory. But she'd grown and changed. Moved on. He had, too. He'd loved and married another woman. He hadn't pined his life away for her.

"You'd be the one caring for Beebee," Reid added. "I have to finish this book. You wouldn't see much of me."

"That," said Nina dryly, "could be a blessing."

"I don't know," Amy said. "I'll miss Beebs too much. I've never been apart from her for more than a day."

"You can come out on the weekends or whenever you have time off," Nina said. "I could bring her in to see you."

"Don't I get a say?" Tara demanded. "I live here, too."

Nina, Reid and Amy turned to look at her. As if uncomfortable with the attention now that she had it, Tara blustered, "The kid wakes me up early every morning. She makes a huge mess that I end up cleaning half the time. There's baby junk all over the downstairs bathroom and toys cluttering up the living room…." She trailed away, as if aware she sounded petty.

"I'll try to keep her out of your way," Nina said.

"Beebee's your niece," Reid admonished Tara gently. "You could be a little more flexible."

"She adores *you*," Amy said.

"That's because I give her meat," Tara retorted, still prickly. "She'll go to anyone who feeds her."

Silence fell. Nina gazed at the faces around the table. Tara was disgruntled; Amy, worried; Reid, brooding. There was no way out of the trouble brewing but to ignore the difficulties and plow ahead as if the matter were settled.

"For goodness sakes, it's not that big a problem," Nina declared and before anyone could raise further objections, she added, "Sunday I'll come and get Amy and Beebee. We'll visit my parents then Amy'll move into my apartment and I'll move out here."

"HELLO! MOM, DAD?" Nina knocked and entered her parents' house, grateful to feel a waft of cool air from their new air-conditioner hit her cheeks after coming out of the blazing sun. Enticing aromas of cinnamon and sugar filled the house. "Come on," she called to Amy, climbing the steps with Beebee in her arms.

Dora hurried out of the kitchen, still wearing a flour-dusted apron and drying her hands on a tea towel. "Nina, is that you?" Then she saw Amy and Beebee and she stopped still, her hand to her chest. "Oh my. You must be Amy." Dora blinked back tears as she came forward, arms outstretched to hug her grand-daughter.

Amy returned her hug warmly. "Nina's told me so much about you, I feel I know you already."

"Then you can tell us all about yourself," Dora said. "Come in. I've just made a coffee cake." Beebee had been watching Dora solemnly through this exchange. Now Dora turned to her and smiled. "This little doll must be Beebee."

"Dolly!" Beebee held up her soft toy for Dora to see.

"Come to Great-grandma," Dora said, pulling Beebee from Amy's arms.

"She makes strange," Amy warned quickly. Nina covered her ears.

"You won't make strange for your great-grandma, will you?" Dora said to Beebee and sure enough Beebee nestled happily into her arms. "Come see what I've got in the kitchen," Dora said, carrying her into the other room. "Do you like cookies? I made some just for you. Great-grandma's a mouthful for a little snip like you. You can call me Grammy." She paused her running commentary to call out, "Leo! The girls are here."

Leo came in from outside and gave Amy a hug then held her at arm's length to study her. "You're the spitting image of Nina when she was your age. But it's more than just coloring. You have the same smile, the same expression in your eyes. Amazing."

"Genetics covers a lot of ground, doesn't it, Dad?" Nina murmured. "She talks as much as me, too."

"Oh, no," Leo groaned with a twinkle in his eye. "That'll make three generations of yakkers."

"Cookie!" Beebee said suddenly. "Dolly want cookie. Dolly hungry. Me hungry, too."

"Say please, Beebee," Amy reminded her.

"Make that four generations," Leo added with a long-suffering expression.

"Sit down," Dora urged. "Have something to eat. Amy, you look like you're starving."

"Watch out," Nina said to Amy as they took their places around a table loaded with coffee cake, cookies and lemonade. "She'll have you fattened up in no time."

The small kitchen was crowded but no one seemed to mind. Amy ate two pieces of coffee cake and managed between bites to answer Dora and Leo's many questions about her role as a film extra.

When a tentative query about Jim and Elaine met with a cool reply, Leo tactfully changed the subject. "If you're done eating, do you want to bring Beebee outside?" he said to Amy. "I've rigged up a swing in the old plum tree in the backyard."

"That sounds like fun, doesn't it, Beebee?" Amy brushed the crumbs off Beebee into the sink and followed Leo out the back door.

Nina stayed behind with her mother and cleared dishes off the table. Setting a pile of side plates on the counter, she gazed through the window at Amy sitting on the swing holding Beebee in her arms while Leo pushed. Beebee's belly laugh could be heard across the yard.

"Beebee's adorable and Amy's lovely," Dora said, joining her. "And you were worried Amy wouldn't like you."

"It's turned out better than I expected," Nina admitted. "On the surface, at least. I sense that Amy is troubled about me giving her up as a baby but she hasn't said anything. I'm afraid to bring it up and ruin our rapport."

"Give yourself time," Dora advised. "Build a relationship before you tackle heavy issues." She paused as she ran hot water into the sink to wash the dishes. "How's Reid?"

Nina picked up a tea towel. "He's fine. You could have warned me Amy was staying with him."

"Is he still handsome?" Dora asked, throwing her a glance.

"Yes," Nina admitted. "More than ever." More assured, more mature, more sexy, more everything.

Dora rinsed a glass and put it in the draining tray. "Maybe you and he will take up where you left off."

"Not likely!" Nina dismissed her mother's suggestion with a short laugh. "We've been apart for nearly twenty years. He's been married and I've had other relationships."

"None that counted for very much," Dora said. "You've said so yourself."

"True," Nina conceded, placing the glass she'd just dried in the cupboard. "But whatever Reid and I had is over."

"Well, I think it's a pity," Dora said mildly. "You two used to be so much in love. Now that you're both older and wiser you might be able to resolve your differences and get together again."

Nina faced her mother, ignoring the growing cluster of dripping glasses in the draining tray. "Some things are too big to be resolved. He didn't seem to care about Amy when I was pregnant with her, at least not till it was too late. But as soon as the Hockings took responsibility, he wanted to be part of her life. He got to see Amy as she was growing up. He had visits and photos, spent birthdays with her and holidays. In all that time he never contacted me even to say that he'd seen her and that she was well and happy. How do I forgive him for that?"

Dora's gentle eyes filled with sadness. "Oh Nina. You gave Amy up for adoption even after Reid asked you to marry him. I know his mother pressured you into it but you could have fought to get her back even after you'd signed the papers. Did it never occur to you that maybe he found it impossible to forgive *you?*"

CHAPTER FIVE

REID SETTLED INTO his high-back leather chair and booted up the computer. He'd deleted the scene where Luke was being tortured but he still had to figure out a way to get Luke out of the warehouse when the place was surrounded by enemy soldiers. The soldiers knew he was in there and were biding their time, playing cat and mouse with him. Luke had to make his move soon or he'd be too weak from loss of blood to even crawl. The heating ducts? No, there wouldn't be a heating system in a warehouse. The roof? Again, no. Soldiers were stationed on all the surrounding buildings.

Nina ought to be back soon from taking Amy to her apartment, he thought, looking at the clock in the computer's toolbar. Then she would move in here with her shampoo in the shower, her lingerie in the laundry and her laughter lingering in the air. He wasn't quite sure how was going to handle her living in his house. She wasn't even in residence yet and already she was distracting him.

Forcing his fingers to move, he typed the first thing

that came to his mind. *The cat sat on the mat. Matt sat on the cat. The cat scratched Matt...*.

At his feet, Daisy raised her muzzle from his bare toes and let out a deep woof. Suddenly she got up and, nudging open the door with her muzzle, loped from the room, her nails clicking on the hardwood floor.

"Shut the door," he yelled but as usual Daisy paid no attention. A moment later he heard Nina talking to the dog. Her voice seemed to have a magnetic effect on Reid, drawing him out of his chair, out of his office and into the family room.

Seeing him, Nina made shooing movements with her hands. "Go back to work. Just pretend I'm not here."

As if. Reid glanced around. "Where's Beebee?"

Nina smiled brightly. "Beebee's still in the car."

"Is she refusing to come out?" Reid asked, noting the strained sound in Nina's voice. "She does that sometimes." Reid had *known* something like this would happen. He almost felt sorry for Nina except that he was going to have to bail her out again. "You've got to learn to deal with her," he remonstrated. "She needs to be shown gently but firmly who's—"

"I *am* dealing with her." Nina moved past him toward the kitchen, a light floral scent wafting in her wake. "Just return to work and don't worry about a thing. I'm going straight back out to her. And before you say anything about leaving her in a hot car, I've got the air conditioning on."

Reid watched her walk swiftly away from him, her

hips and legs outlined against the light coming through the French doors in the family room. Tearing his gaze away, he walked in the opposite direction, to the front door.

"Don't you go to her," Nina warned. Even though she could no longer see him, she seemed to know what he was thinking. "*I'm* babysitting."

Reid stopped in the doorway and trained his gaze on the car. "You can't leave Beebee for more than a few minutes. She can unlock anything."

"Not the car's child lock, she can't," Nina said. He could hear her rummaging in the fridge.

Beebee's face and hands appeared against the back window. Already she was out of the car seat Nina had bought for her. Reid slipped his bare feet into a waiting pair of sandals, ready to give chase at a moment's notice. "Don't bet on her not figuring that out, too."

Nina came back with a handful of sliced salami and Daisy trotting hopefully at her heels. Ignoring Reid, Nina went back out to the car, aimed her electronic key and released the locks with a beep.

Beebee scooted to the other side of the car but Nina just stood there calmly holding out a slice of meat. "Come Beebee. Come and get some salami."

Reid had to hand it to Nina; she was resourceful. "Amy wouldn't like you doing that."

"Amy's not here," Nina said.

"Why don't you just open the door and pick her up?" Reid said.

"She'll scream and, frankly, I'm not in the mood." Nina waved the salami closer. "Here, Beebee."

The temptation proved too much for the toddler but she was canny, too. She slid across the leather seat, reached out the open door to snatch the salami out of Nina's hand and darted back into the safety of the car. Reid chuckled to himself at the way Nina's back stiffened. But she just held out another slice of meat and called softly, "Beebee, I've got lots more lovely salami."

Beebee eased over and reached out. Nina stepped backward one pace. Beebee paused, then slid forward a little farther. Nina leaned closer. Beebee's hand shot out and grabbed the meat before she retreated to the far side of the back seat. With the patience of David Attenborough luring the shy mountain gorilla from its leafy hideaway with a banana, Nina held out her last piece of salami.

Beebee was getting cocky now, Reid could see by the mischievous gleam in her eye as she slid boldly to the edge of the car seat. Before she could grab the meat, Nina grasped her by the hands and pulled her out onto the driveway then quickly shut the car door.

Triumphantly, Nina turned to Reid. "I told you I could get her out by myself."

"Don't look now," Reid said, chuckling. "But she's running away."

Nina whirled around. "That little monkey!"

She caught Beebee before she got near the road but it was humiliating having Reid stand there laughing at her. Of course as soon as Nina picked Beebee up, the girl opened her mouth and began to scream. Grim-faced, Nina marched up the steps, past a grinning Reid and into the house.

What now? She wasn't going to ask Reid for help again, not with him acting so superior. She went into Amy's room, shut the door and slid to the floor with her back against it. Opening her arms, she let Beebee go. The little girl dropped to the ground and carried on screaming. Her face turned red, then purple. Nina started to get worried. What if she had a seizure? She was just about to pick Beebee up when she noticed the child eyeing her during a pause for breath, as though checking to make sure Nina was paying attention.

"Oh, so that's your game." Nina stuck her fingers in her ears and made herself comfortable. "You're going to wear yourself out before you wear me out," she said conversationally. "You might as well save your breath."

Reid banged on the door. "What are you doing to her?"

"Teaching her a lesson. Go back to work."

"With this racket going on?" he muttered.

By the time Beebee stopped crying, Nina's nerves were worn to a thin frazzled edge. Finally the toddler lay on the floor, heaving deep sighs and hiccuping, making Nina feel like the wicked witch. Beebee gave one last sob of utter pathos, her gaze flicking again to Nina's to see if she'd noticed, then went limp.

"You're an actress, like your mom." Nina dragged

the unresisting child into her arms but it was like ma-
neuvering a sack of potatoes. "You should get an
Academy Award for that performance."

She smoothed damp tendrils of reddish hair away
from Beebee's face and saw that Beebee was asleep,
worn out by her tantrum. In spite of the aggravation
Nina's heart melted. Staggering to her feet, she lowered
Beebee into her crib. Then she pulled a light blanket over
the girl then tiptoed from the room.

Nina went down the hall to the kitchen and family
room. Reid's office door was firmly shut, letting her
know in no uncertain terms that he didn't want to be disturbed.

Nina put on a Norah Jones CD and made herself a
cup of coffee. She sipped it standing at the kitchen
counter, her gaze drifting repeatedly to Reid's closed
door. It seemed to challenge her. How could he sit by
himself in a small room all day with no one to talk to?
If it was her, she'd go crazy. He *must* need a break.
Surely if she brought him a cup of coffee he'd take a
few minutes to drink it and chat.

She poured another cup and added cream and two
sugars, just the way she remembered he liked it. She
was outside his office and raising her hand to knock
when the door swung open.

Reid's white T-shirt and khaki shorts set off his
deep tan and for a moment Nina just looked at him in
admiration. He seemed startled to see her then frowned
as if he wasn't quite sure who she was and what she
was doing in his house.

Nina offered him the cup of coffee. "I thought you might want a break."

His frown deepened. Silently he took the cup. Moving past her, he turned off the music and stared out at the bay while he absently sipped his drink.

Humph. Not even a thank you for the coffee. Undeterred, Nina came to stand beside him. "How's the writing going?"

"Huh? Oh, not so good," he admitted, blinking. "I got Luke out of the warehouse but he's cornered in an alley surrounded by enemy soldiers."

"Why don't you give him one of those things that hook onto the tops of buildings so he can pull himself out of danger," Nina suggested.

Reid shook his head. "He's afraid of heights. He'd never do that."

"Right, I forgot," Nina said. "That's the weakness that always gets him into trouble."

Reid threw her one of his quirky close-mouthed smiles. "You read my books."

"One or two," she replied casually before falling silent to ponder Luke's situation. "I know! A beautiful woman dressed as an enemy solider marches him out of the alley under the noses of his would-be captors. They think she's one of them but really she's a double agent."

"I suppose Luke falls madly in love with her," Reid added dryly.

"Well, why not?" Nina huffed. "I've always thought you needed a love interest in your stories. You might get more women readers."

His eyebrows rose as he considered the possibility. He paced away, head down, then stopped to look out the window again. Nina had a feeling his gaze was focused inward, not on the beach. "They could have wild, animal sex, their passion fueled by the atmosphere of danger," she added.

Reid turned, eyes alight. "Not a bad idea."

The way he said it made her think for a moment that he meant him and her. The thought of wild, animal sex with Reid almost made Nina spill her coffee. Until she realized he was already striding back to his office and shutting the door behind him.

"Do I get an acknowledgment?" she called. Then sighed at the futility of trying to communicate while he was working. She might still feel the attraction but Reid was oblivious to everything but his book.

Alone again, Nina prowled the room, wondering what to do. She couldn't even take a walk on the beach in case Beebee woke up. Checking the kitchen clock, she saw the toddler had been asleep for an hour. She'd also slept in the car on the way home from the city. If she had too much nap time she'd take forever to settle tonight.

Nina crept into Beebee's room. The curtains were drawn and the light was dim. She glanced at the crib and her heart dropped to her stomach. Oh, no, Beebee had escaped again! Then Nina heard a sound and spun around.

Beebee was seated on the carpet next to the dresser, rummaging through the contents of Nina's makeup bag. Powder dusted the little girl's blue-and-white striped dress. Her mouth, cheeks and chin were smeared with lipstick. She was trying to open Nina's compact case of different eyeshadows. "Beebee, no!"

Beebee looked over her shoulder at Nina and a guilty smile played over her face. Seeing Nina's horrified expression, Beebee's grin turned impish. Her tiny fingers plucked feverishly at Nina's case, endeavoring to open it before Nina got to her.

Nina approached with caution. Was Beebee getting back at her for letting her scream? How much cunning did toddlers possess? Nina was starting to see Beebee as a small wild animal, not dangerous so much as unpredictable. Possibly untamable.

"Beebee, give me the case." Nina spoke firmly while advancing slowly, hand outstretched.

Beebee crawled a little farther away and sat down facing away from Nina, still trying to open the case. If she succeeded in digging her tiny fingers into the soft lavenders and grays and smearing them over the pale carpet… It didn't bear thinking about.

Nina gave up waiting for Beebee to hand over the eyeshadow and lunged, grabbing the case and trying to wrest it away. The toddler's grasp was surprisingly strong. Beebee opened her mouth as if to scream until Nina gave her a stern look and she seemed to think better of it. Perhaps the child was capable of a rudimentary form of learning after all.

Having regained possession of the compact case, Nina quickly stuffed the rest of the scattered cosmetics back into her makeup bag. It was astonishing how much was involved in handling a small child and how lacking she was in the appropriate skills. She discovered a newfound respect for mothers. Her friends' children always stayed in the background during dinner parties, coming out only to say good-night in their jammies, all clean and cute and well-behaved. Was it only she who lurched from one mini-crisis to the next?

She scooped up the miscreant and bore her off to the bathroom where she wiped the lipstick and powder off Beebee's face. Then she carried her back to the family room. "What do you want to do now?"

Beebee imperiously flung an arm straight ahead, pointing at the beach, visible through the long wide windows. "Beach!"

"Okay, the beach, it is."

Nina found Beebee's pink two-piece bathing suit. "I've got one almost exactly the same," she said, ridiculously pleased. "We can be twins."

And although she'd never understood mothers who dressed themselves and their daughters the same, Nina felt an undeniable pride and delight in walking onto the beach hand in hand with Beebee in matching pink bikinis.

REID FROWNED AT THE MONITOR, stuck again. A female spy was all very well but what kind of woman would bowl over a cool customer like Luke Mann? She'd have to be smart, for sure. Spies needed to be nondescript so as not to draw attention to themselves so she couldn't be beautiful. What the hey, this was his story, he could do what he liked. She would be blond, he decided, with deep blue eyes and a dimple in her right cheek when she smiled.

Movement outside drew his attention away from the screen. Nina and Beebee were going down to the beach wearing what appeared to be matching pink bikinis. Reid suddenly had trouble swallowing over a lump in his throat as an image of himself and Nina as a young married couple with their little girl popped into his mind. If only...

What? Wipe out Tara and Carol as if they'd never existed? He couldn't even if he wanted to, which he didn't, not in a million years.

And yet...

His gaze was drawn back to Nina. She'd dropped over the retaining wall and had turned around to offer a hand to Beebee. His breath caught at the fullness of Nina's breasts, the slender lines of her waist, the gentle flare of her hips—

Wait a minute. What was that small circular object above her right hip? It didn't look like a scar and he didn't recall her having a birthmark. Reid squinted but the thing was too small to see clearly at this distance. He reached for the binoculars he kept on the bookshelf for bird-watching and trained them on Nina.

Damn. She'd gotten Beebee down and was walking away. No, she was coming back for the plastic shovel Beebee had dropped. Reid stood up, adjusting the lenses to bring the smooth skin above her pelvis into clear view. The mark definitely hadn't been there when he'd know her last. It was…a tattoo. A tattoo of…a red rose.

Reid dropped the binoculars from his eyes. A rose. That was *their* flower. Not just any roses, either. Red roses, the color of passion and true love. He'd given her a single red rose on their first date, six roses on their one-month anniversary of going out, eight on her birthday as a stand-in for eighteen, which he couldn't afford, and a whole dozen when she'd been in the hospital having Amy.

After Nina, he'd never been able to give Carol, or any other woman, roses. Carol's flower had been freesia, sweetly scented, delicate and fragile, wilting easily.

He noticed suddenly that Nina's gaze had shifted and she was looking straight at him. Reid quickly trained his binoculars on a clump of cattails in the marshes behind the dike, trying to make it appear as if that's what he'd been looking at all along.

She must have had the tattoo put on after they'd broken up. So she must have still been in love with him in spite of the hateful words they'd flung at each other in the hospital. Years later did she regret letting him under her skin, so to speak, or did she still have feelings for him?

Thoughtfully, Reid put away the binoculars. He sat at his computer and began to type.

Maria was a natural blond with striking blue eyes but to Luke her most intriguing feature was the rose tattooed above her right hip....

WAS REID SPYING ON HER? Nina glanced over her shoulder to double check but he'd swung the binoculars over to the pumping station on the dike. That man looked for inspiration in the most unlikely places.

Nina took Beebee's hand and led her to the path through the rocks. Beebee stopped to investigate a crab that had scuttled beneath a rock. Nina crouched to look, too, but her mind wasn't on the tiny crustacean.

If Nina had known where Amy's adopted parents lived, would *she* have moved to Halifax and maintained a connection with Jim and Elaine Hocking so she could watch her daughter grow up? Or would she have been too afraid of the pain she would feel every time she said goodbye? Too cowardly to watch her baby girl call another woman Mommy?

Nina had to give Reid credit—he'd had a lot of guts to put himself through that year after year. Not only that but he'd uprooted himself from his parents and moved clear across the country to be near Amy.

Beebee turned over the rock with her plastic shovel. Half a dozen small crabs scurried through the film of seawater to burrow into the mud below neighboring rocks. Beebee's face glowed with surprise and delight. She prodded Nina's arm, wanting to share this amazing sight. "Cabs!"

"Crabs," Nina agreed. She lifted another rock and

captured one of the tiny crustaceans. "Hold out your hand," she said and dropped the creature in Beebee's flat palm.

The crab ran up Beebee's wrist. The little girl squealed with excitement and the crab dropped back to the safety of the rocks. "We have to put all the rocks back where they were because they're the roofs of the crabs' houses," Nina explained, fitting the rocks back into their hollows.

Nina rose and took Beebee's hand and continued down the path through the rocks toward the shallows. At the first splash across her toes, Beebee balked. "No!"

"But Beebee, sweetheart, the water is nice," Nina said, freely perspiring in the heat of the blazing sun. She gazed longingly at the stretch of water deep enough to cool off in, tantalizingly out of reach beyond the next sandbar. "Just try it. For Nina?"

Beebee shook her head, mulishly thrusting out her bottom lip and frowning. "Beebee play in sand."

"Fine," Nina said, giving up. She glanced toward the house but there was no sight of Reid at the window.

She hoped he hadn't witnessed her retreat up the beach in the face of Beebee's opposition. He already believed she didn't know how to look after children and, foolish or not, what he thought mattered to her.

She might not be able to cure Beebee of her fear of water overnight, she mused, settling onto the blanket to watch Beebee dig. But with patience she might get there. In the meantime she would do her best to prove in other ways that she was capable of being a good mother.

Not just to Reid but to herself.

CHAPTER SIX

Luke was so entranced by the rise and fall of the
rose tattoo on Maria's hip as she walked naked
toward him that he forgot she was a double agent.
Slowly he unbuckled his belt and dropped his
pants. In doing so he committed the cardinal sin
of an intelligence officer—he let down his guard.

REID SAVED HIS WORK, feeling both exhilarated and exhausted, as though he'd run a marathon. Usually it
took him all day to grind out ten pages. He'd just done
fourteen pages in three hours, a record for him.

Introducing Maria had added a new and exciting
element to his story. Unfortunately for the free world,
hanging out with Maria was proving to be more interesting to Luke than completing his mission. Sure he'd
escaped the warehouse but he'd missed the rendezvous
with his contact in the French government.

The next installment would have to wait until
tomorrow. Reid shut down the computer and emerged
from his office, his stomach growling and his mind on
the smells of cooking coming from the kitchen.

Nina was stirring a pot on the stove. She'd put shorts on but still wore her bikini top. Reid winced at the painful-looking burn on her back and shoulders. "There's aloe-vera gel in the bathroom."

"I already helped myself." She nodded at the bottle on the counter.

Reid came closer to see what she was stirring. "What's for dinner?"

"Broccoli soup," she said. "You were right, Amy wouldn't like me feeding Beebee meat. I'm going to cook nothing but vegetarian meals while I'm here."

Broccoli soup. Ugh. The milky green-flecked goop in the pot reminded Reid of cow's cud. Would his resolution to eat more healthily be sufficient incentive to make him force this down?

"You don't have to cook," Reid said. "You have enough to do looking after Beebee. Tara and I are used to feeding ourselves and one or two extra is nothing."

"It's no trouble," Nina assured him. "I'm so busy at work that I eat out a lot. I kind of like playing house."

The scene did have all the traditional domestic trappings, Reid thought. The woman in the kitchen, the baby at her feet playing with pots and pans, the man arriving from work. Beebee gave him a toothy grin and banged the spoon on the bottom of a pot.

Nina seemed to realize it at the same time and laughed awkwardly. "Appearances can be deceiving, can't they? Looking at us now, anyone would think...but we're not."

"No, we're not." His eyes met hers. What was *she* thinking?

Nina flushed and turned back to the stove. The skin on her back where she'd applied the gel was slightly shiny but the area between her shoulder blades was a dull flaming red.

"You missed a spot with the aloe vera," he said. "I'll get it for you."

She made a sound of protest, which Reid ignored. He picked up the bottle and squirted gel on his hand. Nina's hands stilled on the pot she was stirring, as if she was holding her breath. He hesitated a moment then placed his fingers on her hot burned skin. He felt her shrink at the sudden coolness then relax as he began to spread the soothing gel.

It felt good to touch her, bringing back memories of that first summer on the beach. Hot days. Hotter nights. The patch of bare skin was now well covered but his hand lingered on her back, smoothing and re-smoothing the slippery gel. For over a decade Reid had thrust regrets over losing Nina from his mind. All possibilities for them had ended when he'd married Carol.

"Do you think we'd still be together today if we'd kept Amy and raised her ourselves?" she asked, uncannily echoing the direction of his thoughts.

He paused, his eyebrows lifting in surprise. "What makes you ask that?"

"I don't know. Just thinking."

"About what?" He resumed stroking her back, moving his hands in leisurely circles.

Unconsciously mirroring his actions, she stirred the pot ever more slowly. "People, how they change and grow. Relationships, how love fades…or deepens, depending." She hesitated, then asked, "Do you think you've changed over the years?"

"Well, I have to run and work out to keep in shape, I'm getting the odd gray hair—"

"No, I meant, who you are inside?" she said.

"The essence of who I am is the same," he replied thoughtfully. "I understand myself better. Over time and with experience, I've gained perspective."

"In other words, you've learned something from your misspent youth," she said lightly. After a pause she added, "So what do you think? Would we have gone the distance?"

Reid's fingers fell away from her back and curled into his palm. One thing he believed with the utmost certainty—if Nina hadn't given up Amy, if she'd married him, nothing could have made him leave her.

He hesitated too long. Nina turned the heat down and moved away from the stove. "Maybe we weren't really in love," she said. "Maybe it was just puppy love."

Puppy love scampered away at the next infatuation; it didn't linger quietly, infusing memory with a bittersweet mixture of joy and pain. Feelings that had lain dormant for years tugged at Reid's heart. But he couldn't bring himself to speak them aloud.

"Let's try a different question," he countered, watching her take soup bowls out of the cupboard. "If we met for the first time now, would we fall in love?"

"But we're not meeting for the first time." Tucking

the bowls in her arm, with her other hand she gathered a fistful of cutlery from the drawer and went to the table. "We've got truckloads of baggage, not to mention that we were always very different from each other. If anything, the differences are more accentuated now that we've matured."

"So in your mind," he said, feeling his way, "we wouldn't fall in love if we met today and if we'd married years ago we would have grown apart?" He wasn't sure what he wanted from her—a denial or a confirmation.

"I didn't say that." She moved away from him around the table, distributing bowls and dropping spoons and knives haphazardly.

Reid followed, placing the dishes at an even distance from the edge of the table. "How *do* you feel?"

Nina stopped short and faced him, close enough to touch but her blue eyes were wary. "What do you want me to say, Reid? That there's still an attraction between us?"

"There's only one way to find out." Before he could think twice, he kissed her. The spoon he was holding fell out of his hand and clattered onto the table and the hard rims of the bowls she clutched dug into his abdomen. He felt the incredible softness of her lips and the heat radiating from her sunburned cheek. Years slipped away and he was twenty again. Passion flamed with astonishing swiftness as the kiss deepened, breathtaking in its sweetness and intensity.

Finally Nina drew back with a gasp. Reid blinked, slightly startled to find himself in his ordinary surroundings—the vase of marigolds on the counter that Tara had picked yesterday, Beebee banging the wooden spoon on an upturned pot, the hot breeze floating in through the open window bringing with it the smell of the sea.

Nina, wide-eyed, lips still parted, looked as shell-shocked as he felt. "What was *that?*"

Reid rubbed the back of his neck. "I think we just raised a whole new set of what-ifs."

"Oh, no we didn't." Nina recovered with a brisk shake of her head and pushed past him, almost throwing down the rest of the bowls. "I'm here to take care of Beebee, not to dredge up the past."

"That kiss was very much in the present." Reid put a hand on her shoulder, turning her. "Did you, or did you not, feel something just now?"

"What I felt isn't the point," Nina said as she broke free again. "The situation is difficult enough without complicating it by us getting romantically involved. You had Amy's early years, which I will never have, and spending time with Beebee shows me with heartbreaking clarity how much I missed. A kiss, no matter how hot and soul-stirring, is not going to resolve those issues."

"So we'll ignore what just happened between us, is that it?" Reid demanded.

Beebee, sensing the tension, began to cry. Reid picked her up.

"Look at what our arguing is doing to her," Nina said. "We can't resume a flawed relationship while we're responsible for our granddaughter. What if things went wrong again? We can't risk letting our personal problems interfere with our ability to care for Beebee." Nina turned away, touching the heel of her hand to her eye. "Let's just keep it simple, shall we?"

Reid found a tissue and wiped away Beebee's tears. On a multitude of levels, he agreed with Nina's assessment; he didn't know why it annoyed him so much to hear her say it.

"Is dinner ready?" Tara said, coming into the room.

"Yes," Nina said. "Could you finish setting the table, please?"

Reid strapped Beebee into her high chair then took his place at the table. Nina ladled out the thick green broccoli soup. Tara turned her disbelieving gaze on Reid as if to say, *Do we have to eat this?*

Reid gave her a helpless shrug and picked up his spoon. His mind wasn't on the green goop; he was thinking about what Nina had said. *Hot. Soul-stirring.* Knowing how she felt, how was he supposed to keep things simple?

He concentrated instead on tasting his soup and, just as he'd feared, had difficulty swallowing. Doggedly he persisted. He was Luke Mann being fed indigestible swill in a foreign prison. Words and phrases formed in his mind to describe the experience so he could later put them on paper.

"You're very quiet," Nina commented into the

silence, glancing from Reid to Tara. "Do you like the soup?"

"If green was a flavor, this would be it," Tara muttered.

"I'm sure it's very nutritious," Reid added politely. He wiped Beebee's mouth with the damp cloth lying on her tray. She alone was eating with gusto. Baffling were the vagaries of taste.

Tara took another spoonful then pushed her bowl away. "I'm not very hungry."

"I heard you playing your violin today, Tara," Nina said. "You're very good. Are you in the school band?"

"Orchestra."

"I played the trumpet for a while when I was in school," Nina went on. "I had some idea I would be the next Louis Armstrong and form a jazz band." She laughed. "Turned out it was a lot harder than I thought. I really admire anyone who can master a musical instrument."

Reid waited for Tara to make some response to this. When she remained mute, he gave her a quick frown and said to Nina, "Tara's been studying violin for eight years."

Nina glanced at Tara, who was looking down at her bowl. "Does anyone want any more soup?"

"I'm full," Reid said, patting his stomach.

"No, thank you." Tara rose and took her bowl to the sink. "Dad, could you drive me to the mall? I, uh, need a few things from the drugstore."

Reid eyed her innocent expression, certain this was

a ruse. If so, he was prepared to go along with it. Sure enough, instead of heading for the pharmacy, Tara begged him to take her to the Dairy Queen. A half hour later, he and Tara were tucking into cheeseburgers and fries. For a few blissful moments, life really was simple.

"That soup was disgusting!" Tara exclaimed between hungry mouthfuls. "I almost gagged."

"Don't you dare tell Nina we came here tonight," Reid warned. "We don't want to hurt her feelings."

"Just because Amy's a vegetarian doesn't mean *we* have to eat green slime." Tara stuffed a French fry into her mouth and gave vent to more complaints. "Nina's always talking! When she's not singing along to the radio, that is. She never stops trying to make conversation with me. She makes Beebee scream."

"She's trying to be friendly to you and a good carer for Beebee," Reid replied. "Cut her some slack."

"I just want everything to go back to normal," Tara said plaintively. "I want Amy and Beebee to disappear and Nina to go back where she came from. You and I never have any time together anymore."

"We're here, now," Reid reminded her.

"I know." Tara broke off a piece of bun and squashed it between her fingers. "But I miss the evenings when it was just you and me watching TV or reading or playing cards."

Reid made a noncommittal movement of his head. He could argue that their lives had been *too* quiet. That they needed shaking up a little. Still, she was correct that the times they spent together had become less frequent. "Amy's my daughter, too. She and Beebee are part of our lives."

"What about Nina?" Tara asked sullenly. "Is she back in your life, too?"

"She doesn't want a place in my life." For some reason that made him feel a bit testy.

"I wouldn't make any bets on that. I've seen the way she looks at you when she knows you're not watching," Tara said then added, "You still like her, don't you?"

"Sure I like her," Reid said. Nina looked at him? He would have liked to question Tara further but he knew he couldn't.

"As a friend or something more?" Tara demanded.

The white-hot chemistry between them still existed; their kiss this afternoon had proved that. *Would* they fall in love if they were unencumbered by old emotional baggage? He couldn't honestly say. Her giving Amy up for adoption, him accepting her refusal to marry, had changed their lives forever.

Reid shrugged. "Friends."

His comment seemed to be the reassurance Tara was looking for because she went on to the other subject currently preoccupying her. "Have you thought about the Manga workshop at the community center starting next week? I'd really like to take it."

"What about your violin? You should be practicing for your Conservatory of Music exam," Reid said. "Today is the first time in days that you've played."

"I can do both," Tara insisted.

"I know you," Reid said. "Once you take on a new hobby, you get obsessed."

"The way you are with your writing, you mean?" Tara countered.

Reid chose to ignore that. "Remember when you took up scrapbooking? You spent so much time at it you almost failed your grade six violin."

"So?"

"So, your mother set a lot of store by your music," Reid reminded her. "She wanted you to get your teaching certificate. I thought you wanted that, too."

"I do," Tara insisted. "But I'm also interested in Manga. Some of the stories are really complex, about angels and demons and philosophical dilemmas." She fished in her shoulder bag and produced a well-thumbed Manga comic, which she slapped down on the table beside him. "You can't condemn it until you read it."

Reid recognized his own words being thrown back at him, the ones he'd used to convince Tara to read Charles Dickens. "Okay, I'll have a look at it when I finish my book." He glanced at his watch. "Right now we'd better get home. Beebee will be ready for bed and she likes me to read her bedtime story."

Tara made a big slurping sound at the bottom of her milkshake to express her displeasure. "Yeah, sure. Anything for the kid."

NINA UNDRESSED BEEBEE and stood her in the dry bathtub so she could sponge her down. Wiping broccoli soup out from between fingers as small and flexible as cooked macaroni wasn't easy but not as traumatic as what she was doing now—tipping cupfuls of warm water over Beebee's head to get the green stuff out of her hair.

Beebee pushed fretfully at the cup, splashing the contents over Nina, soaking her pale pink cotton blouse.

"Beebee!" Nina wailed. "You are going to learn to love water or—"

"Or what?" Reid poked his head through the open bathroom door, took one look at Nina, dripping with water, and chuckled.

"I see you and Tara are back from the mall." Nina's gaze flickered over him. "Is that ketchup on your shirt?"

Glancing down, Reid rubbed at the reddish smudge. Instead of answering, he scooped up Beebee's dirty clothes. "Do you have anything you want washed? I'll put on a load of laundry before I read Beebee her story."

"I was going to read to her," Nina said. "You're working, right?"

"I'm finished for the day," Reid replied. "Although if you want to do the honors, go ahead."

But when Nina had Beebee all ready for bed, it was Reid the little girl wanted to read her a book. Nina tried not to feel hurt just because she'd spent the entire day looking after the child and not once had Beebee displayed a fraction of the affection she showed Reid.

Nina curled up in a white wicker chair with blue
cushions and leafed through a magazine, listening though
she was pretending not to. Reid had a distinctive voice,
low and a little rough. Glancing up as she flipped through
the pages, she studied his face. How could he not know
that she was attracted to him? And that kiss! She would
have to be on her toes over the next few weeks not to
spend too much time with him, or get too close. Finally,
she had her chance to be a mother and a grandmother;
she wasn't going to blow it by getting distracted by Reid.

"…and they all lived happily ever after." Reid
closed the book and stood up with Beebee in his arms.
"Time for bed, monkey-face."

Beebee giggled. "I not monkey."

"Yes, you are." He tossed her in the air and caught
her until she giggled and screamed with mirth. "You're
a funny little monkey."

Watching them, Nina smiled involuntarily. Reid
was a natural with children. But he was also getting
Beebee wound up. She glanced at her watch; half an
hour past the time Amy had said to put Beebee to bed.
Uncurling from the chair, she stood and reached out.
"Bedtime, Beebee."

The little girl clung to Reid. He shrugged apologetically. "Maybe I'd better put her to bed."

Covering her disappointment, Nina bent to kiss
Beebee on the top of her head, aware of Reid's hands
and his scent of skin and cotton and French fries
mingling with Beebee's baby shampoo. "Good-night,
Beebee," she whispered. "See you in the morning."

Reid started to carry Beebee away. "Oh, and Reid," Nina said. He paused. "Next time you go for a hamburger, take me with you."

He laughed and met her gaze. "Will do."

CHAPTER SEVEN

TARA RETREATED TO HER bedroom the next day after lunch with her sketch pad, a black Fineliner and a set of colored felt pens, and started copying one of the drawings in *Candy Candy,* one of her Manga books.

She'd just done a particularly tricky bit with the girl's eyes when she heard a knock at her door. Her ink-stained fingers stilled above the sketch pad. "Yes?"

"I've brought your clean laundry," Nina called. "May I come in?"

"I guess so." Tara was seated at her desk. As Nina pushed open the door, Tara leaned forward, moving her arm to cover her sketch pad.

Nina glanced over curiously as she placed the pile of folded tops and shorts on Tara's dresser. "What are you drawing? Is that your Manga?"

Trust Nina to barge in here and start poking around. Anyone with half a brain could see that Tara didn't want her gawking at her work. Tara said nothing and waited for her to leave.

Naturally Nina couldn't take a hint. "You've got great color sense," she rambled on, glancing from

Tara's teal-and-fuchsia bed linen to the black-and-fuchsia patterned curtains. She moved across to Tara's desk to pick up the Manga comic. "Is this what you're doing? May I see?"

Didn't this woman have a clue that she wasn't wanted? Grudgingly Tara moved her arm to reveal the picture of a big-eyed Manga girl with flowing yellow hair she was copying from the comic. "It's not very good."

Nina looked from Tara's drawing to the original. "Yes, it is. I think you have talent. Why don't you do your own?"

Tara just shrugged.

"I mean it," Nina continued in that phony encouraging voice. "You've got her face exactly right. You could write stories to go with them. That would make your dad happy."

Suddenly Tara was furious with Nina, sticking her nose in where she wasn't wanted. Telling Tara what to do with her life. "What do *you* know about making my dad happy? And why are you doing my laundry. You're not my mom."

Nina looked taken aback. "I know that. I was just trying to be helpful."

"Don't bother. You're not going to get anywhere with my dad by sucking up to me." The words seemed to jump out of Tara's mouth. Her pulse beat at a sickening rate. She was *never* rude to adults but she couldn't seem to help herself with Nina.

Nina's face fell. "What on earth do you mean?"

"Don't get any ideas about my dad," Tara said. "He's not looking for another wife. He's still in love with my mom." If he had to have friends, he should be hanging out with his guy friends like Rod who he played golf with sometimes, not taking up with an old girlfriend. Especially not *Nina*. Mom would have hated that.

Nina sat on Tara's bed, her face very serious. "I'm not trying to 'get' anywhere with your dad. I'm here to look after Beebee while Amy's away."

Sure she was. Tara had noticed her father was different when Nina was around, more animated, more talkative, almost flirtatious. Seeing him respond to Nina hurt. Tara wanted to squash any possibility of a romance before Nina got her hooks into him.

"My mom and dad were perfect for each other, like soul mates. Dad swore to me when she died that he'd never get married again because he'd never love anyone else the way he'd loved my mom." He'd never actually said that but who cared? Letting Nina know her place was more important than the strict truth.

"Your mother's death must have been terribly sad for you, too," Nina said. "I'm so sorry."

Her gentle voice triggered unexpected tears. Crap. Blinking furiously, Tara turned back to her drawing. A drop fell on her picture, smearing the color. "Shouldn't you be changing Beebee's diaper or something?"

"She's having a nap but you're right, I should go check on her." Nina rose and passed behind Tara, touching her shoulder lightly on her way to the door. "If you ever want to talk…"

"Thanks but no thanks." Hearing the door shut behind Nina, Tara tore the blotched page out of her sketchbook and crumpled it in her hand.

Nina made her way slowly down the stairs, disturbed by Tara's hostility and resentment. Somehow she needed to let the teenager know she wasn't a threat to her mother's memory. True, Reid had kissed her and she had responded in a way she hadn't experienced since, well, since he'd last kissed her over eighteen years ago. But according to Tara, Reid loved his wife deeply. He and Carol had had years in which to develop the companionship and lasting bond Nina had once dreamed of with Reid.

Feeling slightly depressed, Nina checked on Beebee, who was still napping, then made her way back to the family room. She sank onto the wicker couch and put her bare feet up on the coffee table, exhausted. A combination of broken sleep, running around after an active toddler and a diet of vegetables and rice had her worn out. She lay her head back on the cushion. She would just shut her eyes for a few minutes….

"White wine?" Reid asked, jolting her awake. He placed a chilled glass of rich golden liquid in her hand and set a plate of cheese and crackers on the coffee table.

"Am I dreaming?" Nina asked, sitting up and rubbing the sleep out of her eyes. Beebee was awake and playing with Daisy in the open space between the furniture and Reid's office. "Does Beebee need a change?"

"No to both," Reid said. "Sit back and relax."

Nina glanced at her watch. It was only four-thirty and Reid usually wrote until five. "You're not working?"

"It's Friday," he said, taking a piece of cheese and cracker. "We both deserve a break. I'll put on the barbecue and we can have a relaxing evening."

With a few sips of wine, Nina's fatigue slipped away. The thought of a thick juicy chunk of chargrilled meat had Nina salivating. Of course Reid might have meant barbecued vegetables and tofu but she prayed not.

Sure enough, when she picked up the plate of cheese and crackers and followed Reid to the kitchen a moment later, he was turning over two thick steaks in a marinade.

"What about Tara and Beebee?" Nina asked, savoring the smell of red wine and herbs. "Aren't they eating with us?"

"Tara and her friend Libby are upstairs but they're leaving soon to have dinner at Libby's house then they're going to a movie," he said. "I'll give Beebee something to eat more suitable to a person with six teeth."

Reid reached past Nina to put the fork in the sink and his bare forearm brushed hers, the warmth of his touch bringing back memories of yesterday's encounter. Nina moved to the other side of the kitchen, rubbing her arm to remove all trace of sensation. She'd insisted, rightly, on keeping romance out of the picture and she'd better stick to it. From a safe distance, she asked, "Can I do something to help?"

"Everything's taken care of." Reid poured a packet of prepared salad mix into a wooden bowl and got a bottle of dressing out of the fridge. He went back to the vegetable crisper for a bag of potatoes. "Amy called a little while ago to say she'd come out tomorrow."

"Beebee will be happy to see her after a hard week trying to train her grandmother." Nina perched on a bar stool and sliced off a small wedge of Brie.

"She was short with me on the phone," Reid said as he started to wrap the potatoes in foil. "Everything I do or say now seems to rub her up the wrong way."

"Give her time," Nina advised, though her heart went out to him. "She'll come around."

"I don't know," Reid said. "She hasn't budged on the Hockings."

"She's had a shock and cut herself off from everyone she's ever cared about," Nina said. "Her life is changing rapidly. Once she settles down again she'll see things differently."

"How can you be so sure?"

"Well, I guess I can't."

"I only ever wanted the best for her."

Nina shrugged helplessly. "I know."

Reid placed the potatoes in the oven and closed the oven door with the air of closing the subject as well.

"How's the book going?" Nina asked, taking his cue.

"Luke is headed in a new and unexpected direction," Reid said. "The story could turn out to be the best thing I've ever done or—" he gave a twisted smile "—it could be complete garbage."

"I doubt that," Nina said. "What's this new direction Luke's going in? It sounds intriguing."

"Sorry, I can't say," Reid told her. "Talking about it might kill the creative spark." He picked up his glass of wine. "Let's go outside. It's cooled down a touch."

Adirondack chairs were grouped around a wooden table on a paved patio to the right of the French doors. Daisy padded out after Reid and Beebee followed Daisy. Nina felt a welcome breeze caress her bare arms and lift her airy cotton dress. With a satisfied sigh she settled onto one of the cushioned chairs overlooking the bay. "This is nice."

"Dad?" Tara appeared in the doorway. "I'm going now. Bye."

"Tara," Reid called her back. "Have you introduced Libby to Nina?"

"It's okay," Nina said in an undertone.

Tara heaved a theatrical sigh. "Nina, this is Libby."

Libby, a plump girl with short brown hair, stepped out from behind Tara and waved. "Hi."

"Hello, Libby."

"Libby's taking the Manga course," Tara said to her father. "Can't I?"

"I'm still thinking about it," Reid said.

Tara made a face. "Come on, Libby. Let's go."

"Bye, Tara, Libby," Nina said. "You girls have fun at the movies."

"Yeah, whatever," Tara flipped a hand in a dismissive wave.

"I'm sorry." Reid frowned and shook his head as the pair disappeared. "She's a great kid, really. This whole business with Amy has thrown her off balance."

"You don't have to apologize for her," Nina said. "Tara's a lovely, talented girl." She hesitated. "My being here probably doesn't help."

"What do you mean?" Reid turned to look at her.

Nina hesitated. Should she tell Reid about Tara's outburst earlier that afternoon? If he confronted Tara, the girl would know Nina had gone to her father and think Nina was complaining or interfering instead of merely being concerned. "Nothing, I guess. Just that I sense she doesn't enjoy having strangers staying in her house."

"It'll do her good to interact with people more," Reid said. "I was pleased when she said she was seeing Libby tonight. She tends to keep to herself too much."

"Maybe you should spend more time with her," she suggested mildly. "She needs you more than you think."

"Tara's always been very self-sufficient. She knows exactly what she wants and where she's going."

"She's a teenager. Sometimes they lose their way," Nina said. Not that she was an expert but she did remember what it was like to be fifteen. "Why are you so against her doing the Manga course?"

"I'm worried she'll stop playing music," he replied. "Her mother set a lot of store on Tara going as far as she could with it. I know it should be up to Tara but I promised Carol I'd encourage her to keep it up."

Nina sipped her wine. "Tell me about your wife. What was she like?"

Reid stiffened at the question. Yet he ought to have expected it sooner or later. Being with Nina again had brought thoughts of Carol close to the surface; the contrast between the two women was so great. But how to reply without betraying Carol's memory?

"She wrote children's books under her maiden name, Carol Greene," he said at last. "Very good ones, well received. She won a Canadian Literature prize."

"I didn't know that," Nina said. "Is writing what drew you together?"

"Partly," Reid said. "I met her in a creative-writing class. Later we formed a writer's group who critiqued each other's work. She was a good partner. She knew what it was like to be a writer, you see. So she left me alone when I needed to work."

"Your professional lives meshed," Nina commented. "What was Carol like as a person?"

Reid's gaze was drawn to a teenage couple strolling across the sand to the water's edge. Their arms were linked around each other's waists, the boy's hand caressing the girl's hip as she leaned in to him. Then they stopped and turned to each other in a passion-filled kiss, hands roaming each other's bodies, oblivious to passing strangers. A vicarious surge of desire passed through Reid. He could almost taste Nina's lips, feel her warm skin.

Reid dragged his gaze back to the glass in his hand as he thrust away inappropriate thoughts. "Carol was a wonderful mother," he said. "A loving wife."

"She sounds lovely," Nina said lightly. "What else? Was she outgoing, reserved…what?"

He glanced at Nina. Her expression was composed but was that a tightening around her eyes that hadn't been there a few moments ago? Why was she asking these questions?

"Carol preferred to stay in the background, an observer rather than a doer," Reid said. "She held us together as a family. She was quiet and graceful… musical, too." He gave a self-deprecating chuckle. "Tara certainly doesn't get her talent in that arena from me."

Reid fell silent. There was more he could say, about Carol's insecurity and jealousy, the bouts of passive-aggression, the passion that never quite caught fire and gradually dwindled. How much of that was his fault for not loving her wholeheartedly? Carol's warmth and companionship made up for minor failings that were only human and entirely forgivable. Even though he'd tried not to let his past affect their marriage, she'd known he'd never gotten over Nina.

"Once you've experienced a really deep love and then lost it," Reid said, almost to himself, "it's difficult for anyone else to measure up."

Nina's sigh mingled with the cool onshore breeze

that moved the light fabric of her dress. "You must have loved her very much."

Startled, Reid realized she'd misinterpreted his words. He *had* loved Carol, but that's not who he'd been talking about just then. He was tempted despite himself to set Nina straight. The balmy evening, Nina's warmth and grace, the amorous couple on the beach, were all leading his thoughts in one direction. But if she knew what he felt about her, she'd run a mile.

He roused himself. "I'd better get those steaks on."

CHAPTER EIGHT

TARA EMERGED FROM HER bedroom and stood at the top of the stairs. Amy's tinkling laughter floated up, interspersed with Nina's constant interruptions and only the occasional low rumble from her dad. Yakkety, yak, yak! How Amy and Nina kept up that endless flow of conversation Tara had no idea. She was tempted to join them but she'd end up sitting there with nothing to say, looking like a dope. So she crept down to the third stair from the top. She was hidden from view of those in the family room but she could listen.

Amy was going on about her experiences on the film set—the makeup, the costumes, the movie people.

"Ralph Devenson, a producer from L.A., was there yesterday," Amy said excitedly. "He's looking for an unknown face to star in his next movie. He picked me out of the crowd in the coffee-shop scene. He gave me his card and said he'd call me to go to Hollywood for an audition."

Amy was the only one Tara could see. She was bouncing up and down like Beebee when she was given a candy. But who wouldn't with an opportunity

like that? Maybe Amy would become a big star. She
was certainly beautiful enough. She had that larger-
than-life glow that made people look her way the
moment she came into a room. Nina had it, too. Tara
felt small, pale and mouse-like by comparison.

"What's this other movie about?" Nina asked.

"It's a…love story," Amy told her. "This guy and a
girl meet while walking their dogs in the park."

"Not much of a plot," Reid muttered. Tara could
picture him frowning and rubbing his jaw, the way he
did when he was being skeptical.

"It's a chick flick, right?" Nina said encouragingly to Amy.

"Uh, yeah, sort of." Amy quickly went on. "It's
being filmed on location in Malibu. I don't know who's
playing the male lead yet. I hope it's someone gorgeous like Orlando Bloom."

"I'd be interested to read the script," Nina said. "Did
the producer give you a copy?"

"Not yet," Amy told her. "The script should be fi-
nalized by the time I get to L.A."

"Can I see this Devenson character's card?" Reid
asked.

"I don't know what I did with it," Amy said. "You
probably wouldn't have heard of him, anyway. It's not
a big-budget movie. More of an…arthouse film."

Tara almost gave herself away by snorting with
laughter. Arthouse! Still, it was a movie and it sounded
like Amy was going to be in it.

"You need a green card to work in the States," Reid

interjected again. "And to join the Screen Actors Guild."

"Ralph will take care of all that," Amy said impatiently. "He does it all the time."

Tara took note of the tension between Amy and their father. She couldn't help resenting her for being dismissive of her dad yet at the same time gloating because the golden girl was turning out to be not so nice.

"Why was he looking for actors in Vancouver?" Reid persisted. "There must be plenty to choose from in California."

"He liked *me*," Amy said aggrieved. "Is that so hard to believe?"

"Not at all," Nina said. "But how is it that filming is getting underway so quickly? Preproduction can take months if not years."

"You two are so suspicious!" Amy jumped up and strode into the kitchen. Tara leaned back on the stairs, out of sight. "The lead actress had to drop out suddenly and Ralph needed someone to fill in. I was lucky enough to be in the right place at the right time."

Nina asked, "Where will you stay?"

"Ralph will meet me at the bus station," Amy went on. "He said I can stay with him until I find a place."

"You barely know the man," Reid protested. "He may expect more from you than you're prepared to give if you know what I mean."

Even Tara knew what her father meant.

"It's not like that," Amy said, now seriously

annoyed. "He's married. His wife is used to putting up visitors from out of town. They have a big house in the Hollywood Hills. I'll probably be going to all sorts of parties and meeting other directors and agents. It's a foot in the door, the chance of a lifetime," she added. "I'm still pinching myself. It's almost too good to be true."

"If it seems too good to be true then you have to wonder if it's real," Nina said.

For once Tara agreed with Nina. Call her a skeptic but Tara didn't believe the story of the wife for one minute.

"I don't think you should go," Reid said bluntly.

Amy's chin jutted, making her look even younger than her years. "Just because you're my biological parents doesn't mean you can suddenly start telling me what to do."

There was a silence in which Tara imagined her father exchanging a glance with Nina, as if they were real married parents and Amy was their daughter that they had some control over. Just like that, her feelings toward Nina turned again. Amy, she could possibly get used to in time. Her dad had made a mistake when he was young and, now that Tara had time to think about it, she could see that he'd done the right thing by not abandoning his baby daughter. But Nina didn't belong in this house. She should see Amy on her own instead of using Beebee as an excuse for worming her way back into Reid's life.

"Amy," Reid said. "Don't you think you should

check Ralph Devenson out before you run off to L.A. with Beebee and get yourself into a situation you can't handle?"

"I came across Canada on my own," Amy said angrily. "I can get to L.A. on my own."

"I have contacts in the TV industry," Nina said. "If you stayed in Vancouver I could help you get a job at the studio. It would be something small at first but you could study communications and eventually work your way up the hierarchy. Acting is so competitive. Very few people make it to the top or even make a living. There are all sorts of other opportunities in the industry such as producing and directing, set design."

"That would take years," Amy objected. "I've been offered a movie role. Why should I wait?"

Getting bored of the whole argument, Tara leaned forward to get a better view of Amy. She'd changed her style since she'd been on the movie set. She wore makeup now, for one thing, lots of it. Creamy soft eye shadow, thick black mascara and glistening lip gloss. Amy was already so beautiful it wasn't fair that she was able to enhance her looks even more. If Tara looked like that, would her dad notice her more?

With a little effort, she could look as good as Amy. Only edgier. Eyes lined with kohl and lips colored blood-red, a little Goth, a little punk. Tara was tired of looking like a nerd who played the violin, wore shapeless clothing and got straight As in school. Inside she was bursting with possibilities. Sometimes she felt as if she could be any one of a million different Taras, depending on which way she decided to go. It was hard to choose.

Tara rose and started back to her room. Passing the bathroom, she glanced through the open door and her mouth twisted in annoyance. Amy's toiletries were strewn all over the vanity, her makeup spilling out of a large paisley patterned bag. A lipstick had fallen onto the floor. If Beebee got hold of that she'd make a huge mess.

Tara went inside the bathroom and picked up the lipstick. The name on the bottom said Rose Wine. She put it back in the bag then couldn't help herself from looking at the others. Cotton Candy, Passionfruit Fizz. They sounded exotic and enticing.

Tara looked over her shoulder. No one around. No one coming. She uncapped Midnight Passion and hastily smeared a thick line of deep crimson around her lips. The lipstick was much darker than she'd expected. Startled at the effect, she leaned away from her reflection in the mirror.

Undeterred, she reached for the liquid eyeliner and drew out the black glistening wand, not quite sure how to apply it. Closing one eye she pulled the lid taut and touched the wand to her skin.

"What are you doing?" Amy's voice made her jump.

Tara's hand jerked, smearing a blotch of black across her eyelid. She dropped the wand and it clattered into the sink, spreading black onto the white ceramic. Fumbling, she tried to cram everything back into the makeup bag. "Nothing. I was just—"

Tara gave up trying to explain and scrubbed at the lipstick with a wet washcloth. Caught, red-handed, or red-lipped, in this case. Talk about feeling like an idiot. Tears pressed against the backs of her eyes, mortifying her. She wiped the cloth across her lids to disguise the moisture further smearing the black eyeliner.

"No, no, no," Amy said, rushing over. She wrenched the washcloth out of Tara's hands. "You don't do it that way."

"So I'm not a Hollywood star," Tara snapped. "I only wanted—" She broke off, afraid of sounding pathetic and met Amy's gaze in the mirror, her cheeks flaming. "Sorry. I shouldn't have."

"It's all right," Amy said, brisk but gentle. "If you wanted to try my makeup you just had to ask."

"I'm sorry," Tara repeated, wishing she could slink away, back to her room.

Amy got out a jar of cleansing cream. "Use this to remove the makeup," she said, busily dabbing it onto Tara's lips. "Here, you do your eyelid—I don't want to get it in your eye—then swab it off with a cotton ball."

Tara did as she was told. Now that she'd gotten over her initial shock at being caught, she was burning with embarrassment because Amy was being so nice.

"That's better," Amy said, eyeing her critically. Tara was edging past her on her way out the door when Amy added, "You know, you've got really nice eyes."

Tara hesitated, torn between wanting to put as much distance as possible between herself and the scene of her humiliation and the equally strong desire to hear she was attractive. "I do?"

"They're gorgeous, large and almond-shaped," Amy went on. She lifted Tara's thick chestnut hair off her shoulders and piled it on top of Tara's head. "You could look like a young Sophia Loren."

"I could?" Tara said wistfully.

"Do you want me to give you a makeover?" Amy asked. "I've learned so much this week, I'd love a chance to experiment on someone."

"Could you give me cheekbones?" Tara asked.

"It would be a snap." Amy clicked her fingers with a tinkling laugh. "Wait till Reid and Nina see you. They won't recognize you."

"Cool!" Tara said happily.

Amy arranged her makeup on the counter and got Tara to sit on the closed toilet seat while she perched on the edge of the bathtub. Unscrewing the eyeliner, she said with a small smile, "This is fun. I've always wanted a sister."

So have I. Tara closed her eyes and felt the cool thin liquid flow along her lash line.

"I WONDER WHAT'S KEEPING AMY," Reid said to Nina. Amy had gone upstairs, supposedly to the bathroom, and half an hour later she still hadn't come down. He'd barely got the words out when he heard both girls coming down the stairs.

"Ta da!" Amy said and stepped out from in front of Tara.

Reid took one look at his younger daughter and sucked in his breath. If not for the Gap T-shirt, he wouldn't have recognized her. Her eyes were outlined in black in an upward sweeping shape and shades of purple eye shadow from lilac to midnight gave depth to her large dark eyes. Her cheeks were hollowed out and her aquiline nose and cheekbones emphasized. Her lips were a soft raspberry pout and her hair was piled on top of her head and falling in loose ringlets around her slender neck.

"You look twenty-five!" was all he could think of to say. There ought to be a law!

Tara broke into a brilliant smile. "Thanks!"

Reid scowled; he hadn't meant it as a compliment.

"Very sophisticated," Nina added tactfully. "You have classic features, Tara. We should take a photo."

Nina actually sounded as if she approved! Reid glanced at her but she simply widened her own lightly made-up eyes in innocent challenge, so he turned to his other daughter. "Did you do this, Amy?"

Amy raised her chin. "There's nothing wrong with experimenting. It's just for fun. I hope you're not trying to tell me what I can and can't do."

From the moment he'd picked her up at the bus station this morning she'd been cool and defensive with him. It hurt, after a lifetime of warm memories. "Maybe I don't have any right to tell you how to comport yourself," he grumbled, "but Tara is another matter."

Nina leaned over and said in an undertone, "Lighten

up, Reid, or you'll make this into a bigger deal than it needs to be."

It wasn't just about the makeup; it was about Tara growing up too quickly. Soon boys would be flocking around....

"I'm fifteen," Tara said, as if she'd read his mind. "I'm old enough to wear lipstick and mascara. All my friends do."

"Yeah, well, I'm not ready to be a grandfather again!" He strode into his office and shut the door. He opened it again and poked his head out. "Don't you dare go out of the house like that."

He booted up his computer and stared at the blank screen but he couldn't think. He'd lost Amy and now he was going to lose Tara if he wasn't careful. What was happening to his little girl? She was becoming a woman, that's what. Pretty soon he wouldn't understand her at all.

LIGHT STREAMED THROUGH A GAP in the curtains, waking Nina. Blinking, she glanced around at the unfamiliar walnut dresser and desk. Amy had stayed overnight in her and Beebee's room, so Nina had slept in the spare bedroom upstairs. A glance at the bedside clock told her it was 4:30 a.m.

Nina shut her eyes again but found she didn't feel in the least sleepy. Rising, she pulled back the curtains and saw that the rising sun had turned the snowy peak of Mount Baker bright pink. The bay was glassy and the sky the pearl-gray of a clear dawn. Since she didn't have to look after Beebee when she woke up, Nina was free to go out on her own in the cool of morning.

She pulled on a pair of shorts and a stretch-cotton shirt and tiptoed downstairs. She was sitting on the wicker couch putting on her running shoes when she heard Reid's voice coming from his office. Who on earth would he be talking to at this hour?

Reid opened the door and his eyebrows rose in surprise at seeing her. He was wearing a sleeveless shirt and jogging shorts. "What are you doing up so early?"

"Going for a run on the dike," she said, letting her gaze slide over his bare muscled arms and legs. Run? Had she really said that? She *never* ran. Brisk walking, yes, but running was for athletes.

"Great, we can go together." Reid opened the front door and gestured her to precede him to the street. He immediately went into a slow jog.

"Don't you warm up first?" Nina asked, reluctantly picking up her pace.

He glanced around in surprise. "This *is* a warm up."

"Don't let me hold you back." Even pumping her arms and lengthening her stride, she could barely keep up with him. She hated to see what would happen when he actually started running. "Who do you call so early?" she puffed.

"The New York stock market opens at 4:00 a.m. our time," he said. "I was talking to my broker."

Nina's eyebrows rose but before she could ask him anything more, they passed through the gate onto the dike and Reid shifted gears, accelerating into an easy lope that bore him steadily away. At twenty paces, he jogged backward and taunted her. "Miss Nosy."

"I'm not nosy," Nina exclaimed, piqued into running after him. She gave it up almost immediately as he shot ahead. "It's my job to ask questions."

His low chuckle floated back to her on the early morning breeze. By the time she'd reached the end of the dike twenty minutes later, Reid had run to the far end of the park and back. His tanned skin was sheened with perspiration and his breath flared his nostrils as he slowed to a jog beside her.

"Let's go back this way," he suggested, steering her off the raised gravel dike and onto one of the criss-crossing sandy trails through the wetlands. Birds piped in the bushes and a rabbit hopped across the trail into the long grass.

Nina's mind was on New York. "How long have you dabbled in the stock market? I suppose your father gave you a few thousand to play with when you turned twenty-one?"

Reid threw her a sardonic glance and mercifully slowed to a walk. "When I sold my first book I put a portion of my royalties into shares. Writing can be a precarious way to earn a living so I wanted to have as many safeguards as possible, especially after I quit my job as a teacher."

"Do you ask the broker's advice or make your own decisions?"

"Both," Reid said. "At first I relied totally on his

advice but after a couple of big losses I decided I wouldn't invest in anything that I didn't personally investigate. So now I study the market and consult with him before buying or selling. I've built up a sizable portfolio."

"You were always such a dreamer," Nina said. "I never would have guessed you'd end up doing something so money-oriented. Breeding tells in the end."

"I was trying to make sure my family was secure through my own efforts—*not* my father's connections," he added pointedly.

Nina raised open hands. "I apologize. No more cracks."

"But to tell you the truth—" Reid was forced to move closer as they went through a narrow gap between bushes and she could smell the faint aroma of sweat and clean male body. "—the element of risk is an adrenaline rush, a secret thrill."

"My, my," Nina said, grinning. "Reid Robertson admitting to a guilty pleasure. Better stay away from casinos."

The path narrowed further and he paused to let her go first. When they were walking abreast again, she said, "Your books must be doing well if you have enough money to invest. Was it hard to get published at first?"

"I wrote seven complete manuscripts before I sold," he said. "Writing until midnight after teaching all day was tiring so in that sense, yes, it was difficult."

"You must have wanted it badly."

"I did," he said simply. "For myself and—"

"And what?"

"Nothing." Reid stopped on the wooden footbridge over the deep-sided canal. "Look," he said and pointed out a mother duck and her clutch of ducklings gliding past beneath them. Nina stood by his side and leaned on the rail, watching the ducks.

"What made you go into television?" Reid asked.

"My guilty pleasure is the sound of applause," she replied. "I'm just a ham at heart."

"You're incredibly good at what you do," he said. "People open up to you and say things I bet they never dreamed of admitting on national television."

And yet she couldn't unlock the secrets of her own heart. Nina stared down at the rippling wake created by the ducks' passage. "After giving up Amy, I didn't ever want to be in a situation again where I couldn't afford to keep my baby. My parents sacrificed so I could go to college. I went into television thinking I could make a damn good living in front of the camera."

"You were always so outgoing whereas I had my nose in a book," he said. "It's a wonder we got together at all."

"How did that happen again?" Nina asked with a laugh. As if she didn't recall every tiny detail of that day at the beach. She just wanted to see if he did.

"Don't tell me you don't remember nearly drowning after you fell off the log raft and were swamped by the wake of a passing motorboat?" he said.

"I only pretended to be drowning," she admitted. "How else could I get the handsome lifeguard to notice me?"

Reid snorted. "I couldn't fail to notice you in that fluoro-green bikini."

Nina grinned. "I paraded past you so many times I thought I'd wear a groove in the beach."

"What do you think I was looking at through those binoculars up there on my lifeguard stand?" he said. "It wasn't the seagulls."

Nina cast his profile a sidelong glance, enjoying the easy banter. Feeling her scrutiny, he met her gaze and she felt herself being sucked back into his spell. Was it the height above the water or gazing into his eyes that was making her feel dizzy? Was she in danger of falling, or just falling in love? All over again.

Pushing away from the rail, she jogged off the bridge and back to the dike. "Last one home's a rotten egg."

"You're on." Reid breezed past easily, only to drop back and literally run circles around her all the way home, making wry comments that had her laughing so hard she ran out of puff.

As she slowed to go through the gate at the end of the dike, Nina realized they'd spent the entire time together without discussing Amy and Beebee. For a brief time it had just been her and him, the way it used to be.

TWO DAYS AFTER THEIR leisurely morning on the dike, Reid was gulping down coffee as he paced the kitchen waiting for toast to pop. Nina quickly buttered a piece and handed it to him. "I don't understand how you can forget that you were scheduled to give a writing workshop until this morning."

Reid slurped at the coffee and wolfed down the toast in three bites. "I simply got the weeks mixed up. It's not a problem. The workshop's all prepared. I've given it before." He glanced at his watch. "I'm going to be late."

"Don't you mark things on your calendar?" Nina spread peanut butter on another piece of toast for Beebee and placed it on the tray of her high chair.

"I do but then I forget to look at it." Reid put his cup down and brushed crumbs from his hands into the sink. "With all that's been happening lately plus getting behind on my book, the workshop slipped my mind. It couldn't have come at a worse time."

"Have you made a decision about Tara's Manga course?" Nina asked. "It starts today."

Reid cursed. Then he began piling papers into his briefcase, stuffing them in crumpled when they spilled out. "I don't have time to think about that now."

Nina followed him out to the front door. Tara wasn't her daughter and she had no right to interfere but she couldn't help feeling as though she were seeing things that Reid wasn't with regard to his younger daughter. "Maybe you should talk to her. I think she's feeling offside with so much of your attention going to Amy." *And to me.*

Looking completely harassed, Reid paused on the

doorstep. "Tara's always been the center of my life. She knows that."

"I wouldn't be so sure." Nina adjusted the light cotton wrap over her short nightie and glanced both ways down the street. What would the neighbors think if they saw her standing here in her nightgown?

"I've really got to go. See you this afternoon," Reid said and kissed her on the lips.

Nina blinked in surprise. The quick peck had to be a reflexive action. An old habit of kissing the wife goodbye before going to work. Except that she wasn't his wife or even his girlfriend. Hadn't they agreed, no more kissing? This kiss didn't have the passion of the other kiss but the touch of his mouth and the scent of his aftershave aroused a tingling in her breasts and invoked thoughts that were anything but domestic.

Reid himself seemed startled by his action. "Er, that was...I didn't mean to...not *intentionally*—"

"Bye, *honey*." With a bemused smile at his confusion, Nina waggled her fingers.

His clean-shaven jaw coloring, Reid hurried off to his car, leaving Nina laughing softly. Then humming to herself, she shut the door and went back to the kitchen. She turned up the radio and sang along to a top-forty tune.

"Where's Dad gone?" Tara greeted her in dismay as she ran down the stairs from her bedroom. She crossed the room and turned the music off.

"He's giving a workshop in Vancouver," Nina said. "Didn't he tell you?"

"No!"

Nina sighed. Relations between Reid and his daughters were definitely dysfunctional at the moment. Amy had gone back to Nina's apartment after two days of ignoring Reid. Tara had taken to wearing lipstick and mascara day and night in what appeared to Nina as an act of defiance against her father. Reid had responded by retreating to his office, claiming he had to work on his book.

"He left without telling me whether I can take the Manga workshop," Tara went on as she paced the kitchen. "I have to have the money in by today."

Don't interfere, Nina told herself. On the other hand, what was the big deal about doing a course? It wasn't as though Tara were asking to study Manga in Japan. But if *she* tried to help, Tara might refuse. There might be another way…. "Actually, he mentioned it to me."

"To you!" Tara replied. "Why would he do that? It's not like you're his wife or anything."

Nina counted to ten, telling herself the girl was upset and it had nothing, this time, to do with her. "Reid's had a lot on his mind lately, what with Amy and Beebee—"

"Amy, Amy, Amy. It's all about Amy," Tara said bitterly, collapsing into a chair. "Or Beebee. What kind of stupid name is that for a kid, anyway?"

Beebee, hearing her name, offered Tara a soggy finger of toast. Tara smiled despite herself and shook her head.

Nina felt compelled to defend Amy and her child. "Amy is Reid's daughter, too, and he feels a responsibility toward her. But he hasn't forgotten you. He told me you could go to the Manga workshop. He left money and asked me to give it to you."

"Really?" Tara straightened. "When did he do this?"

"This morning," Nina fibbed then remembered she didn't have much cash in her wallet. "I mean, last night. But I spent the money on groceries—"

"What!"

"Don't worry," Nina hastened to reassure her. "I'll go to the bank today. You can come with me and from there we'll go to the community center to sign you up. Okay?"

"Cool." Tara's smile crept back, transforming her sullen expression. "I knew Dad would come through in the end. I'm going to call Libby." Tara turned and ran up to her room.

Nina breathed out a sigh of relief and hoped that Reid would approve. Parenthood was like putting out spot fires—as soon as one crisis was under control, another flared up.

CHAPTER NINE

"NUMMIES!" BEEBEE CRIED from her high chair and stretched out her hand, opening and closing her fingers in anticipation.

"It's almost ready." Nina frantically blew on the dish of homemade macaroni and cheese to cool it down.

Making the macaroni had taken longer than Nina had expected and Beebee was wild with hunger, banging the tray and crying. The rusk Nina had given the tot to tide her over had been tossed angrily to the floor where Daisy prowled, shark-like, for scraps.

Nina heard the front door open and Reid come in, home from his workshop in Vancouver. She plucked a few pasta elbows off the top and placed them on Beebee's tray. The little girl picked up a piece with her fingers and stuffed it in her mouth with a baleful teary glance at Nina.

"Hi, sweetheart," Reid said, coming into the kitchen.

Nina spun around. Oh. He was talking to Beebee.

"Hi, Nina," he added. "Where's Tara?"

"She's at Libby's for dinner and is staying overnight," Nina replied. "Um, by the way—"

Beebee banged her tray again, demanding more food.

"Will dinner keep?" Reid said, dropping his briefcase in his office before heading for the stairs. "I'm going to have a workout."

"Sure. I let Tara—" Nina started to tell him about the Manga course.

"Nummies!" Beebee shouted.

"Here you go." Nina put the bowl on her tray and hurried to the stairs. Reid had disappeared.

Over dinner Nina forgot about Tara's Manga course as Beebee continued to dominate her and Reid's attention. Afterward Reid cleaned up while Nina put Beebee to bed. Nina returned to the family room to find Reid with a photo album open on his lap. "Between my writing and you looking after Beebee, I haven't had a chance to show you pictures of Amy when she was young. Do you want to do that now?"

"Oh, yes." Nina sat next to him on the couch. "Does she look like Beebee?"

"A little." Reid opened the first album and pointed out a photo of a six-month-old blond, blue-eyed baby. "I think she looks more like you."

Nina leaned closer, eagerly drinking in the features of the daughter she'd never known until a few weeks ago. Reid took her through pictures of Amy at various stages and ages, skipping quickly over the few pages that included Carol, a dark-haired, slight woman who always seemed to have a serene smile on her oval face. Nina laughed at five-year-old Amy dressed up in a long flowing dress and tiara and holding a sword.

"She wanted to be the princess *and* the rescuing knight," Reid explained. "She was always acting out some little play she'd invented. I guess it's no surprise she grew up wanting to be an actor."

"She's absolutely adorable," Nina said wistfully, turning the page. There were photos of Amy playing with a cocker spaniel, Amy in a Girl Guide uniform, Amy in front of a cabin with a lake in the background. Nina came to a photo of Amy at about sixteen years old wearing a party dress in blue organza with a big artificial flower pinned to her strap. Standing next to her was a tall youth with thick chestnut hair who was gazing not at the camera but at Amy with profound adoration.

"This was her first formal dance," Reid said. "That's Ian. I've never met him but I remember talking to Amy on the phone beforehand. She was so excited because it was their first date."

The photos were a stark reminder to Nina of how much of her daughter's childhood she'd missed. With a deep sigh, she swiveled to face Reid. "Why *didn't* you contact me? You had all these photos of our daughter. Did you imagine I wouldn't want to see them? That I wanted to forget she ever existed?"

"Isn't that what you intended when you gave her up for adoption?" Reid shifted away from her on the couch. Their closeness dissolved in an instant and tension formed in its place.

"I didn't *want* to give her up," Nina said. "Your mother convinced me it was the right thing to do. For you, for us, for Amy." Bitterly she added, "It turned out she was only thinking of you. She used my love for you to break us apart. I was too naive and trusting to realize it at the time."

"You should have talked to *me*."He got up to pace away. "We could have worked something out together."

"You were three thousand miles away shut up in your ivory tower," she snapped. "I was on my own, dealing with the reality of being eighteen, broke and pregnant. And I *did* tell you what I planned."

"A week before the birth!" he exclaimed, spinning back to her. "It hit me like a bolt out of the blue."

"If I'd told you sooner I might have screwed up your whole school year."

"Instead you screwed up my whole life! Both of our lives." Frustrated and angry, Reid raked both hands through his hair. "When you did finally tell me, I begged you not to do anything irrevocable until I got back. But you gave her up anyway."

"I wanted our baby to grow up in a loving home with a mother *and* a father," Nina defended herself hotly. "The Hockings were good people and they wanted a definite answer on the adoption. I couldn't leave them hanging—will she, won't she?"

"Why do you think I rushed back? Because I wanted to marry you!"

"Only because I had the baby," she cried. "As

soon as Amy was out of the picture, you didn't want me anymore."

"Because of what you'd done." Reid's voice cracked painfully. "And what you said."

Nina stared up at him, scared by the black, hollow look in Reid's eyes. She'd said so many things in the emotional aftermath of birth and giving up the baby. "What was that?"

"'Go away, I never want to see you again,'" he reminded her of her dreadful words. "'*I hate you.*'"

Nina felt sick at the memory. She *had* hated him at that moment, with every atom of her body and soul. She'd also loved him with a consuming fire that was too big for her to put into words. Even now she could feel the terrible pain of those conflicting emotions tearing her apart.

Wrapping her arms around herself, Nina rose and moved away, putting distance between them. "I'd given up our baby. I'd lost your love. My life had emptied out. I didn't know what I was saying."

"I thought that's why you gave her up," Reid mumbled. "Because you didn't want me anymore."

"*No.*" Nina shook her head, stunned. "Never that." She dragged in a breath. "Giving Amy up was hard but just as difficult was watching your love for me die right there in that hospital room with the smell of baby powder and milk reminding me every second of the family we could have had if we hadn't been so young and foolish."

Pain and empathy flowed from Reid. Understanding swept through Nina. He'd experienced the same anger and grief, the same loss as she had. Not just of Amy but of their love. The love they'd thought would last a lifetime.

Tears came unexpectedly. As her legs began to buckle, Reid's arms were around her.

"Nina," he whispered, his warm breath ruffling her hair while he held her in an anguished embrace. "Oh, Nina. I'm so sorry. For everything. For not seeing what my mother was doing to you, for not being there to support you, for fighting when we should have been loving." His voice broke and she could hear his indrawn breath, ragged and hoarse. "You'll never know how much I hated not being with you while you were giving birth, not being in time to stop the adoption."

"I'm sorry, too," she said, trembling. "I should have called you sooner. We didn't just fail each other. We failed our child. We should have raised Amy together."

They clung to each other. Nina wept the tears she'd denied herself for years. Reid's back was racked with silent sobs. After what seemed an age, Nina's crying gradually slowed to sighs and her sorrow eased to a gentle ache. The bitter salt of her tears turned sweet with shared suffering and Reid's embrace filled her with a warmth that went beyond comfort.

Nina became aware of his arms loosening but not letting her go. He pressed small soothing kisses onto her hot moist eyes, murmuring words of support and reassurance. Nina's hands crept from Reid's shoulders to smooth back the shock of unruly dark hair that fell over his forehead. His face was close to hers and his lips moved lower to kiss away the tears that streaked her cheeks.

Reid drew back slightly, his gaze never leaving Nina's. Warmth rose suddenly between them. The past receded and became a distant memory. Nina's mouth parted as Reid's lips settled onto hers with heart-stopping tenderness. With a sigh, she shut her eyes and let herself melt into the kiss. Her limbs weakened but that didn't matter because she was cradled in Reid's iron embrace, molded to his chest and thighs. She came alive as she hadn't for nearly two decades. It wasn't just her baby she'd lost when she'd lost Reid. She'd also lost the glorious driving heat and soaring passion of their love.

Even as her body urged her to press closer, to give in to her and Reid's obvious desire, something held her back. A part of her brain refused to blur and lose itself in the physical. She tried to ignore it but that was impossible. Niggling and annoying, a little voice told her that forgiving each other for the past didn't solve current issues or necessarily pave the way for the future.

Then she broke the kiss as she realized the voice wasn't just in her brain. Beebee, down the hall, was crying for her mommy. Confused and conflicted, Nina pushed Reid away. "Beebee's calling."

"We'll get her in a minute." Reid's hands moved restlessly over her back and arms and he tried to kiss her again.

"We shouldn't be doing this." Nina tore away to peer down the darkened hall for a glimpse of a tiny figure with flaming red hair. How could Reid hear that cry and not feel an almost physical urge to tend to the child immediately?

Then the phone rang and Reid groaned. Nina seized the opportunity to break free and hurry down the hall to Beebee. As she opened the bedroom door, Beebee's cries grew louder. The little girl was standing in her crib, rubbing at her eyes and crying. In the background, Nina heard Reid pick up the phone and say hello.

"Beebee, honey, what's the matter?" she crooned, reaching over the side of the crib for the toddler. "Did you have a bad dream?"

"Want Mommy," Beebee wailed and struggled inside Nina's grip. "Where my Mommy?"

"Your mommy's coming home tomorrow, sweetheart," Nina said. "Don't worry, Nina's here. Nina will take care of you until Mommy gets home." She walked around the room, jiggling Beebee up and down in her arms the way she'd seen Reid do. "Nina won't let anything bad happen to her little Beebee."

Beebee sucked in a deep breath and gave Nina a hard stare that somehow combined suspicion with a grudging willingness to trust. "Ni-na?"

Nina stopped short in delight at hearing Beebee say her name for the first time. "Yes! Nina. That's me."

And then Beebee put her little arms around Nina's neck and rested her head on Nina's chest. Her face was hot and wet with tears but Nina felt something deep and warm curling around her heart as the toddler cuddled next to her.

Reid appeared in the doorway. "Is she all right?"

"She's fine," Nina whispered then paused. "I'm going to stay with her a while. Don't wait up."

Nina saw the disappointment in Reid's face and felt the same. Now that they'd found healing and resolution, she wanted to go to him. But Beebee needed her and the little girl took precedence.

REID LEANED BACK in his office chair and gazed up at the ceiling, hoping inspiration would strike. There was nothing to see except two dead flies resting in peace behind the frosted-glass light fixture.

He'd worked all morning and hadn't written more than two pages. The problem was, he'd come to a screeching halt over Luke's next move. What was Luke going to do about Maria—take her into his confidence and agree to meet her contact? Or tear himself away from her distracting beauty and finish the mission solo? The deeper Luke got behind enemy lines, the harder it was for him to operate on his own, so an ally would be useful. But Maria had her own agenda and linking himself too closely with her could bring about his downfall.

Jeez, it was hot. Reid plucked his damp T-shirt away from his chest. And quiet. Why *was* it so quiet? At this time of day, Tara should be practicing her violin.

Rising, he emerged from his office. Nina was sitting at the dining table dressed in a halter bikini top and a short skirt. Her burn had already faded into tan and her blond hair seemed to have lighter streaks from the sun. She was typing away at her laptop. "What are you doing?"

"Working on ideas for future shows," she told him then cast him a sunny smile. "I'm thinking about interviewing a successful local author."

"I know one who'd be happy to talk if you timed the interview for when his next book comes out."

"December, isn't it?" Nina made an entry on her computer. "I think that could be arranged."

Reid tore his gaze away from the V of freckled tanned skin curving over the top of her bikini. "Where's Tara?"

"She's at her Manga course." Nina tapped away as she spoke. "Have you looked at that book she gave you yet? It might be helpful if you know what she's talking about when she gets home."

"What? No, I haven't read any idiotic comic." Just the mention of Manga made Reid irritated. "I don't recall giving her permission to do the course."

"Uh-oh." Nina paused to think and a sheepish expression stole across her face. "I meant to tell you about that. Are you sure I didn't tell you and you just didn't hear? You know how distracted you get."

"I think I would have remembered that," Reid declared. "Where did she get the money?"

"I gave it to her."

"*You!*" Reid went to the fridge for a cold drink. Nina had an inherent right to be involved with Amy and

Beebee, but Tara was his responsibility. "You should have checked with me."

"You were at your workshop," Nina explained. "A decision had to be made so I made it. I thought you should support Tara's interests."

"She should be practicing her violin," Reid said. "Or reading books, not comics."

"I've seen plenty of books in her bedroom," Nina said. "But this isn't about the stories. In case you hadn't noticed, and it's clear you haven't, she wants to illustrate."

"I always hoped she'd be a writer."

"Like you?" Nina asked.

"Like her mother. Tara's very like Carol."

Nina went quiet the way she always did when Carol's name came up. He sensed that Nina thought he was still grieving for Carol and he didn't know how to tell her he wasn't, without sounding callous or unfeeling.

"Well," he said awkwardly. "I guess her taking an art course isn't the end of the world. I'd better get back to work."

"Reid," Nina called, making him pause. "Beebee will be up from her nap soon. I'm going to take her to the water park in Ladner. Do you want to come?"

Before he could reply that he had to write, the patter of small feet could be heard coming down the hall.

Nina smiled indulgently. "Speak of an angel…"

Beebee ran into the room and stopped. Her face was flushed with heat and damp tendrils of hair stuck to her cheek on the side she'd been sleeping on. She saw Reid and her face lit. "Weed!"

Reid scooped Beebee up in his arms and lifted her high in the air until she squealed with delight. Then he tucked her in the crook of his arm and pushed damp curls off her cheek. "Nina's going to take you to the park."

Nina rose and rubbed circles over Beebee's back while she smiled at Reid. "She might go in the water for *you*."

Reid narrowed his eyes at this blatant appeal to his devotion to Beebee. Or was it his male ego? This kind of distraction was exactly what he'd been afraid of when Nina had moved in. But what a distraction—she looked damn sexy in that bikini. On the other hand, taking a break might allow his subconscious to come up with a solution for Luke. "Maybe I could spare an hour or two."

He went upstairs and changed into board shorts and a T-shirt, and came back down to find Nina packing cold drinks and snacks into a small cooler. She'd put on a light blue tank over her bikini top and the bright pink bottoms showed through her white miniskirt.

Nina crouched to slather sunscreen over Beebee's bare arms and legs. The little girl braced herself on the ever-patient Daisy and did her best to stand firm as the gentle force of Nina's smoothing motions made her rock on her plump tottery legs.

"All done." Nina plopped a sun hat on Beebee and reached for a tote bag stuffed with towels. "Let's go."

Beebee took off down the hall, jogging for the front door. She glanced over her shoulder and laughed.

"Beebee, you little imp!"

Chuckling, Reid picked up the cooler. One day Nina would figure out that Beebee was playing a game with her.

Twenty minutes later, Nina, Reid and Beebee walked across a broad green lawn toward an oasis in the haze of the scorching afternoon. Shrieking children played in shallow pools and fountains, and spraying nozzles cast miniature rainbows across the mist enveloping the water park.

Nina dropped her tote and spread out a blanket on the grass in the shade of the broad limbs of an oak tree. She was about to strip off her skirt when she noticed Reid watching and remembered the tattoo. After the emotional outpourings of the previous night, she wasn't prepared for another revelation of her feelings so soon.

She gave Reid a wink and said to Beebee, "You stay here with Reid. I'm going to play in the water."

Nina took Beebee's yellow rubber duck and without a backward glance, she walked away, not even turning around when she heard Beebee say, "Ducky!" in surprise and consternation at the loss of her toy.

Nina sat on the edge of the toddler pool where children Beebee's age were happily splashing and began to play with the duck. She felt a little silly— okay, make that a *lot* silly—but she persisted even though Reid was openly grinning. Beebee had taken out her plastic bucket and shovel and was happily playing on the blanket. Clearly the child couldn't care less if Nina wasn't there as long as she had Reid.

Nina was ready to give up when Reid rose and stripped off his T-shirt. His tanned shoulders and arms, toned from working out with weights, matched his strong legs. Nina found it impossible to look away when he started walking toward the pools. Beebee glanced up, noticed he was leaving and, with a startled cry, ran after him.

Still ignoring Beebee, Reid walked past Nina and sat in the middle of the pool where the water came halfway up his thighs. "Ah, that's better."

Nina glanced back to see how Beebee was taking this when, without warning, a spray of water hit her in the chest and face. Too late she saw Reid slice the surface with the flat of his hand and send a second blast of cool water in her direction. "Why, you—"

Beebee, hit by a few drops of spray, stopped in her tracks and, with a worried frown, looked from Nina to Reid.

"See how much fun playing in the water is, Beebee?" Reid said innocently, sending a third spray at Nina. By now her T-shirt was soaking wet and water dripped from the end of her nose. "Doesn't Nina look funny?"

Reid laughed. Beebee smiled uncertainly.

Nina grinned and planned her counterattack. "Watch this, Beebee." She took the girl's bucket, scooped it through the water and dumped the contents over Reid's head. "That ought to cool you down."

Beebee's infectious chortle rang out, making Nina laugh, too, at the sight of Reid sputtering and gasping.

"Me do." Beebee grabbed the bucket out of Nina's hands. Seemingly unaware of what she was doing, she stepped into the pool to pour water over Reid's head.

"I said you would get her in the water," Nina said with satisfaction.

"You're so clever," Reid said then instructed Beebee, "Now Nina."

Beebee dipped the bucket again and pointed to a spot next to Reid, indicating to Nina she should sit down in the middle of the pool. Resigning herself to a further dunking Nina sat in the water and allowed a giggling Beebee to pour a bucketful over her head.

Nina pushed the wet hair from her eyes and turned to Reid. "Is this what they mean by making sacrifices for children?"

"There's no dignity in parenting a toddler," Reid said. Then he lifted his eyebrows. "But when's the last time you had this much fun?"

Water droplets glistened on his tanned chest. His shoulders gleamed and he'd never looked so appealing as he did at that moment. Nina saw his gaze drop from her eyes to her mouth then drift lower. Glancing down, Nina noticed that her bikini top was visible beneath the transparent wet T-shirt plastered to her chest. The curve of her breast, the outline of her nipples, everything was on display. Instead of feeling exposed, she felt a surge of excitement at Reid's obvious interest. Nina stood up, pulled the T-shirt over her head and tossed it onto the grass.

Then she relieved the little girl of her bucket. "Beebee's turn."

Laughing, Beebee backed away, stumbled and sat down abruptly. Her laughter faded as she found herself in water up to her waist and she could only stare wide-eyed as Nina came toward her with the bucket of water.

"Beebee get wet like Nina and Reid." Nina smiled encouragingly and spilled the water gently over Beebee's shoulders and back.

Beebee's mouth opened and closed; she was obviously too shocked to utter even a cry. Nina drenched Reid and herself again. Beebee giggled and waved her arms, inadvertently splashing the water. Surprised, she glanced down and this time deliberately hit the water with the flat of her hand. Droplets sprayed over her body and hit Reid and Nina. Reid skimmed the flat of his hand gently over the surface and sent a small spray across at Beebee. Nina held her breath.

Beebee chuckled. Reid sprayed her again. She splashed Reid. Her chuckle developed into full-fledged laughter. She stood up and sat down with a bigger splash, laughing with uproarious delight. Soon the three of them were engaged in an all out water fight, shrieking and laughing and spraying water everywhere. Beebee was right in the thick of it, having the time of her life.

Nina's gaze was continually drawn to Reid. His

broad smile and his rich deep laugh reminded her of the days when they'd been carefree and in love, barely more than children themselves. Today was one of those rare perfect days when she was completely happy in an uncomplicated way.

In a sensual undercurrent to the innocent fun, she was aware of her body and conscious of Reid's wordless flirtation as they played with Beebee. His hand touched her bare wet waist, her shoulder brushed against his, his arm went around her and Beebee as she cuddled the child. His nearness set up a tension that had her nerves singing and her fingertips tingling with the urge to skim them over his taut abdomen or massage his muscled shoulders.

Finally Beebee started to flag and Nina caught Reid's eye. He seemed to have noticed Beebee's fatigue at the same time for he immediately nodded and picked Beebee up to carry her out of the pool.

Beebee protested briefly but gave up at the promise of juice and a snack. They returned to the blanket under the oak tree and Reid dug in the cooler for Beebee's food and drink. With a bottle of juice in one hand and a cheese stick in the other, Beebee was content.

Nina toweled off. She hesitated with her fingers on the button of her soaking wet miniskirt. She envied Reid his board shorts made of a thin material that dried almost instantly.

"You can't lie on the blanket in that wet skirt," Reid said, noticing her indecision. "Don't worry. I've already seen your tattoo through my binoculars."

"You *were* spying on me that day!"

Reid laughed. "I was just bird-watching."

So he knew. She was wearing her heart on her sleeve, or in this case, her hip. She unzipped her sopping skirt and drew it off then tossed it at his grinning face.

He caught the skirt and deflected it onto the grass without taking his gaze off her bikini-clad body. "You're lucky I have quick reflexes."

"You mean, *you're* lucky." She dropped to the blanket on the other side of Beebee but the child immediately crawled over her to get to her toys, leaving Nina facing Reid with nothing between them. He handed her a bottle of flavored mineral water and she welcomed both the distraction and the chance to slake her thirst.

"Ah, that's better." Nina lay on her side, head propped on an elbow. "EeBee-bay's ost-lay er-hay ear-fay of ater-way," she added in a conspiratorial whisper.

"I don't think you need to bother," Reid said, chuckling. "She's gone to sleep."

Nina looked over her shoulder. Beebee had lain down among her buckets and shovels and shut her eyes. Tiny bubbles issued from her half-open mouth and her small back rose and fell peacefully.

"All that play tired her out," Nina said softly.

Reid nodded and reached over Nina to move Beebee's empty bottle onto the grass and pull a plastic sailboat out from under her leg. He regarded Nina intently for a moment then finally spoke. "There's something I think you should know. I loved Carol...."

Nina felt a stab of pain then immediately berated herself. Of course he'd loved his wife; she would think less of him if he hadn't. But why was he bringing it up?

Then he added quietly, "But she wasn't the love of my life." A heartbeat passed in silence. Shadows moved over his face as he looked long and deep into her eyes. "*You* were."

Reid edged closer and brought his mouth down on hers, easing her onto her back. His head and shoulders blocked out the flickering diamonds of light shafting through the branches of the tree. His kiss was as warm as the day, as soft as the gentle breeze that caressed her bare midriff. Nina had tried to ignore how much she wanted him but now there was no denying she craved intimacy.

Reid shifted closer still, until his legs brushed hers. His hand slowly slid across her shoulder and down her arm, lightly brushing the outer curve of her breast. While his tongue conducted a delicious exploration of her mouth, his fingertips drifted lower, tracing the inner curve of her waist until they rested on her hip.

He broke the kiss to inspect the spot his fingers had found unerringly—her tattoo. His voice was husky when he asked, "Why a rose?"

"You know why."

"Tell me."

"To remind me of our love." She punctuated her words with kisses because the raw look in his eyes was too much witness. "Our baby. The passion we shared. And lost."

"And found again." Reid pressed his hips into hers, heedless of the public setting and the baby sleeping next to them. His deep kiss woke every slumbering desire in her body. When her blood was at fever pitch, Reid lifted his head. "Let's go home."

CHAPTER TEN

NINA SWIFTLY GATHERED UP their belongings, folded the blanket and tossed the garbage in the cooler. Reid placed Beebee in her arms, still sleeping, then carried the cooler, towels and blankets back to the car.

The ten-minute drive to Beach Grove through town and farmland had never seemed so long. As she slowed for a ninety-degree turn, Nina felt Reid's hand on her thigh. A jolt of electricity ran through her that nearly had her swerving over the white line.

"Sorry." Reid looked anything but apologetic.

"Careful, or we'll end up in the ditch," she replied, shuddering at the deep channels on either side of the road.

In spite of her caution, his sense of urgency was matched by her own. She glanced in the rearview mirror and saw that Beebee was still slumped in her car seat. She usually napped for an hour and a half but maybe today with all the exercise and fresh air...

"She should sleep for at least another hour," Reid said, reading her mind. "How long does Tara's Manga class go?"

"Till four-thirty. Then she was going to walk home, say another fifteen or twenty minutes." Nina met his gaze. "That leaves us a window of roughly forty-five minutes."

Reid ran his hand up her leg and squeezed gently. "Long enough."

Back at the house Reid carried Beebee in, ordering Nina to leave the cooler and towels for now. He gave Nina a quick kiss. "Go up to my room. I'll be right there."

Passing the mirror above the hall table, Nina caught a glimpse of herself and paused, jolted by the reality she'd glimpsed. For the past few hours she'd been the young woman out of her past. Now staring back at her was the woman she'd become. Peering closer she examined the tiny lines at the corners of her eyes. Did Reid notice those when he kissed her or did he see her eighteen-year-old self?

Then there was her body…. *That* definitely wasn't eighteen anymore. She stepped back and looked at her profile, sucking her stomach in. She'd gone up only one dress size in nineteen years; not *too* bad.

"Just like a woman—can't pass a mirror without stopping to check herself out." Reid's hands slid around her waist and locked in front as he came up behind her.

"I was just…my hair is such a mess—" Nina broke off, embarrassed at being caught out. "Okay," she said, laughing. "I was wondering if I looked…older."

"It would be strange if you didn't." Reid met her

gaze in the reflective glass. "But you're as beautiful as ever. If anything, you're *more* beautiful." He kissed the side of her neck and a tremor ran through her that had as much to do with his next words as his touch. "Let's go upstairs."

One step behind Nina, Reid watched the sway of her hips and charted the delicate slant of her shoulder blades. He wanted to take the stairs two at a time but he forced himself to climb sedately. Restraint, that was what he needed, to show her he wasn't a callow eighteen-year-old anymore. He would *not* pick her up and throw her onto the bed like some caveman, no matter how much he wanted to rip her bikini off.

At the top of the stairs she stopped and turned, taking him by surprise by throwing her arms around him and almost pushing him back down the stairs. Her breasts pressed against his chest, firm yet tantalizingly soft as well. The halter straps were tied with a bow that came undone in a tug. And he hadn't lost his touch when it came to undoing the catch on the lower strap single-handed.

Her bikini top dropped away, leaving her breasts naked and him breathless with their full roundness and high, tight nipples. He took one in his mouth and sucked until his shorts were straining at the front seam and he was so hard it was painful. How many nights had he lain awake and imagined making love to Nina? Not just in the past two weeks but over the years. Especially since Carol had died, but if he were honest, before that, though he would never have cheated on his wife, not even with Nina.

Now he was on his own, Nina was in his arms and he was about to go out of his mind if he didn't shed his shorts and strip off her bikini bottoms—

"What was that?" Nina whispered. "I thought I heard something."

Reid tried to focus on listening but his attention was entirely taken up by the visual and tactile splendor of Nina's breasts. "I, uh, I can't…hear…anything." He could barely speak, either. Her skin was soft and smooth, lighter where her bikini top hadn't allowed tanning.

"I guess it's nothing," Nina said. "It's too soon for Tara to be back. If Beebee was awake she'd be running through the house by now."

"She's out like a light." Reid steered Nina into his bedroom and started to shut the door then changed his mind and left it ajar so they could hear Beebee when she awoke.

Nina had never been shy about her body or making love, and now she was more confident than ever. Reid found the way her brazen blue eyes challenged him extremely sexy. With a teasing smile she slowly rubbed her breasts back and forth across his chest then slipped her hand inside his shorts. His body responded with a jerk that tightened her grip and almost had him climaxing.

"It's been a while since I've been with a woman," he gasped. "Touching is…too much." Words, which he was usually so adept with, failed him. He slid his hands down the back of her bikini bottoms and pushed them off, leaving a trail of kisses until he was kneeling before her, his tongue parting a nest of soft blond hair to bury itself in her folds.

"Oh, Reid," she said in a husky murmur. "I love what you do to me."

All Nina's yearning fantasies came true as Reid tumbled her onto the bed. He stripped off his shorts and stood over her naked and so gloriously male that she wanted to laugh aloud with sheer happiness. They were together again!

She opened her arms to him and he lowered himself on top of her. Every cell in her body came alive with the slight abrasion of his chest and leg hair. She ran her hands over his muscled shoulders, down the dip in his lower back and gripped his firm buttocks. He smelled of sun and heat and desire. The hard erection pressing between her legs was sending her mindless with lust.

"Condom?" she breathed, in between kisses.

He stretched an arm out and opened the bedside drawer for a small box. With a groan he upended it on the mattress. Nothing fell out. "There are none left!"

"What?" She couldn't believe her ears. Her body tensed but the surging blood didn't ebb. "I thought men were never without protection."

"I ran out."

"You ran out!"

"Last March. I told you it's been a while."

"I know, but Reid, that's plenty of time to restock.

What if you needed one?" She dug her nails into his shoulders in frustration. *"Like now."*

"I'm not in a relationship and I don't go around cruising singles bars," he said, his voice tight with the strain of maintaining control. "Don't you have any?"

"No, I don't," she said through her teeth. "It's been even longer for me."

He shifted and his hardened penis pressed more firmly against her clitoris. Every cell in her body went from singing to screaming for release with an aching, throbbing need that drowned out rational thought. Reid was finally naked, on top of her, and she couldn't have him? She wanted to sob. It was so unfair.

"I'll just have to be careful," Reid said.

"Careful?"

"To pull out in time. I can do it, I promise."

Oh, she was tempted! If she just opened her legs a little wider he'd be inside.

"That's irresponsible," she said primly, even as her thighs involuntarily edged farther apart. Her whole body was taut and his was rigid. The least movement by either of them sent waves of desire flooding through her. She could feel him tremble all over with the effort of not pushing into her. "Imagine if Amy or Tara copied our example."

"Don't even mention their names in this context. They're not going to know what goes on in this bedroom," he ground out. "But you're right, unprotected sex *would* be irresponsible, especially given our history." He made a move to get off her.

"Just one more kiss first," Nina begged, knowing she was being stupid.

He hesitated, then lowered his mouth to hers. His tongue swept inside with a sensual plunge that made her arch up and push the head of his penis within the entrance to her vagina. Nina gasped as white heat swept her body. Instinctively she arched again. He sank into her, blazing hot, filling and stretching her.

"Oh!" Nina gasped.

"We…can't." His gaze burned into hers with an agony of longing and regret as he started to withdraw.

Nina groaned at the loss. Once again her body betrayed her. Desire overrode every ounce of self-restraint she possessed and only one impulse ruled her— to fuse body and soul with the man she'd loved her entire life. Her hips jerked upward again, forcing Reid deep inside her. Nina came with a shattering intensity. Her climax sparked his and Reid shuddered and groaned, his body pulsing.

He never had a chance to pull out, Nina realized in a postcoital haze. Three amazing thrusts and they'd gone up in flames.

"Oh God," he mumbled into her neck. "I can't believe we did that."

"My fault," she said, hugging him tightly. "I practically forced myself on you."

"You did, didn't you?" Reid said with a flash of his irrepressible grin before he quickly sobered. "We're old enough to know better."

"And young enough to do it again?" she teased.

"No!" He was very definite about that.

"Look, let's not stress out about this," she said. "Neither of us is promiscuous so disease isn't an issue. That leaves pregnancy, which is…unlikely…given the time of my cycle. At least we've only done it once."

"All it takes is once," he reminded her.

Nina heard the front door open and close. "Tara's back early!"

Reid muttered a curse and rolled off her only to pull her with him in a tangle of sheets and legs.

"Hey, Dad! Where are you?" Tara's excited voice drifted up the stairwell as her footsteps hurried through to his office then back along the hall. "Wait till you see my drawings!"

Nina struggled to free herself but the sheets were wound around her and Reid, binding them. Tara started up the stairs.

The door pushed open. Tara stood there, her face alight with excitement. "Dad?"

Nina sank back onto the pillow, just barely resisting the urge to pull the covers over her head.

Tara took in the scene and her smile turned to disbelief and horror. "What's going on?"

"I can explain—" Reid started.

"Don't bother. It's obvious," Tara cut him off. "So this is why you agreed to let me do the Manga workshop—so you and her could spend the afternoon in the sack."

"*She,*" Reid corrected automatically. "You and she."

Nina winced.

"I don't give a damn if it's *she* or *her*," Tara raged. "The bitch had sex with you in *Mom's bed*." With that she turned on her heel and ran from the room.

"Tara!" Reid bellowed. "How dare you use that kind of language. Come back here and apologize!"

Down the hall, her bedroom door slammed shut. The next instant Beebee, awakened by the noise, began to wail.

Nina freed herself from the sheets and scouted around the floor for her bikini. She found both pieces and pulled the bottoms on but her shaking fingers couldn't do up the catch on the top. Beebee's cries became louder. Then the toddler's bare feet could be heard pattering down the hall.

"Let me." Reid did her straps up then pulled her into his arms and whispered in her ear. "It'll be all right. I'll talk to Tara."

Nina kissed him and ran downstairs to Beebee, lifting the little girl in her arms. "Did you wake up and find nobody there? Don't worry, sweetie. Nina's here."

Cuddling the little girl, Nina walked through toward the kitchen to get a cold drink for Beebee. She wiped the toddler's face with a clean cloth then headed back to the bedroom to change Beebee's diaper. As she passed the stairs, her gaze drifted up. If Nina had been in any doubt about Tara's feelings toward her, the teenager had just made it perfectly clear how much she resented Nina. It seemed unlikely Tara would ever accept another woman in her father's life, least of all Nina.

Upstairs, Reid knocked on Tara's door. "It's me."

"Go away." His daughter's voice was muffled, as if she was crying facedown in her pillow.

He sighed and went in. "Tara, we have to talk."

She turned her head to the wall, hugging her ancient stuffed hippo with the faded pink fur to her chest. Reid sat on the edge of the bed and pulled back the long chestnut hair that covered her face to reveal reddened eyes and tear tracks on her cheek.

"Sweetheart, I'm sorry you got a shock just now. We didn't expect you back so soon."

"I got a ride with Libby's mom." Fresh tears squeezed out of Tara's eyes. "How could you go to bed with Nina? You told me when Mom died that you would always love *her*."

"And I will," Reid assured her, placing his hand on her shoulder. "That doesn't mean I won't ever fall in love again."

"It's too soon," Tara protested, rolling over to look at him. "Only two years. You must not have loved Mom very much if you can get over her that quickly."

"It's been three years. I loved your mother very much," Reid said. That was the truth and yet Tara's comment struck close to the bone, assailing him with a pang of guilt. But there was more than one truth. "I'm a man, healthy and relatively young. Not a monk."

"I suppose if it was just sex with Nina that wouldn't be so bad," Tara said hopefully.

Reid frowned. He'd been very discreet with the two women he'd had brief no-strings-attached affairs with since Carol's death and as far as he knew, Tara hadn't been the wiser. Maybe if he'd been more open she'd have gotten used to the idea of him seeing other women and wouldn't be so judgmental. Because, he suddenly realized, he wanted more than just a clandestine fling with Nina.

"My feelings for Nina don't negate or in any way diminish my love for your mother." He could see Tara wasn't convinced. Her opposition was more deep-seated than simply a reluctance to see him with another woman. "It's Nina, herself you object to, isn't it? Why do you dislike her?"

Tara's ink-stained fingers tugged at a loose thread on the hem of her pillowcase. "She's so chirpy all the time, asking me how I am, questioning what I think and how I feel about this and that."

He was so surprised, he laughed. Tara had picked on one of the things Reid loved about Nina; she brought him out of himself. "Isn't that better than not caring? She's concerned about your happiness. She wants to get to know you." He paused, still certain there was more to Tara's antipathy. "You don't *want* to like her."

The thread on the pillow hem pulled loose, taking out several inches of stitching. "Mom didn't like her."

Reid put a hand on Tara's, stilling her fidgeting fingers. "Unless you want to mend that, can you please stop? What do you mean, your mother didn't like Nina? She never met her."

"Whenever she saw her show on TV she used to

scowl and turn it off. Whenever *you* weren't around, that is. Once she said, 'I can't stand that woman.'"

Reid recalled the times they'd watched Nina's show together. Carol always made complimentary remarks about Nina's appearance but she hadn't fooled him; she'd been fishing to see if Reid still found his old girlfriend attractive. He'd tried to reassure her, as he did now with his daughter.

Taking Tara's hand, he touched her cheek, forcing her to meet his gaze. "When your mother was alive, all the time we were married, she was the only woman in my life."

"And now?" Tara whispered.

"Now, we'll just have to see how things work out." He knew he was being evasive but he could hardly tell Tara he was serious about Nina when the change in their relationship was so recent. "I care about Nina. We have history. We have a daughter and a granddaughter together."

Tara's gaze fell and her lower lip wobbled. The hem thread ripped out another three inches. Reid could have kicked himself for bringing up another sore point but maybe it was better to talk things out.

"You're my daughter, too," he said. "I love you and that will never change, no matter how many children I have."

"You're going to have *more* kids?" Tara said, dismayed.

Had he actually said that? He hadn't been thinking it, unless subconsciously. "No. I don't know," he said, confused. "Having Beebee around has made me remember how much fun you were as a little girl." That earned him a smile, which Reid returned before releasing her hand with a parting squeeze. "Why don't you show me your drawings?"

"Okay." Tara wiped her eyes and sat up to reach for a manila folder on her desk. She pulled out a handful of pen-and-ink drawings and handed them to Reid. "They're not very good because I've only just started."

Reid leafed through the drawings, surprised at what Tara had accomplished. "They *are* good. I'm amazed, actually. I didn't realize you were so good at art."

"I've always liked it but you and Mom were so set on me learning the violin that I never had time to draw," Tara said. "Thanks for giving me the money to take the course."

Reid glanced up from the papers in his hands. He could use some points right now but he had to give credit where credit was due. Goodness knows, Nina could use some good PR right now, too. "I didn't. Nina did."

"But she said—"

"She was covering for me." At Tara's surprised expression he added, "You see, she *is* genuinely nice. She didn't want you to think I'd forgotten you."

A mixture of emotions washed across Tara's face as she struggled to reconcile this picture of Nina with the one she'd built up in her mind. But although she was shaken, in the end she settled back into her old scornful, resentful attitude.

"She was trying to suck up to me," Tara said, gathering her drawings to return them back to their folder. "No matter what you say I'm not going to like her. I can't wait till Amy comes back so Nina will leave."

NINA HEARD THE DOORBELL ring as she finished changing Beebee's diaper. Reid was still upstairs with Tara so she went to answer it. A gangly young man of about twenty stood on the doorstep. He had a shock of messy brown hair, soulful green eyes and a smattering of freckles across the high bridge of his bony nose.

"I'm Ian," he said, extending a hand. "Is Amy here?"

"She's in Vancouver." Nina stepped back to open the door wider. "Come in. I'm Nina, Amy's biological mother."

Ian's eyebrows rose. "She said she was going to find you but I never thought she'd do it this quickly. Has she met her biological father?"

"Er, yes." Nina went to the foot of the stairs and called up, "Reid, can you come down? Ian's here."

How calm she sounded when in reality thoughts were racing through her head. How would Amy react to Ian's arrival? Would he want to take Beebee away? Could they stop him if he did?

She led the way into the living room and moved a pile of Beebee's picture books off the couch so he could sit. "Please excuse the mess. I haven't had a chance to clean up since Beebee did her last whirlwind tour of the room."

Ian's face lit at the mention of his little girl. "Beebee's here? Can I see her?"

"She's in her room, playing. She just got up from her nap and I was changing her when you arrived." Nina had no sooner spoken than Beebee's voice could be heard talking to her dolls in her room across the hall. "I'll go get her."

Beebee was sitting on the floor in her clean diaper, bouncing a doll up and down. When she saw Nina she looked up and smiled. "Dolly having bath."

Then she lifted her arms to be picked up. It was the first time she'd ever done that with Nina. "You little darling." Nina cuddled the toddler as a sudden burst of tears and laughter flowed together. "Whatever happens, I want you to know that I love you very much."

Beebee pressed chubby fingers into Nina's cheek where the tears had left a trail.

"Don't worry. I'm not crying." Nina blinked away the moisture and smiled. Then she put Beebee in a clean sundress and brushed her hair. "You want to look pretty for your daddy."

"Daddy!" Beebee went running out of the room and stopped short in the hall, wondering which way to go.

"Hey, Beebs!" Ian emerged from the living room and crouched so Beebee could launch herself into his arms. He swung her high in the air and hugged her. Even with his eyes closed Nina could see the love on his face as he held his little girl close. And when he spoke, his voice was rough with tears. "I missed you, kiddo."

"Me play in water," Beebee said proudly. Squirming out of his arms she ran into the foyer to get the bath toys Nina had dropped there when they'd come home. Ian's gaze followed her, his open honest face creased with the cheeky grin Beebee had inherited.

"Ian," Reid said, coming down the stairs. "Nice to meet you." His gaze was cautiously welcoming as he shook Ian's hand. "Did Nina tell you…?"

"She told me she was Amy's biological mother—" Ian's eyes widened then narrowed. He looked at Reid and said in a wondering voice, "*You're* her father."

Reid nodded. "After Amy ran away I thought Jim and Elaine might have told you."

"They never said a word about that when they gave me your address." Ian glanced from Reid to Nina. "I didn't know you two were together. I thought from what Amy said that you gave her up for adoption because you were too young to marry."

"That was a long time ago and much has happened in between. It's a long story." Nina glanced at Reid. When he nodded, she said, "Come and sit down. We'll fill you in."

They adjourned to the living room. Ian, nursing a cold beer, sat back on the couch with Beebee playing at his feet and listened while Nina related the history of Amy's birth and adoption right up to the present.

"So you two are back together," Ian deduced, filling in the gaps.

Nina glanced at Reid and exchanged a small warm smile. It seemed incredible that less than an hour ago she'd been in his bed, making love to him for the first time in nearly twenty years. She wanted to slide over and drape her hand possessively across his thigh but, was it her imagination or did some of the wariness he was displaying toward Ian extend to her as well? Had his talk with Tara given him second thoughts?

"We're…getting to know each other again," Nina said. "I'm here mainly to look after Beebee while Amy's away so Reid can continue to work on his book. I'm sorry you missed seeing Amy today. Will you be staying long in Vancouver?"

"I came for Beebee's birthday next week," Ian said. "And to convince Amy to come home. When will she be back?"

"She's staying at Nina's apartment in Vancouver," Reid said. "She got a bit part in a movie."

"A movie!" Ian exclaimed with a whistle of admiration. "That's always been her dream. Can you give me the address? I'll go see her there."

"I'm afraid we can't do that without speaking to Amy first." Nina had an awful feeling Amy wouldn't voluntarily agree to see Ian. But now that Nina had met him and seen how much he loved Beebee, she felt more than ever that he deserved a second chance.

Downcast, Ian picked at the label on his beer bottle while Nina pondered how to get him and Amy together. Then an idea came to her. It was brilliant; it was huge; it would solve everyone's troubles all at once.

"Reid," she said, barely containing her excitement. "Can I see you in the kitchen?"

CHAPTER ELEVEN

"YOU'RE OUT OF YOUR MIND," Reid said when Nina explained her plan. "Amy will never agree to such a thing."

"How could she refuse to come home for Beebee's birthday party?" Nina's eyes were shining and her words tumbled out in a rush. "I know having a lot of people around is the last thing you want when you're trying to finish your book. I promise, you won't have to do a thing except give me moral support. And show up on the day, of course."

"That part I have no trouble with," Reid said, suppressing a smile at Nina's animated appeal in spite of his misgivings over her idea. "Bringing everyone here without telling Amy is what worries me. Ian and the Hockings—"

"I like Ian," Nina interjected. "And I'm sure the Hockings will be delighted."

"I agree on both counts," Reid said. "But Amy said she doesn't want to see them and we need to respect her wishes. You'd be asking for trouble bringing those people here without her knowledge or permission."

"Beebee didn't want to go in the water until we

coaxed her in," Nina reminded him. "Now she loves it. Children don't always know what's good for them. It's the parents' role to guide them."

"Amy's an adult, not a child," Reid said. "She still hasn't forgiven me for lying about being her biological father and I don't intend to add to my sins by throwing a party she wouldn't agree to."

"I'll accept full responsibility," Nina assured him. "Just let me have the party here, where Beebee's comfortable. I want everyone to come—Ian, the Hockings, my parents, your parents—"

"Whoa, whoa, whoa." Reid held up his hands to slow her down. "Have you forgotten that your parents and mine never got along? Their political beliefs are on the opposite ends of the spectrum and I bet your dad is even more set in his ways than ever."

"If *your* father will refrain from looking down his nose at people who work with their hands then I'll tell *my* father not to make inflammatory remarks about the 'born to rule' mentality," Nina said.

"I can see it now," Reid muttered. "One big happy family."

"Everyone loves Beebee," Nina went on as if he hadn't spoken. "Celebrating her birthday gives us an opportunity to get Amy together with her family."

"I don't know," Reid said, shaking his head.

"Please, Reid?" Nina pleaded, taking his hand. "I haven't done anything for my daughter her whole life. Let me try to reconcile her with those who love her."

"Have you thought about how you'd feel if you

succeed so well that she goes out of your life again, perhaps forever?"

Frowning, Nina bit her lip. "I'll risk it."

Reid shook his head again as he gazed at her, a small smile playing around his mouth. "You're really prepared to sacrifice your own happiness for what you think is best for Amy and Beebee?" Nina nodded. "Do you know what kind of person does that?"

Nina shrugged helplessly. "A fool?"

"A mother."

"Oh, Reid, that's the nicest thing you've ever said to me." She threw her arms around him. "Does this mean we can have the party here?" This time he nodded. "You won't regret it."

"I hope *you* won't." Reid slid his arms around her waist and kissed her. "I'm going out to the movie set tomorrow to tell Amy about Ian. I'll mention the party to her, then."

"Dad, have you seen my Manga comic—?" Tara broke off as she came into the room and saw him and Nina locked in each other's arms, yet again.

"I took it to read," he said.

"Yeah, right." Tara snorted. "I can see you're getting a lot of reading done. I need it back to draw from."

Reid disentangled himself from Nina's embrace. Behind Tara, Ian entered the kitchen with Beebee on his shoulders. "Tara, this is Ian, Beebee's father. Ian, Tara, my daughter."

"If he's Beebee's father, then he can take her and go, right?" Tara said, looking from Reid to Nina.

"No!" Nina exclaimed. "We can't let Beebee go anywhere without Amy's permission."

"I'm not leaving Vancouver until I've talked to Amy," Ian said, tightening his grip on Beebee's ankles.

"Reid is going to see her tomorrow," Nina told him. "We'll have a birthday party for Beebee here. Amy will come out for that."

"Do you hear that, Beebs? You're having a party," Ian said to his daughter. "Until then I'll hang out with you every day."

"He's not staying with us, too, is he?" Tara demanded of Reid.

As Reid hesitated, Nina whispered, "He misses Beebee so much."

"Do you have a place to bunk while you're in town?" Reid asked Ian even though he'd already resigned himself to the inevitable.

"I was hoping you could recommend a cheap hotel," Ian said gamely.

"You can stay in our spare room," Reid told him.

"Thank you, sir," Ian said. "I won't be any trouble."

"Dad, the Manga comic," Tara reminded him.

"Reid, we'll need to set a date for the party."

"Later," Reid said firmly, holding up his hands to ward them off. "Right now I have to rescue my hero from a seductress, foreign mercenaries and an untreated bullet wound. Compared to what's going on in this house, Luke's problems are a walk in the park."

THE DARK GREEN MOUNTAINS of West Vancouver rose steeply ahead of Reid as he drove up the winding road toward Capilano Canyon where Amy had told Nina they were filming that weekend. Reid parked several blocks away from the Capilano Suspension Bridge and proceeded on foot to the area taped off by the movie people. The cool moist air scented with fir and cedar was a welcome change from the heat at sea level.

The narrow footbridge spanned a chasm three hundred feet wide and hung two hundred feet above a rocky stream. At any other time Reid knew the swaying bridge would have been crowded from end to end with jostling tourists clutching the metal cables and gaping at the long drop. Today it was empty.

At the near end of the bridge, a small crowd of on-lookers were cordoned off, watching for glimpses of the leading actors. A couple of trailers were parked along the side of the narrow road. Inside the cordoned off area more people milled, presumably extras like Amy. Cameras and sound equipment were standing by at the head of the bridge but not much appeared to be happening. At the far end of the bridge another group of extras waited.

Reid walked around the perimeter, peering into the crowd. He couldn't see Amy. A man in a baseball cap with a walkie-talkie glued to his ear moved toward the extras. "Standby on set. Tourists, move onto the bridge."

Reid watched the extras start across the bridge from both ends accompanied by cameras mounted on motorized wheels. When the groups met in the middle, the man with the baseball cap spoke into his walkie-talkie again. A commotion at the far end of the bridge resolved into someone being chased through the crowd. It was a woman pursued by two men in balaclavas, brandishing guns. Reid craned his neck along with everyone else. The trio wove through the tourists who parted in a panic, screaming and gripping the cables as the narrow bridge swayed wildly.

"Cut!" the man in the baseball cap yelled suddenly. "Where's the damn helicopter?" His walkie-talkie crackled. He listened for a moment then said in resigned disgust to the waiting actors, "Take five, everyone. We're waiting on the helicopter."

Immediately the tourists went back to being extras. The leading actress headed for her trailer and the villains pulled off their balaclavas, prompting a collective murmur from the crowd of onlookers and the clicking of many cameras.

A young woman in jeans and a skinny pink top with a camera slung around her neck detached herself from the crowd and ducked under the cordon to approach Reid. "What are you doing here?"

Reid smiled though he was hurt by Amy's accusing tone and defiant expression. At one time him coming to her first film shoot would have been a moment of celebration. Now he wasn't even welcome. "I need to talk to you. Have you got a minute?"

"I guess so," Amy said reluctantly.

They walked away from the bridge to a quiet park bench overlooking the canyon. The moment they sat,

Amy said, "What is it? Nothing's wrong with Beebee is there?"

"No, nothing like that." Reid leaned forward and rubbed his palms together. There was so much he wanted to say he hardly knew where to start. "Ian came to the house yesterday."

Under her pancake makeup, Amy visibly paled. "What did he want?"

"To talk to you. He wanted to see Beebee, too," Reid added. Nina had told him of Amy's doubts about the strength of her feelings for Ian and, while Reid sympathized with her, he also empathized with a father missing his little girl.

"Did you tell him where I'm staying?" Amy asked.

"Nina and I wanted to check with you before we gave him your address or phone number," Reid told her. "Although I must say, we both liked him and Beebee was thrilled to see him. Will you talk to him?"

"We're working ten- to twelve-hour days," Amy said. "Mostly just standing around and waiting but it's tiring. I can't cope with emotional stuff at the end of the day."

"You can't avoid Ian forever," Reid said. "He's the father of your child." Reid paused. "Do you love him?"

Amy ignored the question and concentrated on disentangling a strand of long hair from the camera straps. Reid found it impossible to tell what she was feeling.

"What about Saturday?" he went on. "You are coming out for Beebee's birthday, aren't you? And by the way, how come you didn't tell us about that?"

"I was going to but I forgot."

"Did you?" Reid asked. "Or did you know that such a milestone in your baby's life should be shared with Ian and the Hockings and you were ashamed because you'd run away from them?"

"You know what?" Amy turned on him suddenly. "You don't have any right to tell me what's right and what's wrong."

"Someone has to," Reid said equally angry. "And who has more right than one who cares about you?"

Amy subsided to chip at a corner of her pale pink nail polish. "Ralph Devenson called. He wants me to come to L.A. this weekend for an audition."

"Nina's planning a party," Reid said, deciding not to mention at this point just how big an event it was turning into. "Ian's come all the way from Halifax just to see you. Couldn't you arrange another time for the audition?"

"What if there is no other time?" Amy's hands clenched into fists. "What if Ralph gives the part to someone else? You don't understand how much I want this. I *have* to go."

"Beebee—"

"Beebee doesn't even know what day it is," Amy said. "She'd be just as happy if her birthday is celebrated the following week."

"Nina doesn't want to leave it too long. Ian has only a week off before he has to fly back or he'll lose his job."

"I didn't ask him to come." Amy looked down as she twisted her hair around her finger.

"He loves you," Reid said quietly. "If you keep pushing him away eventually he'll think you mean it and give up."

"How do you know I *don't* mean it?" Amy had a glint of tears in her blue eyes.

"Just think about it, okay? Ian's staying with us for now. Call him." Reid tried to take her hand but she pulled away and folded it in her lap, protected from his touch. Reid flexed his fingers across his thigh, pretending he wasn't cut to the bone. "The Hockings will be thinking about their grandchild's birthday, too." He paused. "And they're thinking of you. Every time I talk to Elaine all she wants is to know if you're well and when you're coming home."

Amy was silent then, in a faltering voice, asked, "D-did she say how Jim is? He was having some medical tests done but they hadn't gotten the results before I left."

"She mentioned he'd had a gall-bladder attack but it's not serious," Reid said. "You should call and find out for yourself."

"Why should I?" Amy said, antagonistic again. "They—"

"Imagine how you'd feel if some day Beebee turned against you." Amy's head came up swiftly and the painful flinch in her eyes told him the shot had gone home. "That's how they feel now."

Amy let out a long sigh. "I'll think about it."

"That's all I ask." Reid started to reach over to squeeze her hand then decided not to risk another rejection.

A thumping whir of a helicopter could be heard in the distance. Amy blotted her heavily mascaraed eyes carefully with a tissue and glanced over at the film crew. "I'd better get back to the set."

They rose. Amy squinted at Reid, shielding her eyes from the sun. "Why did you come all the way out here anyway? You could have phoned Nina's apartment."

"I wanted to give you something." Reid reached into the breast pocket of his shirt and pulled out the gold bracelet. "Recognize this?"

"My bracelet!" Amy exclaimed as he handed it to her. "I loved this bracelet. I cried when I lost it. Where did you get it?"

"I found it in a box of your clothes and toys that Elaine had passed on to Tara after you'd grown out of them," Reid said. "I kept it."

"If I'd known Mom was giving it away, I never would have let her even if I was too old for it." Amy fingered the tiny pink stones.

"I guess Elaine didn't realize it meant something to you," Reid said. "I thought you might like it for Beebee."

"I'll save it for when she's a little older." Amy slipped the thin gold chain into the pocket of her jeans. She rose and stood there a moment in an uncomfortable silence. "Well, I'll see you."

His heart a painful lump in his chest, Reid watched her start to walk away.

A few paces off, Amy stopped and turned to him. Shoulders hunched, arms angled awkwardly, she dug the toe of her running shoe into the dirt. "Thanks...for bringing the bracelet, I mean."

"Sure." Reid forced himself to smile though his eyes were burning. "Go on now. Knock 'em dead."

NINA WAS SEATED at the kitchen table going over the guest list when she heard the front door open and close. Reid was home from seeing Amy.

"All quiet, I see," Reid said, coming into the room. He put a hand on her shoulder, glanced around quickly, and bent to kiss her.

Nina thrilled to the touch of his lips but as he drew away she felt disappointed they could have no more than a fleeting embrace. Ian was here even when Tara was out and, though he could have no objection, she and Reid could hardly disappear upstairs to make love.

"How did it go?" she asked as he sat down next to her.

Reid shrugged. "So-so. Movies and acting jobs are consuming all her waking thoughts right now." Reid glanced at the list and frowned. "Who are Peter and Helena?"

"Ian's parents," Nina said. "They live in Kelowna where Peter owns a butcher store and Helena is a teacher. I thought we should invite them."

"Go ahead," Reid said glumly. "The more the merrier."

"You're a regular Eeyore today," Nina said. "What exactly did Amy say?"

"She's not ready to talk to Ian although I'm hoping

she'll change her mind when she's had a chance to think about it."

"What about the party?" Nina asked anxiously.

"She's set on going to L.A. this weekend for an audition," Reid said. "Can you postpone the event a week?"

"Actually, that would be better. The Hockings were going to have trouble leaving on such short notice. I'll let them know right away."

"I'm glad they're coming," Reid said. "After talking to Amy, I think she wants to see them but she's finding it hard to back down from her tough stance."

"My parents won't have any problem changing dates," Nina said then made a face. "I'll have to call your mother back so she can check her social diary again."

"You talked to my mother?" Reid asked. "How was that?"

Nina made a show of double checking her lists. "Fine."

"Meaning?"

Nina leveled her gaze at him. "She pretended she didn't remember me."

Reid muttered under his breath. "I can't believe she's still acting that way. Don't worry I'll speak to her."

"No, don't," Nina said quickly. As long as Reid was on her side, she could cope with his mother. "I'm a big girl now."

"Does she want to meet Amy and Beebee?"

"Oh, yes," Nina was happy to tell him. "She was already planning what to buy for Beebee's birthday present."

Reid rolled his eyes. "I can just imagine."

NINA STOOD AT THE FRENCH doors, unashamedly watching Amy and Ian on the beach. Amy had come home to see Beebee before she flew to L.A. and in doing so hadn't been able to avoid Ian. Not that she was liking it. A good three feet of sand separated them and no amount of reaching out by Ian seemed able to bridge the gap. Beebee was splashing in the shallows between sandbars with Daisy, happily unaware of the fraught situation between her parents.

"What do you think they're saying to each other?" Nina asked Reid. When he didn't reply, she glanced over her shoulder to where he sat on the wicker couch, engrossed in his work. "Did you hear me?"

"Who are you talking about?" Reid said, frowning as he scribbled changes on the hard copy of his rough draft.

"Amy and Ian. Who else?"

"I haven't got a clue," Reid murmured.

"Do you think he'll be able to talk her into letting him go to L.A. with her?" Nina persisted.

"He can't even talk her into taking a walk on the beach," Reid replied. "Why would she take him to L.A.?"

"She said she might be down there all week. I hope she doesn't miss Beebee's birthday party," Nina fretted. "Everyone's going to be there, even Ian's parents. And the Hockings. I thought she took that news well, didn't you?"

"That's because all she can think about is the audition," Reid said. "I still don't think she should go."

"I feel uneasy, too, but I've decided I'm simply being too protective. She *is* nineteen. Lots of young people travel and work on their own at that age. I think we should support her ambitions."

"How do we know this producer is even legitimate? Some stranger tells her to come to L.A. and off she goes. I don't like it."

"I asked my research assistant at the station to dig up some information on him," Nina said. "She should phone back today or tomorrow."

"By then it could be too late," Reid said. "Amy's flying out this afternoon."

Movement on the beach pulled Nina's gaze back to Amy and Ian. "Oh! He's moved closer. He's putting his arm around her. He's— Aw shoot. She pushed him away. Now she's turning toward him, saying something…I can't make out if she's frowning or sad."

"The binoculars are in my office," Reid said.

Nina ignored his faintly sarcastic tone and retrieved the binoculars. She trained them on the young couple only to find that Amy was facing the water again, her narrow back straight beneath her flowing blond hair. Ian had followed Beebee into the pool between sandbars.

"Darn," Nina muttered. "Whatever they were saying to each other I missed it."

JOAN KILBY 197

"Leave them alone," Reid said. "I'm sure when they figure out what they're going to do they'll let us know. Can't you find something else to do besides spying on your daughter?"

Nina put down the binoculars and came to sit beside Reid on the couch. "Who's Maria?" she asked, reading over his arm.

Reid edged the manuscript out of Nina's line of sight. "Someone who, like you, is too nosy for her own good. She'll probably get shot in the end."

"She's the double agent I suggested, isn't she?" Nina guessed, reaching up to play with the lock of dark hair falling over Reid's forehead. "Does Luke fall in love with her?"

"He gets tangled in her devious schemes," Reid replied, going on with his reading. "To his detriment."

"I don't believe you." Determined to get his attention, Nina trailed the tip of a finger down the strong bones of Reid's brow and cheek to his jaw. "I'll bet she's really his salvation."

"We'll have to see about that," Reid said. "It's not over till it's over."

Nina stroked from his jaw around to the back of his neck and began massaging. "You finished the first draft. You must know how the story ends."

"I haven't written the last chapter," Reid said. "I'm working through the book again to refresh my memory about Luke's goals and motivation."

"To save the free world, I thought," Nina said, idly slipping a hand beneath Reid's shirt collar. He had incredible powers of concentration not to notice her caresses. "You've been working since 6:00 a.m. Don't you need a break?"

Reid muttered something under his breath.

Ah, she was finally getting to him. "Pardon?" Nina said. "I didn't catch that."

"Nothing."

"Maybe Luke should work on having *personal* goals." Nina edged closer, draping her arm around his shoulder and placing the other hand on his thigh. "That would be a first for a Luke Mann story, wouldn't it?"

At last, Reid lowered the thick sheaf of dog-eared paper. "It's really hard to think when you're touching me like that."

"Like this, you mean?" Nina stroked her hand up his thigh.

With a groan, Reid turned to her. The manuscript slipped off his lap to the floor and separated into hundreds of individual pages.

"I hope that's paginated," Nina murmured as he pushed her down on the couch. His lips met hers, and she sank deep into the cushions with him stretched out on top of her.

"Nina?" Amy's voice penetrated the sensuous fog surrounding Nina's brain. "It's time for me to go to the airport. Would you mind driving me?"

Nina pushed on Reid's chest and struggled to sit up. If Amy thought it was strange that they were making out like teenagers on the couch, she didn't show it.

"Uh, sure," Nina said, straightening her shirt.

Ian followed Amy into the house. His thick chestnut hair was sticking on end as if he'd been plowing his hands through it. "Amy, please. I don't want you to stay with that guy all by yourself."

"You're just jealous. You follow me around like a lovesick puppy. I need space."

"And I need you and Beebee," Ian said. "When you come back to Halifax, I want us to move in together again."

"I told you, Beebee and I are staying in Vancouver. You can—" She broke off and flapped a hand dismissively. "Oh, I don't care what you do!"

"Fine! If that's the way you want it, we're through!" Ian sat down and dragged on his socks and tennis shoes with angry jerking movements. "I have begged and pleaded with you. I've told you I love you a million times. And this is the way you treat me. I've had enough." He got up and jabbed a finger at Amy's face. "First thing Monday I'm applying for joint custody."

"Oh, you're full of big talk," Amy blustered, hands on her tie-dyed hips. "You wouldn't dare."

"You're wrong," Ian countered, his voice low and dangerous. "I just might get sole custody considering you're abandoning your daughter to run off to Hollywood."

Amy paled as she realized he was serious. "Ian, please tell me you wouldn't try that."

"Beebee's my child. I'm not letting her go out of my life." He bent to hug Beebee, who'd begun to cry at the angry sound of her parents fighting. His arms eased away even as Beebee clung to him. His voice breaking, he said, "I love you, Bonnie. I'll see you soon."

Bonnie? Nina exchanged a glance with Reid.

"Ian, wait!" Amy called out. "Where are you going?"

"To find myself a lawyer." The front door closed behind him.

"I can't believe he actually left me." Amy's eyes were round with shock.

"Go after him," Nina urged.

"No." With an effort Amy pulled herself together. "I'm going to L.A."

CHAPTER TWELVE

NINA WAITED UNTIL SHE GOT onto the highway curving between farmland and greenhouses before she spoke. "He won't try to take Beebee away from you. He knows you're a good mother and that Beebee loves you. He wouldn't do that for her sake."

Amy frayed a strap on her woven bag, pulling apart the colorful threads with tense fingertips. "I've never seen him like that before. He's always so good-natured."

"If you push people too hard they push back." Nina paused. "After I had you, I pushed Reid away because I had all sorts of doubts—about his feelings for me, about our ability to raise you, about the way his parents felt about me. Later I regretted—"

"Are you going somewhere with this?" Amy interrupted. Her voice held a brittle edge. "Because frankly, I can't see the connection to me and Ian."

"My point," Nina said patiently, "is that if I'd had more faith in Reid and in myself, if I'd had more faith in our love, we might have stayed together. Love means being able to compromise."

"You think I'm being selfish, don't you?" Amy accused.

"I didn't say that," Nina replied, trying to maintain an atmosphere of calm. "Do *you* think you're being selfish?"

"Stop it!" Amy said. "You have no right to act like you're my mother after giving me away as a baby."

Nina couldn't speak for a moment as she dealt with the pain Amy's bitter words inflicted. "I told you why I felt I had to give you up," she said quietly. "I know you're lashing out because you're worried about Beebee and what Ian might do—"

"Stop acting like you know me!" Amy snapped tearfully. "You don't know me."

"*You* came looking for *me,* young lady!"

"Only to satisfy my curiosity," Amy retorted. "I've done that."

Oh God. Nina felt tears burning the backs of her own eyelids and wished she'd held her tongue. This wasn't going well at all. In fact, it was hard to see how Amy could be more hurtful. Nina gripped the wheel and stared straight ahead, blinking rapidly to avoid wiping her eyes and letting her daughter know just how vulnerable she was. But Amy was hurting, too. She was mixed up and upset over her fight with Ian. She had to care more about him than she was willing to admit. Then, too, maybe Nina had come on too strong.

"I'm sorry," Nina said at last in a strained voice. "I have no right to give you advice. I haven't had any practice at being a mother. Okay, I know, I'm *not* your mother." She dragged in a deep breath and slowly let it out. "Anyway, I've screwed up my love life in the past so who am I to tell anyone else."

Nina put the headlights on as they entered the tunnel under the river. Fighting with Amy left her feeling gloomy. The hum of cars bouncing off the hollow concrete was oppressive. Career-wise she'd done well. Friends, too. Which reminded her, she ought to touch base with a few people soon. But love? How long would she and Reid last this time?

Amy reached for a tissue from the box on the console and blew her nose. "I don't know who I am," she said, her voice small and bleak. "I don't know where I'm going."

Nina wished her hurt and anger would simply dissolve in the face of Amy's distress. She wished she could reach out with an infinite capacity for love. She wished she were a better mother. She wished she were a mother, period.

"Everyone has to figure out who they are regardless of whether or not they know their parents. It's part of life." Almost to herself, Nina added, "None of us really know where we're going—until we reach that fork in the road."

THAT NIGHT, NINA SLEPT POORLY. She awoke around two, her mind churning over her conversation with Amy. Their relationship, which had been going so well up until now, had taken a sudden nosedive. Unlike a mother and daughter who lived together, they didn't have the long history of bonding that would ensure their connection bounced back no matter what hurtful things they said to each other.

Added to that, Ian hadn't returned. Beebee was fretful; Reid was preoccupied with his book, and he and Nina were both worried about Amy being on her own in Los Angeles. Not having the rights and responsibilities of parenthood did nothing to reduce Nina's apprehension over Amy's safety and well-being.

Finally Nina dropped off to sleep only to be wakened a short time later by the birds singing with the dawn. Although she tossed and turned and buried her head under the covers, she never got back to sleep.

Yawning and bleary-eyed, she got breakfast for herself and Beebee. Reid was already in his office and Tara had to choose today, of all days, to practice her violin.

"Shall we go to the beach, Beebee?" Nina asked.

"Beach!" Beebee replied enthusiastically.

At least someone was cheerful this morning, Nina thought, smiling despite her fatigue. She packed up a book for herself and toys for Beebee and spread a blanket on the sand in front of the house. The tide was out so they ranged over the sandbars, collecting cracked shells and bleached sand dollars before finally returning to the blanket. Beebee started shoveling sand so Nina lay down and opened her book. Her eyes were so tired she could barely focus on the sun-dazzled print. She set her book aside and contented herself with watching Beebee shovel scoop after scoop of sand into her bucket before dumping it out and starting all over again.

Nina yawned. The movement of the shovel was mesmerizing. She glanced at her watch. Nearly twelve o'clock. "Are you ready for lunch, Beebee?"

"No," Beebee said, patting the sand smooth on top of her full bucket.

"A few more minutes," Nina conceded. "Then we'll go inside."

Nina yawned again. The sun was so warm, the sand so soft, her eyelids felt so heavy. Her eyes fell shut. It felt so good to relax. Just for a second…

Her eyes snapped open. The blue plastic bucket and shovel were half-buried in the sand. But Beebee was gone.

Nina's heart stopped in her chest. "Beebee?"

Sitting up, she looked around. A few yards away a man and a woman lay facedown on their blanket, eyes closed. On her other side was a pile of discarded towels, books and clothing belonging to the young family playing in the water. No little girl in sight.

Nina checked her watch and got another jolt. It was nearly one o'clock. She'd closed her eyes for what seemed like seconds but in reality she'd been asleep for an hour.

This couldn't be happening. Beebee was nearby, she had to be, maybe just behind that log. Nina jumped up and ran over to look. Her stomach fell sickeningly when she saw the bare patch of sand. There were dozens of logs she could hide behind. Front yards of houses she could wander into.

Maybe she went back to Reid's house. The wild burst of hope this thought engendered was quickly dashed by common sense. Beebee had never once left the beach voluntarily.

Shielding her eyes with her hand, Nina scanned the beach from one end to the other, as far as she could see. No little pink bikini, no flaming red hair. A sob filled her throat with panic. Where could Beebee be? Had she become bored and wandered away? Or had she been snatched, carried off by a stranger. Or had she gone to play in the water, wandered out where it was deep and—

"Beebee!" Nina ran over the rocks toward the water, not even feeling the barnacles slicing into her feet. Splashing across tidal pools, she ran down the sandbar then back onto the beach, calling loudly for Beebee. Everyone she met she stopped to ask, "Have you seen a little girl with red hair in a pink bathing suit?" Everyone shook their heads, no.

Nina jogged along the edge of the water, her gaze constantly sweeping the terrain ahead of her from the top of the sandy beach out to the bay on her right. She came to the end of the beach where the sand petered into mud and another dike rose to separate the head of the bay from the farm fields beyond. Nina turned around and jogged back the way she'd come, feeling an overwhelming need to get to Reid. He would know what to do. At the same time she dreaded what he would say.

By the time she reached the house, her heart was racing and her whole body felt sick with fear. "Reid!" she cried, bursting through the French doors, panting. The family room was empty and his office door was shut. She flung it open without knocking. "Beebee's gone. I shut my eyes for a minute and she just disappeared. She—"

Nina broke off as Reid's high-backed chair swiveled around. Curled up on his lap with a half-chewed digestive biscuit in her hand was Beebee.

"Oh, thank God!" Nina sobbed. "I was so afraid she'd wandered away or gone into the water and drowned…or…or been taken." She shivered, unable to rid herself of the grip of icy fear that had seized her when she'd awoken and Beebee was gone. She hugged herself as if she could never get warm.

"Hey, there," Reid said, concerned. He set Beebee on the floor and rose to put his arms around Nina. "It's okay. I had my eye on you two from the window the whole time."

"Oh, Reid," Nina wailed. A great pain constricted her chest all the way to her throat so she could barely speak. "Why didn't you wake me?"

"I was on the phone. I left the person on hold and dashed out to get Beebee when she started to wander away. I came straight back in," Reid explained. "Nina, sit down. We need to talk about Amy."

But Nina couldn't calm down. She couldn't stop the tears bursting like floodwaters from a broken dam. Now that the danger had passed, she thought she knew what was prompting her outpouring of emotion. Opening her eyes and finding Beebee gone had sent her flashing back to the hospital ward the morning she'd given birth to Amy. After Reid had seen Amy and Nina had sent him away, she'd dropped off to sleep. When she'd woken, her baby was gone. That she'd signed the adoption papers with her own hand and knowingly given Amy up hadn't lessened her anguish. What she hadn't been told was that they would take her baby while she was asleep.

She'd never had the chance to say goodbye.

"It's my fault," Nina cried, hysterically. "I let her go. I lost her."

"Nina, it's okay," Reid said, stroking her back. "You've been working too hard. It's not surprising you fell asleep. Don't be so upset. Beebee's gotten away from both Amy and me at times."

"You don't understand. I didn't know." Nina struggled out of his arms to reach for Beebee. She picked up the toddler and hugged her close to her chest, as if with enough protection and love she could change the past. She hugged Beebee so tightly the child squirmed.

"What didn't you know?" Reid asked, frowning.

Reluctantly Nina loosened her grip on Beebee and the child slipped away and ran to where Daisy was stretched out under Reid's desk. "How forsaken I would feel. How guilty. What that loneliness and guilt would do to my life."

Reid's puzzled expression cleared. "You're talking about Amy."

"My life has been completely taken up by career, friends and travel." Nina wrapped her arms around herself, trying in vain to stop the trembling. "I've filled every spare second going to parties and movies and trips. I've busied myself having a good time so I wouldn't notice the empty spaces, the alone times that not even friends or lovers could fill. I'm close to my parents but I've avoided true intimacy, avoided marriage." She wiped her streaming eyes with the back of her hand. "That guy I told you about, Bill? *He* was the one who wanted children. *I* said no."

"But why?" Reid asked, bewildered.

"I don't deserve a family after giving away my baby." Nina ran her fingers through her hair. "Even though I wanted children more than anything. Almost anything," she amended, thinking of Reid himself and how much she wanted him.

Reid wrapped his arms around her again. "You did what you thought was best. That's all any parent can do."

"It's not enough," Nina muttered against his chest.

"It never *feels* like enough. That's the way life is."

"How can she ever forgive me?"

"Amy had a good upbringing with the Hockings," Reid said, stroking Nina's back. "I know because I saw. She was loved and cared for. She never lacked for anything."

"Except me, her mother," Nina cried.

"She had a mother—Elaine," Reid said. Softly he added, "It's *you* who missed out, Nina. It's natural and understandable that you've suffered over the loss of your child but Amy isn't angry with you. She's only mad at me because I was part of a lie."

"But she must feel abandoned by me."

"You've got to forgive yourself, Nina."

In his arms she went very still. How could she forgive herself unless Amy did?

"SWEETPEA, WHERE ARE YOU?" Nina ran through the dark wood, stumbling over twisted roots and tangled undergrowth in her desperate search. A sob rose in her throat that drifted away on the keening wind. Nina had put her down just for a moment and when she'd looked again, Sweetpea was gone. Gone forever.

"Sweetpea!" Nina said aloud and sat up.

Darkness surrounded her and for a second she was back in the wood, her heart thumping with terror. Gradually her eyes adjusted to the lack of light and she made out the dim shapes of Beebee's crib, the dresser, the window where a faint crack of light from the street lamp shone through.

Nina threw back the covers and went to the crib, her hand over her heart, her breath caught in her throat. The nightmare was still with her, overwhelming rational thought. Not until she saw Beebee curled on her side, her blanket kicked off, did Nina breathe out a sigh of relief.

From the depths of the house, she heard the phone ring. Who could be calling at—she glanced at the clock radio—2:00 a.m.? The phone was still ringing as she hurried down the hall to the kitchen.

She picked it up just in time to hear a drowsy Reid mumble on his bedroom extension, "Hello?"

"Hi, it's me, Amy." Her voice sounded unnaturally bright and bubbly in the quiet dark of night. "I got the part! I'm going to be in the movie!"

"Is everything all right?" Nina asked anxiously.

"Do you know what time it is?" Reid demanded.

"Everything's *wonderful!*" Amy exclaimed. "What time *is* it? Did I wake you?" She giggled. "Sorry!"

"Where are you?" Nina asked. "What's that noise?" She could hear laughter and loud music in the background.

"I'm at Ralph's house. He's throwing a pre-filming party for the cast." Amy giggled again. "It's wild. People are jumping in the pool with their clothes on and some are going in without *any* clothes."

"Have you seen the script yet?" Reid asked.

"I'm thinking of taking a stage name," she babbled on. "How does Amy Holly grab you? Or Holly Hocking?"

"Why Holly?" Nina asked.

"It's my second name," Amy explained.

"The script," Reid reminded her. "Have you seen it?"

"Of course I've seen the script," Amy said indignantly. "I don't have a lot of lines but that's less for me to memorize, right? Don't worry! There really is going to be a movie. I signed the contract."

"Well, I guess that's all right then," Reid muttered.

"I miss Beebee so much," Amy went on. "Can I say hi to her?"

"She's sleeping," Nina said. "We've had a…busy day."

"Is she okay?" Amy asked. "Is she missing me?"

Nina had a sudden attack of confession anxiety about falling asleep while in charge of Beebee. "There's something I should tell you—"

"Nina's taking excellent care of Beebee," Reid broke in. "Don't worry about a thing."

Nina let out her breath. *Thank you, Reid.* "Beebee does miss you," Nina said. "When will you be back?"

"Ralph wants to start shooting right away. I'll have to stay longer." Amy's voice became strained. "What's Ian doing? Tell him—" Before she could say what to tell Ian, Amy's voice drifted away and Nina could hear her talking animatedly to someone else at the other end. A moment later she came back on, still giggling. "I have to go. I'll try to call tomorrow when Beebee's awake."

"Wait!" Nina cried. "What's your number there?"

It was too late; she'd hung up.

Nina listened to the silence, hearing echoes of Amy's voice in the dark. "Reid, are you still there?"

"I'm here." He sounded reassuringly close. "Did she sound strange to you?"

"A little." Nina paused. "No, a *lot*. Do you think she's taking drugs?"

"She sounded more like she's had too many drinks. I hope that's all it is."

"I don't like the sound of that party," Nina said.

"I know," Reid replied. "We can't do anything tonight. Get some sleep and we'll talk in the morning."

Nina hung up the phone and went back to her room. Beebee woke up as she came in and dragged herself to her feet, hanging onto the bars of her crib. "Mommy?"

"Nina's here." Nina picked her up and Beebee nestled sleepily into her arms. She breathed in Beebee's sweet-smelling hair and stood there holding her until long after the little girl fell back to sleep. She prayed that Amy wasn't in danger and wished with all her heart she'd never let her go. Amy Holly Hocking. She hadn't even known her daughter's second name.

REID GRIPPED A COFFEE CUP between both hands and watched Nina pace the kitchen with the receiver pressed to her ear as she listened to what her research assistant had to say about Amy's producer. Nina's deepening frown was doing nothing to alleviate his tense mood.

Ian was seated on a stool next to him, his troubled gaze also fixed on Nina. He'd shown up early this morning to let them know he'd taken the first steps in applying for joint custody of Beebee. But when he'd heard the details of Amy's phone call, his concern shifted to Amy.

Finally Nina hung up and turned to Reid and Ian, her expression grim. "Ralph Devenson makes pornographic movies."

Reid was stunned into silence as the news and all its horrible ramifications sank in. His little girl being stripped and pawed by strange men— He couldn't even think about it without wanting to vomit.

Ian's faint freckles stood out starkly against his white face. "I'm going down there to get her."

Reid shook his head. "I'll go. I'm her father."

Ian's steady gaze was determined. "I would be her husband if she'd let me."

"Let him go, Reid," Nina urged. "He's got a right."

"He's a boy," Reid said. "These people could be thugs."

"Wouldn't she know if it was porn? Why would she sign a contract?" Nina looked ready to cry.

"Maybe they threatened her," Ian said. He looked sick at the thought.

"Then she should go to the police," Nina said.

"The police can't do anything if she signed a contract," Reid replied. "She's legal age in California. And old enough to know better."

"Why are we sitting around talking?" Ian said suddenly, sliding off his stool. "*I'm* going to get her. I can handle myself. I have a brown belt in tae kwon do."

Reid started to protest again but a glance from Nina made him reassess. Ian *wasn't* a boy but a grown man. Nor was he asking Reid's permission. "I'll drive you to the airport."

An hour later Reid dropped Ian off in front of the terminal for international departures with his overnight bag and an address for Devenson's production company that Nina's assistant had unearthed.

"Wait," Reid said when Ian had opened the car door to get out. He fished in his shirt pocket for a folded check and handed it to Ian. "If reason and force fail, money usually does the trick. I've left it blank for you to fill in whatever amount will convince them to let her out of her contract."

"I'll try not to use it but…" Ian stared at the paper in his hand then at Reid. "Is there an upper limit?"

Reid ran a hand through his hair. There was no price too great to pay for Amy's safety but there was a limit to how much cash he could pull together on short notice. "Use your best judgment. If it's over say, ten thousand, contact me first."

Ian nodded. "I'll figure something out."

"Just bring her home safely, for all of our sakes."

Ian gave Reid his hand and shook it with a firm grip that, despite Reid's earlier misgivings, inspired confidence. "You can count on me."

CHAPTER THIRTEEN

NINA STUCK A FAT YELLOW CANDLE in the shape of a 1 on Beebee's birthday cake and stood back to admire her handiwork. The rich chocolate cake leaned to one side but the swirls of chocolate-fudge icing set thickly with Smarties made up for any architectural weaknesses.

"Before you say anything, I want you to know this is a really special cake," she said to Reid who was loading up a cooler with drinks. "Mom always made this cake for me on my birthday when I was a kid. Come to think of it, she still does."

"Me, me," Beebee said, reaching for the cake.

"Yes, sweetie, this is your cake but we won't eat it until later, until your mommy and daddy get back and all your grandparents and great grandparents are here," Nina said. "You can lick the spoon, though. And then it's time for your nap."

"What about me?" Reid murmured as he passed behind her with an empty beer carton. "Can I have a lick?"

Nina ignored the thrill up the back of her neck and

gave him a nudge with her elbow, connecting with the hard muscles of his abdomen. "Go away. I've got too much to do to be distracted by you this afternoon."

"Everything's done," he said, sliding his arms around her waist and kissing the back of her neck. "Beebee's about to go for a sleep and Tara's at her class. All those condoms I bought are going to waste."

Nina glanced at Beebee but the toddler was engrossed in removing every last trace of chocolate from the mixing spoon. "How can you even think about sex when we don't know what's happening with Amy and Ian in L.A.?"

"They're coming home today," Reid said. "That's all that's important."

They'd had a brief call from Ian that morning saying he hoped to bring Amy home in time for Beebee's party but he'd been at a pay phone without enough coins to give them any details as to whether they'd gotten Amy out of her contract, and if so, how.

"Anyway," Reid went on, "how can you think about chocolate cake?"

"It takes my mind off my worries—" She broke off, rolling her eyes. "Oh, I get it. But sex is different."

"How?" Reid demanded.

"It's more…complicated." She and Reid had been keeping their relationship low-key out of consideration for Tara's feelings, but how long could they go on like that? Sooner or later they either had to decide if they were together again and bring their relationship out in the open or… She didn't like to think about the *or*.

Right now, she was having difficulty thinking at all. Reid's hands were moving under her shirt and he was kissing the sensitive skin behind her ear. A tiny moan escaped her lips, a symptom of the buildup of frustration of past weeks that was begging to be released. "Let me get Beebee to bed. And clean up the kitchen. And—"

"And nothing." Reid slid his hands out from her shirt and down her hips, drawing her back against his groin to let her know just how impatient he was. "I'll put Beebee to bed. You throw the bowls in the dishwasher and meet me upstairs."

Forty minutes later, Nina lay sprawled across Reid's naked, sweaty chest savoring the hazy afterglow of lovemaking. "I wish your mother could see us now."

"Please!" Reid groaned. "Thank God you didn't say that before we made love."

"No, really, I've been thinking," Nina said, propping herself up to meet his gaze.

"Bad idea," Reid said lazily, tracing her lips with his finger. "Thinking's dangerous."

"I don't hate your mother anymore," Nina said.

Reid's eyebrows rose but he said nothing.

"However misguided, Serena was only acting out of love for you," Nina went on. "I knew that before but now I see it from a mother's perspective. If I had a nineteen-year-old son at Yale, I'd freak at the thought of him dropping out to marry a girl he'd known only a few months, tied down with a wife and baby." She paused thoughtfully. "Although I hope I'd support whatever my son wanted."

Reid pulled her closer. "You'd be a fantastic mother."

Nina gave him a long slow kiss then pulled away before she lost all impetus to return to the outside world and the coming events. "I'm going to shower and dress," she said. "It's party time."

Nina used Reid's shower then went downstairs to change her clothes. She eased open the door to Beebee's bedroom, trying to avoid waking the toddler before it was absolutely necessary. Her caution was pointless; Beebee had climbed out of her crib and was playing with her toys. Her eyes looked glittery with fatigue and there were tiny circles in the soft skin beneath them.

"Did you even sleep?" Nina scolded her gently. "I wouldn't be surprised if you didn't, with all the excitement around here, but today of all days, you really needed a rest."

Nina gave Beebee a quick bath and dressed her in a new yellow dress with blue smocking. Beebee seemed unconcerned with the enormity of meeting all her relatives but, for Nina, the anticipation of the coming party made her very nervous.

"When is everyone getting here?" Reid asked, coming downstairs, his hair still damp from the shower.

Nina glanced at her watch. Four o'clock. "Any minute. I can't believe there's been no word from Amy and Ian yet."

"Ian said he'd call from the airport when they got in," Reid reminded her.

"I know but I thought they'd be home by now. What if they miss the party?"

Reid wrapped his arms around her and drew her close. "When all this is over we're going to concentrate on us."

"Us," Nina repeated. She liked the sound of that. "What do you have in mind?"

"Something long-term. Permanent." His breath ruffled her hair with a gentle warmth. "Where we're looking toward the future instead of back at the past."

"That sounds a lot like marriage." She pressed her cheek against his chest, filled with a deep contentment. How many times had she dreamed of this very moment and never believed it would happen? Her dreams were so close to coming true.

Reid started to say something when Tara suddenly said loudly, "Isn't anyone going to answer the door?"

"Tara!" Nina sprang apart from Reid as the teenager came into the kitchen. "I didn't know you were home."

"I've been back for fifteen minutes." Tara threw her a narrow-eyed look as she crossed to the fridge, tension crackling from her stiff form and jerky movements.

"Oh," Nina said, only partly relieved. Tara couldn't have known they were in bed together but she could easily have overheard their conversation about marriage.

"Why didn't *you* answer the doorbell if you heard the ring?" Reid said, exasperated.

"It only just rang and I was in the bathroom," Tara retorted. "Anyway, it's not *my* party."

"But it *is* a party so I'd appreciate it if you could lighten up." Reid made an effort to lighten his own tone. "Try to enjoy yourself. Be happy."

"I'll get the door." Nina hurried down the hall, glad to escape the scene in the kitchen.

She opened the front door to a couple in their early sixties—Jim and Elaine Hocking. Elaine held a large square box and beside Jim on the step were two large black plastic garbage bags inside which Nina glimpsed wrapped presents. "Welcome," Nina said. "It's been a long time."

"Nice to see you, Nina." Jim's sparse hair was combed over a large bald patch and he wore a pink shirt under a dark sports jacket. He turned to his wife as they entered the foyer and said with a good-natured grumble, "We've made our entrance. Can I take off this damn jacket now? I'm sweating like a pig."

"Jim!" Elaine admonished him. In her floral silk dress and gold jewelry she had the sprayed and coiffed look of a woman who'd just come from the hairdresser. She laughed nervously and apologized to Nina, speaking quickly and with emphasis. "We're a little *anxious*. We didn't part with Amy on very good terms and it's been *weeks* since we've seen her or Beebee. I was *so* grateful when you called and asked us out for the birthday party."

"I'm glad you could come," Nina said, stepping back as they entered the house. She held her hands out for Jim's jacket and hung it on a hanger in the hall closet. "I don't blame you for wanting to get out of this. The summer has been exceptionally hot."

"I brought an ice-cream cake," Elaine said, holding up the square box. "It's Amy's favorite."

"What a lovely gesture," Nina said. "Thank you! Come in and sit down."

"We were so worried when Amy took off and came out here with Beebee," Elaine prattled on. "Naturally we had certain *feelings* about her contacting her biological parents but we're glad she came to you instead of ending up at the YWCA or some horrible tenement. Aren't we, Jim?"

"Is Amy still mad at us?" Jim asked bluntly as he set his bulging garbage bags down.

"I think she's over the worst of her, um, feelings," Nina said.

"Where *is* our darling girl?" Elaine asked, moving into the living room. "If anything had happened to her, we would have *died*. Did I say how grateful we are to you for looking after her and keeping her safe?"

"It was our pleasure. I'd better get this in the freezer." Nina seized the cake, glad of a reason to exit. What would Jim and Elaine say if they knew their darling daughter had been involved in a porn film? "Reid!" she called out. "Jim and Elaine Hocking are here."

Reid came down the hall, followed by Beebee at a run.

Elaine broke into squeals of delight. "Look Jim, hasn't Beebee grown?"

"Jim, Elaine, good to see you," Reid said. "How was your flight? Come in and sit down."

"Come to Grandma," Elaine cooed, holding out her arms to Beebee. "You remember me, sweetheart. Don't be shy."

Nina left Reid to get the Hockings settled and took the ice-cream cake into the kitchen. She opened the freezer, hoping it had miraculously cleared out since she'd last looked. Fat chance. If she took out a roast beef, two pounds of hamburger and a whole chicken, she just might squeeze in Elaine's cake.

Reid came in and went to the cooler for a couple of cans of beer and a bottle of white wine. "What's all this?" he asked, nodding at the meat on the counter.

"Elaine brought an ice-cream cake," Nina said, lifting the cardboard lid to peek at the yellow and pink swirls decorating the top with Happy Birthday Beebee. "It looks delicious."

"You should see the piles of presents they brought," Reid said in a low voice. "Two bags full."

"Did you tell them where Amy is?" Nina asked as she shoved the cake into the freezer.

"Not yet," Reid said, pouring a glass of wine. "Why?"

"We can't say *anything* about her and the porn film," Nina told him. "Don't even tell Elaine we let her go off to L.A. She'll have *conniptions.*"

"Why are you talking like that?" Reid asked.

"It must be contagious." Nina slammed the freezer door and started loading the frozen meat into the fridge.

"What should we tell them about Amy, then?"

"She went to an audition, which is true as far as it goes," Nina said, improvising. "Ian's gone to pick her up but we don't know exactly when they'll be back."

The doorbell chimed again.

"I'll get it," Nina said quickly. "You deal with Elaine and Jim."

It was Leo and Dora. Nina breathed a sigh of relief at the sight of her parents. "It's so good to see you."

"I made Beebee a cake because I know you're not into cooking," Dora announced, kissing Nina on the cheek. She had on a sleeveless flowing dress in madras cotton and a new pair of leather sandals. She lifted the lid on a plastic cake container to reveal a chocolate cake with fudge icing covered in Smarties. Exactly like Nina's cake except that it had straight sides. "Leo, did you bring in the presents?"

"I got them," Leo said, holding up a wrapped parcel and a red ride-on fire engine with a big pink bow on the steering wheel.

"Thanks for the cake, Mom," Nina said, taking the container and giving her father a one-armed hug. "I'll put this in the kitchen. The Hockings are in the living room. I'll be right out with some drinks."

"I'll give you a hand," Dora said, following her. "If you'd asked, I'd have come out early and helped with the preparations."

"Everything's under control." Nina hurried down the hall so she could put her cake in the pantry before—

"You made a cake!" Dora said, spying the misshapen chocolate mound. "Good for you." She smiled at Nina. "You're getting domesticated. I knew looking after Beebee would be good for you."

"Your cake looks so much better than mine, we'll eat it instead," Nina said.

"With so many guests, two cakes won't go amiss," Dora assured her. She ran her gaze over Nina's face. "You look good. Glowing." Dora smiled slyly. "It's Reid, isn't it?"

Nina's smile widened at the mention of his name. "Oh, Mom, I think this time we're—" She abruptly broke off as Tara glided silently into the room. Laughing nervously she said, "Don't be silly. It's the sun and the salt air. Mom, this is Tara, Reid's daughter. Tara, this is my mother, Dora Kennerly. Let's all join the others."

Tara didn't move from the kitchen. "Dad asked me to get some snacks ready."

"Everything's laid out over there on the counter," Nina said. "Give me a minute and I'll help you."

"No, I'll do it. You go back to the party." Tara sighed over the cheese board with the air of a modern Cinderella.

"Okay," Nina said awkwardly. "If you change your mind just give me a yell."

Nina introduced Dora to Jim and Elaine before re-membering that they already knew each other from when Dora used to clean the Hockings' house. Leo parked the fire engine next to the already alarmingly large pile of presents and took a seat by the window.

Dora went to sit beside Elaine on the couch. "Please, tell us all about Amy as a child. I'll bet she was just like Nina. They look so much alike now."

Elaine needed no more encouragement to chat and Nina began to relax. Beebee climbed on the fire engine and drove it away, a big grin on her face.

"Is that okay?" Leo asked.

Nina shrugged. "Why not?" *She* wasn't going to be the one to take it away from Beebee.

"Where is Amy's audition?" Jim asked Reid, running his fingers carefully through his comb-over. "You didn't say."

Reid cleared his throat. "It's, uh—"

The doorbell rang.

Reid rose with an expression of relief. "Saved by the proverbial."

Jim turned to Leo. "What did he mean by that?"

"Beats me," Leo said. "How's the weather in Halifax? We're having the hottest summer in twenty years."

Nina checked the scene—Dora and Elaine chatting happily about Amy, Jim and Leo politely conversing about the weather, Beebee backing Daisy into a corner with her ride-on fire engine. Everyone looked safe enough to leave alone, so she followed Reid to the front door.

Reginald and Serena Robertson, Reid's parents, had arrived. Reginald wore an immaculately pressed white shirt and camel-colored pants with a knife-edge crease. Serena looked equally cool in a white dress with navy piping. Serena offered her cheek, enveloping Nina in a cloud of expensive perfume and the faint tinkle of her heavy charm bracelet.

"It's been a long time," Serena said, sounding as though it hadn't been quite long enough.

"Hasn't it?" Nina replied with a smile, determined to put her theory into practice and be pleasant.

Serena gave Nina's discreet cleavage a disparaging glance as if to say, *What else would you expect from the trollop who seduced my teenage son,* and with a flick of her manicured fingers summoned Reid. "The cake is in the back seat. Beebee's present is in the trunk. Could you be a dear and assemble it? Reginald is useless with a screwdriver but you have somehow acquired handyman skills. I don't know how you do it."

"Through trial and error mainly," Reid said cheerfully and went out to get the cake and present from his parents' late-model Mercedes.

"You didn't have to make a cake," Nina said. "But thank you."

"Oh, I didn't *make* it," Serena replied with a light laugh at the very idea. She sailed past Nina. "Where's that delightful great grandchild of mine?"

Reginald nodded at Nina with an inaudible greeting and followed his wife into the living room. Reid came sideways through the wide doorway bearing an enormous box.

"Good grief!" Nina exclaimed. "With all these presents Beebee's going to be one spoiled little girl."

"This is the cake," Reid said, offloading it into her arms. "The present is a little bigger."

"How big?" Nina demanded over the top of the cake box.

"Let's just say it'll have to be assembled on the lawn." Reid paused and touched Nina's cheek. "Don't let her get to you."

"I won't." Nina straightened her back and put on a smile. "This day is about Beebee."

In the kitchen, she lifted the cake-box lid to find an enormous sheet cake iced in pink with dozens of red rosebuds strewn across the sides and top.

Tara, arranging quartered sandwiches Nina had made earlier that morning on a glass plate, glanced over, expressionless. "It's twice as big as the one she gets for me every year."

"Beebee has twice as many grandparents," Nina joked feebly. Tara didn't crack a smile. Nina poured herself a glass of wine and took a couple of quick sips. "Shall I take some of those plates in for you?"

"Sure, take credit," Tara said sarcastically, pushing a plate across. "You deserve it."

Nina's jaw froze in a tight smile. She'd made or shopped for the food, decorated the house and organized the entire party all while worrying about Amy, trying to placate Tara and being preoccupied with Reid. Tara had her nose so far out of joint she couldn't see past it. But Nina was determined not to let any unpleasantness mar Beebee's party so she squared her shoulders and, with plates of food in both hands, headed back to the fray.

The living room, as she approached, was a babble of voices. Leo and Reginald were squaring off over federal politics, just like old times, Nina thought, catching a telltale phrase. The women, in their various ways, were trying to attract Beebee's attention; Serena by command, Elaine by cajoling and Dora by getting down on the floor and rolling a ball to the toddler. Reid was moving around the room, keeping everyone's glasses topped up and trying not to take sides.

Nina was wondering why she'd ever thought this was a good idea when the doorbell sounded again.

"Can you get that?" Reid said, moving past her. "I've got to put together Mother's gift."

Nina put the plates of sandwiches on the coffee table and went to the front door.

"Peter Jaremovic." The tall man with the easygoing smile switched a bag from his right hand to his left so he could shake hands with Nina. "This is my wife, Helena. We're Ian's parents."

"I made this for Beebee." Helena presented Nina with a cake in the shape of a turtle with green icing and a licorice-whip smile. "We drove from Kelowna so it's been in a cooler for about six hours. I hope it's all right."

"You really shouldn't have," Nina said weakly. "But Beebee will love it."

"We're so excited to meet Amy and Beebee." Helena's blue eyes sparkled and her strawberry-blond curls bounced on her slender shoulders.

"We've looked forward to this ever since Beebee

was born," Peter added. "We've had photos, of course, but they're not the same."

Nina regarded Ian's mother thoughtfully. "You know, Helena, I thought Beebee took after my mother but now I see she also looks quite a bit like you. She's in the living room. Come and say hello to everyone."

Nina introduced Peter and Helena. The couple, who were roughly the same age as she and Reid, squeezed onto the couch beside Elaine.

"It's a *pleasure* to finally meet you," Elaine said.

"Likewise," Helena agreed, bobbing her head. "We're really hoping Ian and Amy get back together again. He loves her so much. He told us when he called last week he was going to ask her to marry him. We haven't heard from him in days, though. I hope she said yes."

Oh dear, Nina thought.

"That would be wonderful!" Elaine exclaimed. "Jim, did you *hear* that?"

"I'm not deaf," Jim told her patiently.

From down the hall in the kitchen, Nina heard the phone ring and Tara pick it up.

"In my opinion, they're not old enough to marry," Reginald pronounced.

"Puppy love doesn't last," Serena said, adding pointedly, "Does it, Nina?"

"Just because they're young doesn't mean it isn't the real thing," Nina replied evenly. "Young love can grow into something true and lasting."

"Nina." Tara stood in the doorway with the telephone receiver in her hand. "It's for you."

Nina stepped around Beebee and over Dora's legs and took the phone from Tara. She started back down the hall to the kitchen. "Hello?"

"Nina? It's Ian."

"Thank God!" Nina reached for the glass of wine she'd left on the counter and frowned when she saw it was empty. Had she drunk all that? She'd better watch her consumption. "Where are you? Is Amy with you?"

"Yes. We're back at the Vancouver Airport, waiting for Amy's duffel bag to come off the luggage carousel."

"Was it really a porn film? Was she relieved to see you? Did you get her out of the contract?" Nina fired questions at him.

"Yes. Yes. Yes," Ian replied. "We'll tell you everything when I get back. Don't worry about picking us up. The shuttle goes right through Beach Grove and it's leaving in a few minutes."

Nina tucked the receiver under her chin while she corkscrewed open another bottle of wine. "Hurry."

"What's wrong?" Tara asked, coming into the room with an empty plate and a clutch of wineglasses to be refilled. She bumped into the table and sat down abruptly.

"Nothing's wrong. Ian and Amy are on their way." Nina frowned. Tara was acting strangely. "Are you all right?"

"Fine." Tara smiled brightly. "I just misstepped."

"Okay," Nina said. "Thanks for your help today. Reid and I appreciate it."

Tara's eyebrows rose at the suggestion, however oblique, that Nina and Reid were a couple. Nina could have kicked herself. Her only thought had been to make Tara feel valued and she'd taken it the wrong way.

"The mini quiches are done," Nina said, opening the oven door to check on them. "Can you take them out to the living room?"

"You take them. I'll pour more wine," Tara offered.

Something about the way she said it made Nina pause.

"I know whose glass is whose," Tara said, indicating the distinguishing charms around the base of the stems. "You might want to get out there with your camera. Beebee's starting to open her presents."

"Already?" Nina grabbed the tray of mini quiches and hurried back to the living room.

Beebee was seated in the middle of a ring of doting adults who were all handing her presents to open. Her dimpled smile was smeared with candy, which Jim was feeding her from his pocket. Her sticky fingers tore at shiny gold wrapping paper printed with colored balloons.

"I decided it was time for presents," Serena declared, staring imperiously at Nina from the best chair.

"We should wait for Amy and Ian," Nina said, glaring back. "They'll be here in half an hour."

"Beebee *was* starting to tear at them," Dora told her with a commiserating look.

"Fine," Nina said, giving up. They might as well get the presents over with before Beebee got too strung out. She was already starting to act up as a result of all the attention lavished on her.

Beebee had already taken possession of Dora and Leo's ride-on toy but now she opened, with help from Dora, a complete set of Beatrix Potter books.

"I know she's too young for them," Dora said apologetically. "But they were so sweet."

"They're adorable," Nina agreed and whisked them away for safekeeping before Beebee could rip the pages.

Helena gave Beebee a hand-knit sweater and Peter had made her a wooden boat. "For the bathtub," he said.

"Beebee loves to play in the water," Nina told them proudly. "She'll adore the boat."

Beebee would have happily played with the boat then and there but Elaine upended the two plastic garbage bags. A cornucopia of wrapped presents slid out into Beebee's lap and spilled across the carpeted floor. Beebee giggled charmingly and Elaine pulled her onto her lap to assist in opening the parcels. It was a long drawn-out process yielding Beebee four different stuffed animals, multiple dolls, books, clothes, a toy phone, crayons, Plasticene and building blocks.

Nina stifled a sigh and told herself that Elaine's heart was in the right place. Then she glanced at her watch. Forty minutes had elapsed since Ian had called. They should have been back by now.

All through the unwrapping of the presents, the noise level continued undiminished as the adults conversed and Beebee shrieked with delight over each new item. At least Tara had joined the party, Nina thought, watching her chatting animatedly to Helena. Tara's face was flushed and smiling as she showed Helena a Manga drawing.

"Look at *this* dolly," Elaine said, handing Beebee a Cabbage Patch Kids baby.

Beebee took the doll and immediately threw it down in favor of a stuffed zebra. She quickly moved on to something else again, unable to settle on one thing. All her beautiful new presents lay heaped around her but she was too overstimulated to play.

"You've spoiled the child," Serena rasped at Elaine with blatant displeasure. Then she peered out the window to where Reid was assembling her present on the front lawn. "I do wish Reid would hurry up."

Elaine pushed back the curtain to take a peek and snorted. "Talk about spoiling her!"

"How about some birthday cake?" Nina suggested desperately to the group. "Tara, can you get it ready?"

"Which one?" Tara asked.

"Beebee would like a piece of *my* cake," Serena said firmly.

"Bought cakes tend to be dry." Elaine smiled sweetly. "Beebee will need ice-cream cake to wash it down."

"Homemade is best," Dora said. "Cut her a little piece of mine, too, Tara. Children love the Smarties."

"And some of my turtle cake," Helena added. "Please?"

Nina took a deep breath. "We'll have *all* the cakes, please, Tara."

CHAPTER FOURTEEN

TARA RETURNED A FEW MINUTES later and announced, "Everyone can come into the kitchen," so they all trooped through the house to gather around the kitchen table.

Five birthday cakes were rafted together in a vast frosted expanse. Beebee's eyes lit up at the sight and she wriggled wildly in Nina's arms as if ready to launch herself headfirst into the middle of all that of candy-colored goodness.

"Light the candles, quick," Nina said.

When a single candle burned in the center of each cake, a rousing chorus of "Happy Birthday" was sung with camera flashes going off every second.

"Blow out the candles, Beebee!" half a dozen grandmotherly voices encouraged her, complete with actions.

Beebee made a few ineffectual puffs that barely caused the candles to flicker so the grandmothers each leaned over their own cakes and blew for her. Nina, with grave misgivings, placed a dinner plate containing five pieces of cake in front of Beebee. The little girl chortled lustily as though she couldn't believe her good fortune. She took one bite using the spoon Nina gave her then threw it on the floor. Cutlery was clearly inadequate in this situation. Beebee tackled the job the best way she knew how—by stuffing chunks of cake directly into her mouth with her hands.

By the time she'd finished, cake crumbs were strewn far and wide with Daisy doing her valiant best to slurp them off the tiled floor. Beebee had cake smeared through her hair and on her clothes. Nina could have cried for the beautiful little yellow dress with the blue smocking, her present to Beebee. But what really made Nina uneasy was the crazed look in Beebee's eye and her maniacal giggle as she bounced in her high chair, slapping the tray with both hands and chanting, "Cake, cake, cake." She was hopped up on a sugar overdose that would have felled a six-year-old.

Into the mayhem came Reid, a smudge of dirt on his cheek and a screwdriver in his hand. "It's done," he said to Serena.

"Excellent!" Serena came over to the high chair and dabbed at Beebee's chocolatey mouth with a washcloth. "How do you get her out of this contraption?"

Nina rinsed the cloth under warm water and wiped Beebee's hands and face thoroughly, much to Beebee's distaste and Serena's impatience. Then she lifted the tray and brushed the crumbs off the little girl's lap. Spotting pink icing around Beebee's neck, she started wiping again. Beebee twisted away from her and slid out of the high chair.

Serena seized her chance and held out a hand to Beebee. "Come with Great grandmama, darling. I have something special for you. We've saved the best for last."

Ignoring her, Beebee grabbed Daisy's tail and wagged it. Then she set about finding and feeding cake crumbs to her playmate.

"*Come,* Beebee." Serena's tone became preemptory. When Beebee still didn't pay attention, Serena snatched up the toddler, pulling her away from Daisy. Beebee's bright blue eyes widened into twin circles of astonishment.

Oh dear, Nina thought. Before she could warn Serena about Beebee's little quirk, the child's mouth opened and her face screwed up. Nina covered her ears.

The screaming toddler went rigid and Serena very nearly lost her grip. "What's she doing?" Serena demanded of Nina as though it were all *her* fault.

"She doesn't like being grabbed by strangers," Nina said over Beebee's cries.

"I'm hardly a stranger! I'm her great grandmama." Serena marched out of the room and down the hall with the screaming child held before her like a shield.

Nina followed as far as the front steps. When she saw the present Reid had put together, she stopped in her tracks. A gigantic pink plastic kitchen in three wraparound partitions took up half the front yard.

Mercifully, the sight of the pink kitchen surprised Beebee enough that she stopped screaming. But she looked pale and sullen, not fully appreciative of the bounty she was receiving.

"Look, darling!" Serena held Beebee up so she could see then turned Beebee toward her with an enthusiastic jiggle. "Isn't it fabulous? What do you think?"

Beebee opened her mouth but it wasn't to speak, or even to scream. The undigested remains of five kinds of cake erupted in a projectile vomit all down the front of Serena's white silk dress. Great grandmama uttered a distinctly unladylike word. Nina gasped and pressed her fingers over her mouth but couldn't quite quench a burst of laughter.

Serena almost flung the child down on the grass. "Run off and play with your kitchen."

Beebee ran toward the fridge but at the last moment she veered left and headed down the driveway.

Nina's laughter faded in an instant. "Catch her!"

"Me?" Serena cried, wild-eyed and appalled. But she hesitated only for a second before she grasped the situation and tottered after Beebee on her high heels.

A minibus came around the corner just as Beebee took her first step onto the road. Nina screamed. The minibus screeched to a halt with the smell of burning rubber.

The sliding passenger door slammed open and Amy jumped out, quickly followed by Ian. Amy scooped up her child to hold her close in her arms. "Oh, my God, Beebee. You scared me!" She turned to Nina who'd also dashed across the lawn. "What's going on?"

Nina glanced at Serena, who looked as though she was about to have a heart attack if she didn't expire from the guilt of nearly letting her great grandchild get run over. Nina could have pointed a finger in blame; payback would be sweet. But it really wasn't fair. Or politic. "Beebee's wound up," Nina explained. "Too much birthday excitement."

White-faced, drenched in vomit, Serena steadied herself on Reid's parked car and applied a hand to her heaving chest. "I thought that child was going under the wheels. If she'd been hurt, I'd never have forgiven myself."

Nina supported Serena's arm and helped her hobble back up the drive. "It happens to the best of us."

Amy hurried into the house with Beebee clinging to her for dear life while Ian got the luggage out of the minibus. Nina desperately wanted to ask Amy what had happened in L.A. but she didn't have a hope of finding out, not in the short term. She took Serena up to the bathroom so she could clean up and lent her another dress. When she got back to the living room, Amy was engulfed by everyone chattering at her at once.

"Where have you been?"

"It's wonderful to finally meet you."

"You look lovely and so tanned."

"You look exhausted, poor thing."

"Is Beebee's name really Bonnie?"

Ignoring all the questions and comments, Amy walked across the room and straight into Elaine's arms.

"Oh, Mom," she cried. "I'm so glad to see you." She looked at Jim, burst into tears, and he was pulled into the group embrace. "I'm so sorry."

"Don't cry, sweetheart." Slightly bewildered, Elaine patted her back. "Everything's all right. We're *together*."

Nina was surprised. And hurt. A bittersweet ache tightened her chest and made it hard for her to breathe. Then she felt Reid's eyes upon her and she glanced over to see him watching her with a small sad smile on his face. He must have known how much she needed him at that moment for he stepped out of the circle surrounding Amy and her parents and came to her.

His arm went around her waist and pulled her in close to his side. "She's home safe and sound," he murmured. "That's what's important."

Nina leaned into him, grateful for his love and warmth supporting her when she really wanted to collapse. Tara was watching them from across the room but for once Nina didn't care. She was too full of emotion, both relief that Amy was safe and the poignant knowledge that her daughter called another woman Mom, and that was how it should be.

Just when Nina was thinking she'd have to leave the room so no one would see her cry, Amy pulled away from Jim and Elaine and put her arms around *her*, hugging her and saying, "Thank you for everything. I'm sorry about all the things I said. I'm so lucky to have so many wonderful people who care about me."

Suddenly Nina was smiling again with undiluted happiness. But she still couldn't speak, so she just squeezed Amy tightly and let her tears flow.

Nina drew back. Reid was standing awkwardly at her side. He started to reach out to Amy then stopped.

Amy gave Reid a loving smile and moved into his embrace. "Ian told me what you did," she said, her voice muffled against his chest. "I didn't need to pay them off but thank you."

Reid drew back and searched her face. "Did they hurt you?" He spoke so softly no one but Amy and Nina heard. "Or make you do anything you didn't want to do?"

Amy shook her head and wiped her eyes with the heel of her hand. "I'm fine, thank God, although for a while there I wasn't so sure."

Then Amy took a deep breath and turned to look around the room at all the smiling faces. "I'm glad I didn't miss seeing everyone. Thank you all for coming. Beebee's one lucky little girl."

Beebee was in Ian's arms, calm at last, though her rosy cheeks were tearstained. After greeting his parents, Ian had perched on a stool next to Helena's chair but his gaze never left Amy.

What had happened between them? Nina was dying to know. But the buzz of conversation shifted to Amy's audition and the news, astonishing to everyone but Nina and Reid, that she'd just returned from Los Angeles. Amy quickly quelled their interest by saying she hadn't gotten the part.

"Never mind," Dora said, consoling her. "You wouldn't want to live in L.A., anyway."

"Where *will* you and Ian live?" Reginald asked.

There was a silence. Amy went pale.

"We won't be living together," Ian said quietly. "Amy wants some time on her own. Still, we need to decide on a location where we can both spend time with Beebee."

Amy glanced at Ian. "So you did apply for custody?"

"Custody!" Elaine exclaimed.

Murmurs rose around the room. Nina wished she could wave a magic wand and make all the grandparents disappear so Amy and Ian could have privacy. Beside her, Reid took her hand and squeezed.

Ian tightened his embrace of Beebee. "I hope you won't keep me from seeing her." His voice broke and he had to pause for a moment. "But I don't want to put her at the center of a legal battle. I've decided to withdraw my application."

Amy went very still, as if she was afraid she hadn't heard correctly. She didn't seem to see anyone in the room but Ian. "Why?"

"I can see that in spite of…what happened in L.A. you're serious about acting," Ian said. "You should follow your dream. If you need space to do that then I'll give you space. But let's not fight over Beebee."

Amy stared at him, confused and bewildered. "Why didn't you tell me this on the way home from L.A.?"

"It took a while for me to sort all that out." Then he

gave her a wry smile. "Not that I could have got a word in edgewise with you talking nonstop about Hollywood."

"What if *I* changed my mind," Amy said. "What if I want to be with you?"

Ian lifted his head. Mingled hope and caution played across his face. "What are you saying?"

"I was wondering—" Amy's fingers twined together "—if you still wanted to marry me because—" her voice softened "—I want us to be a family." Amy took a deep breath. "If you still want me, that is."

"Jeez, Amy." Ian set Beebee down then rose and gathered Amy in his arms. His voice was a husky murmur. "I'll always want you."

Nina felt tears pricking her eyes and she heard several other grandmotherly sniffles.

"Now that you're getting married, we're back to deciding where you're going to live," Serena declared, interrupting the tender moment with a return to practicalities. "My friend in real estate could get you a good deal on an apartment in Shaughnessy close to us. There are a number of excellent schools nearby."

"Shaughnessy's way out of the price range for a young couple starting out," Leo snorted. "They'd be better off near us on the east side. Although nowadays even that's expensive."

"They can't stay in Vancouver," Elaine cut in. "Amy's home is in Halifax. Ian has a *job* there."

"Not anymore," Ian told her. "I've been away too long and lost it."

"Amy has family in Vancouver, too," Dora ventured hopefully.

"Kelowna has all the advantages of a small town," Helena said. "It's a wonderful place to raise kids. I could babysit. Peter could take Ian on in his butcher shop."

"Vancouver," Serena said firmly. "Amy needs to be near the film industry if she's going to be in the movies. And here on the West Coast we're closer to Los Angeles."

"Whoa, folks!" Ian held up his hands for quiet. "We appreciate your input and the fact that you all want us near you. But it's for Amy and I to decide where we live." He turned to Amy. "I have a friend who owns an organic apple orchard in southern Ontario. He's been asking me for years to come and work for him and eventually form a partnership. It's not far from Toronto. You could take acting classes, or whatever." His questioning gaze turned to Amy. "What do you think? Where do *you* want to live?"

Amy looked around the room at each face in turn. "I love you all…." When her gaze came to rest on the woman and man who'd raised her, her eyes filled with tears. "But…Ian and I should make a fresh start. I won't be ready to go back to Hollywood for a long time." She slid her arm around his waist. "Let's go to Ontario."

Very diplomatic, Nina thought. They'd be more or less in the middle of the country.

Elaine smiled bravely and blew her nose. "You can come home whenever you want."

Amy laughed. "I hope you'll all come to visit us."

Nina went back to the kitchen for coffee and tea. The room looked as if a disaster had struck, with half-empty glasses and dirty plates everywhere. Tara was clearing the table. She set a wineglass down abruptly as Nina entered the room.

"Careful," Nina said mildly. "Those are crystal."

"I know."

Nina filled a tray with china cups of tea and coffee, sugar and cream, and took it back out. She handed around the cups and found a seat beside Amy. "So tell me. What happened in L.A.?"

Amy sipped her herbal tea. "It was like a dream come true at first. I didn't even have to audition. Ralph told me I was perfect for the role. His wife was really nice and they had a maid and a cook and a big house in the Hollywood Hills. The second day I was there, they threw a party and all these glamorous people came that I was going to be working with. I felt like I'd hit the big time." She paused and shook her head. "It's a different lifestyle, that's for sure. They started drinking cocktails at lunch and just kept drinking all afternoon. I tried to keep up. By the time Ralph brought out the contract, I could have signed away my soul and not realized it."

"Was he purposely getting you drunk so you would sign?" Nina asked, appalled. "There must be a law against that."

"He wasn't trying to trick me." Amy cast her eyes down and set her teacup carefully in the saucer. Then she met Nina's gaze. "I knew what kind of movies he made when I went down there."

"You knew he made porn and you still went!" Nina exclaimed. She had just enough presence of mind to keep her voice down to a whisper.

"Shh," Amy begged, glancing around. "Please don't tell anyone. Especially not my parents. Or Reid. I told Ian but only because I had to. Thank God he was so understanding. A dozen times I wanted to call him and ask him to get me out of there but I was afraid of what he would think of me."

"But why would you agree to make a porn film?" Nina tried not to sound judgmental but she was having a hard time being understanding.

"I wanted to be in a movie so badly I shut my mind to the reality." Amy shrugged unhappily. "I told myself it would be a stepping stone to better things. Only when I was on the set and they were preparing to start shooting did I have doubts. I was in the dressing room, looking over the script, and that's when it sunk in what I was about to do. I suddenly thought about what you said about the fork in the road. I knew then I couldn't go through with it."

"What happened when you told Ralph you wanted out?"

"That's when it got scary," Amy admitted with a shiver. "I refused to take my clothes off much less— Well, you know. Ralph got really angry because he had a crew and other actors assembled and I was wasting his time and money. He started shouting at me that I'd signed a contract and if I didn't do what he wanted he'd take me to court. Suddenly no one was friendly anymore and I was afraid he really could sue me for thousands of dollars." Amy paused. "That's when Ian showed up."

"Enter, the cavalry," Nina murmured.

"Exactly." Amy relaxed and smiled. "Ian was wonderful, totally calm but very authoritative. I've never seen him like that before. He took me aside and I told him everything, just as I've told you. Then he went up to Ralph and told him that since I'd signed the contract while under the influence of alcohol it wasn't legally binding and that I had witnesses to the fact that I'd been drunk. He said that if Ralph had anything further to say all future correspondence should be directed to my lawyer. Then he handed over a business card with a lawyer's name on it."

"The lawyer he saw about Beebee's custody," Nina deduced.

"I don't know. I guess so." Amy's gaze rested on Ian and Beebee with love in her eyes. "He doesn't need that anymore."

"I'm glad you've worked things out," Nina said, putting her arm around Amy. "I'm sure you won't regret it."

"Even before Ian showed up at the studio I'd already changed my mind about not wanting to be with him. When he walked out that day, I realized what I'd given up and how much I loved him." Amy smiled sheepishly and shrugged. "He's changed. I've changed."

"You've both grown up," Nina said, hugging her.

Gradually the party wound down. Beebee fell asleep in Ian's arms and Amy put her to bed. Serena and Reginald were the first guests to leave but not before inviting everyone over to their house for dinner before the out-of-town visitors left Vancouver.

"You'd better come, too," Reginald said gruffly to Leo. "Seeing as we have family in common."

"It's about the only thing!" Leo said.

"Oh, you two aren't fooling anyone. You both love to argue," Serena scolded. To Dora she added politely, "We'd love to have you." Then she gave Nina a tentative smile. "You, too."

"Thank you." Nina felt her heart fill with warmth. Forgiveness was so much better than payback.

Peter and Helena were the last to leave after making arrangements to see the young couple the next day. Amy and Ian followed them out then popped back in long enough to say they were going for a walk on the beach.

"We'll clean up when we get back," Amy promised.

"Don't worry about it." Nina said and closed the door behind them. She turned to Reid with a heartfelt sigh.

Reid saw the fatigue and emotion wash over Nina's face and took her in his arms. He held her for a few moments, breathing in her familiar scent and savoring the feel of her next to him. "It was a great party. You were a spectacular hostess." He smiled into her hair. "You even won over my mother."

Nina drew back with a wry smile. "That might be overstating it. Call it an armed truce." She glanced around at the dirty dishes and scraps of wrapping paper strewn throughout the living room. "We might as well get started cleaning up."

Reluctantly Reid loosened his embrace and joined her gathering empty plates. He realized he hadn't seen Tara since shortly after Amy and Ian had gotten back. "Where's Tara?"

"She was clearing up the kitchen when I got the coffee." Nina placed dirty glasses on a tray and gathered up crumpled napkins. "She's trying to be helpful."

"That's nice to hear. I was afraid she'd be jealous and cause trouble during the party." Reid carried his load of dirty dishes down the hall. When he got to the kitchen, he stopped dead in the doorway. Tara was sprawled at the table, her head tilted back and her hair cascading over her shoulders. Before his astonished gaze, she tipped half a glass of white wine down her throat. She was reaching for the bottle to pour herself more when she saw him.

"Cheers," she said tipsily, lifting her glass.

"Tara!" Reid exploded. "What the hell are you doing?"

"What you told me to do. I'm getting *happy*," Tara said, slurring her words. The sardonic smile she threw him was grotesque.

Nina set her dishes down in the sink. She frowned, full of concern. "How much have you had to drink?"

"None of *your* business," Tara said rudely.

"You do not speak to Nina like that," Reid said. "Apologize at once."

"No," Tara said, insolent. She fixed Nina with a mocking glare. "I know all about you and my dad. What I didn't know already I was able to fill in after chatting to Elaine and Serena, even your mom, Dora. People aren't very careful about what they say when they've had a drink. Everything's not as peachy keen as you'd like to believe."

"I don't know what you're talking about," Nina said stiffly. She turned her back on Tara to place plastic wrap over the cakes.

"Then I'll tell you," Tara said with malicious glee. "The only reason Dad's been pretending to be in love with you is so he could use you to get to Amy and Beebee."

"That's ridiculous." Nina stopped what she was doing to stare at Tara, her face pale.

"Tara, go to your room." A cold anger washed over Reid at Tara's behavior but also at himself for letting her jealousy toward Nina get out of hand.

Tara ignored him. "*Is* it so ridiculous?" she asked Nina. "Years ago he gave *you* up but he never gave up Amy. He would never have given up his beautiful blue-eyed daughter. He left Vancouver and *you* and moved to Halifax to be near *her*. He didn't care about *you*."

If possible, Nina's face turned even whiter. "Don't listen to her," Reid said. "She's just trying to make trouble."

"Then there were all the mean things he said about

you to Mom." Tara stumbled over her words but she was clearly enjoying herself.

"What?" Nina demanded.

"You drove him crazy with your talking, talking, talking. 'She never shuts up,' he said to Mom. He said he had the hots for you when he was young but he could never have lived with you." Tara sniggered. "From what I can see, nothing's changed. Why he told me just the other week that his relationship with you is just for sex."

"I said nothing of the kind!" Reid said, outraged.

"You implied it." Tara wagged her finger at him.

"Adults don't mean everything they say," Nina said but Reid noticed she wouldn't look him in the eye.

"And Nina, *you're* only interested in Dad now that he's successful," Tara said, changing her line of attack. "You dumped him when he was poor and a nobody. Mom stuck with him through the tough years while he was struggling to sell his first book. She worked two jobs so he could take a year off teaching and do nothing but write. If it wasn't for her, he might never have gotten published."

Reid's gaze was riveted to his daughter in a kind of paralyzed horror. Where had Tara come up with this twisted version of events? There was just enough truth in what she was saying to make both he and Nina wonder about the other. But it wasn't true! Surely Nina didn't believe any of it.

In a voice he barely recognized as his own, he growled at Tara, "Go to your room. Don't come out until you're sober. You're a disgrace!"

Having done her worst, Tara dragged herself up from the chair and stumbled out of the kitchen. Reid walked to the doorway and made sure she negotiated the stairway. Then he shifted his gaze to Nina. Her eyes were dry but her throat worked as she gazed back at him with a mixture of hurt and anger.

"Surely you don't believe all those things Tara said."

"Did you really complain to Carol that I drove you crazy by talking too much?" Nina asked.

"Well…" He rubbed his hand across the back of his neck, uncomfortably aware of her scrutiny. "Okay, I *did* say something like that once. We were watching your TV show. Carol was jealous of you even though I hadn't seen you for ten years. I wanted to reassure her that I wasn't pining for you."

"A convenient explanation," Nina said.

"It's the truth! I couldn't say all that in front of Tara. She holds her mother up on a goddamn pedestal." In his heart of hearts he *had* pined for Nina. But even though Carol was dead, he couldn't bring himself to be disloyal. "We shouldn't hold each other responsible for things we said and did long ago."

"What about the present?" Nina asked in a strained voice. "Do you really think I'm after you for your money and reflected glory?"

"It never crossed my mind," he said with complete honesty. "You're a success in your own right, which Tara certainly must realize when her brain isn't addled with alcohol and jealousy."

"I *wanted* you to pursue your writing," Nina

insisted. "I didn't want you to give up your studies to take some crap job so you could support me and the baby."

"Or was that just an excuse so you wouldn't have to marry me?" A bitterness Reid hadn't realized he harbored spilled out.

Nina went pale. "Is that what you think? After all we've said and done these last weeks? You still think it's my fault we didn't end up together."

"No," he said, throwing his hands up. "Look at us. She got what she wanted—she got us fighting. All that stuff is in the past."

"Maybe so," Nina said. "But Tara's problems are very much in the present."

"I've been hiding my head in the sand," Reid admitted. "I know, I know, you've been telling me for weeks."

"This isn't going to work."

"What isn't?" he asked.

Moisture welled in Nina's eyes. "You and I."

"Don't be silly," Reid said. "You admitted yourself that what Tara said was all nonsense."

"You can't discount her feelings," Nina argued. "You've underestimated how strongly she feels about another woman taking her mother's place. Not just any woman but *me.*"

"I'll talk to her." Reid paced away to the window, frustrated. "She'll come around."

"No, Reid, she won't. Not while you and I are seeing each other. If I wasn't your first love, we might have a chance but I cast a shadow over her mother's happiness. Tara will never accept me. And if you choose me, she'll turn away from you." Nina came up to him, touched his arm. "Look at me."

She was deadly serious, so serious it scared him. "What is it?"

"I know what it is to yearn for my daughter's love." Nina's pale face reflected that suffering. "I will not be the cause of a rift between you and Tara. We have to stop seeing each other."

Reid went cold all over. "For how long?"

"Indefinitely."

An appalling, paranoid thought came to him. Maybe Tara was right and Nina's feelings weren't genuine. *No.* He shook his head. That's what Tara wanted him to think.

"Now that Amy's leaving, she doesn't need me to look after Beebee anymore," Nina went on, her voice far from steady. "My vacation is over. I need to go back to work."

"But we can still see each other."

"No, we can't." Nina shut her eyes and drew in a breath, as if to gather strength for what was to come. "I'm going to pack. And then I'll leave."

Reid slumped into a chair and gazed out the window at the white gulls wheeling against the darkening sky. In a few short hours his world had fallen apart. Amy was leaving Vancouver before they'd fully mended their rift or gotten to know each other in a new context. Tara had turned into someone he barely recognized and Nina—Nina was the most unfathomable of all. This afternoon she'd been in his bed, making love with him. Now, she was saying she didn't want to see him anymore.

Nina appeared in the doorway with her suitcases.

Reid slowly rose, feeling stiff and old. "You're really going."

Nina stood on her toes and planted her hands lightly on his shoulders. Her lips barely brushed his cheek.

Reid reached out to hold her but before his fingers could clasp her waist, she was slipping out of his reach. She picked up her suitcases and walked quickly down the hall, the soft tap of her sandals on the tiles echoing in his bewildered brain.

Reid stared after her. This was crazy. He and Nina were meant to be together. He couldn't let her go. He started after her, his pace picking up as he moved down the hall past the staircase—

A muffled sound from upstairs halted him. Tara was crying, her quiet sobs just audible.

Nina glanced over her shoulder. "Go to her."

"I'll call you." Reid's glance moved from Nina to Tara's door at the top of the stairs. Another sob caught his heart and squeezed it painfully.

"Please don't," Nina said. "I'm going to be really busy in the next month."

She walked out the door and shut it behind her. A moment later her car engine started.

Reid wanted to run after her but he had no choice but to stay. His daughter needed him. As Nina reversed her car out of the driveway, Reid's shoulders sagged. He heard her drive away as he started up the stairs.

CHAPTER FIFTEEN

"TARA?" REID OPENED HER door and, without waiting for an invitation, walked in.

"Go away!" She lay facedown on her bed with her legs askew, one arm dangling over the side. Her head was turned sideways on the pillow and one bloodshot eye peered through the lank hair hanging over her face.

"No," he said bluntly and stood over her. He'd never been so angry with her in his life. "You swilled enough wine to make a sailor drunk and then spewed out venom at people who care about you."

"Nina doesn't care about me," Tara mumbled.

"Quiet!" Reid ordered. "You be quiet and listen. You made me ashamed of you, something I've never felt before. Nina's tried hard to get to know you, to help you."

"Yeah, right." Tara raised her head then fell back with a moan and rolled onto her side, holding her stomach.

"Yes, right," Reid said. "She thought I was being blind to your needs. She tried to tell me over and over that I needed to pay more attention to you. I was so absorbed in my book and her and Amy and Beebee that I didn't listen."

"No, you *don't* listen." Tara pushed herself up on her elbow. "You never listen to me, that's for sure. I'm the good girl, I do what I'm told. I play my violin and stay out of trouble, nice and quiet. Well, I'm sick of being quiet!" she shouted. "It hasn't gotten me anywhere. Amy gets pregnant and runs away, then makes a porno film and has everyone running around like chickens with their heads cut off—"

"How did you know about the porn film?" Reid demanded.

"I eavesdrop, *okay?* But you could have told me." She paused to burp then pressed a hand to her stomach. "I'm not a child."

"You're not acting very mature—" Reid broke off as Tara moaned again, louder. "Are you going to be sick?"

"I don't know." Tara pushed herself to a sitting position and doubled over, arms crossed. "I'm not feeling so good."

"That's what you get for drinking too much alcohol," Reid lectured. "Maybe next time—"

"Ohhh," Tara moaned. "I'm going to throw up."

"Quick, into the bathroom!" Reid put his arm around Tara and guided her as she stumbled next door. He flipped up the toilet seat and held her hair back while she vomited. "Get it all up or you'll keep feeling sick."

When she was finished, he handed her a warm wet

cloth and then a towel. He was reminded of when she was a little girl washing up for bed and that made him sad at how things changed. By now his anger had dissipated and he felt only disappointment. "Wipe your face. Then brush your teeth."

Subdued, Tara did as she was told. When she'd rinsed her mouth, she straightened and met Reid's compassionate gaze in the mirror. Stony-faced, she looked away.

Reid helped her back to her room then paused in the doorway. "Go to bed. You'll feel better after you sleep it off," he said. "We'll talk tomorrow."

NINA LEFT THE BEACH AND DROVE toward home. Lights twinkled against the blue mountains as dusk settled over the city. Her heart was heavy and her eyes swollen with tears she refused to let fall. It was no good feeling sorry for herself. She'd done the right thing but oh, it was hard. She kept making sacrifices and had nothing to show for it. Part of her had longed for Reid to run after her and stop her, to tell her that nothing and no one would ever come between them again. But he'd done the right thing, too. She wouldn't love him half as much if he didn't put Tara first.

The security light came on as she climbed the steps to her apartment in the West End. When she'd moved in ten years ago, she'd hoped and expected that someday she'd exchange it for a house and a family of her own. *Another dream bites the dust.*

She walked through the house, shaking her head at

the evidence of Amy's occupation. Amy probably thought she'd left it tidy but there was a dirty coffee cup in the living room, flyers strewn over the kitchen table, toast crumbs on the counter and used towels on the laundry-room floor. Kids.

That thought almost sparked tears. Nina fought them back and went through the house, cleaning away the last traces of Amy's presence. She would have photos and letters to look forward to, she told herself, determined to remain positive. She hadn't seen Amy grow up but she wouldn't miss Beebee's development.

Maybe in a few years she and Reid could be friends. She didn't see how they could go back to being lovers or ever marry. Even if they waited until Tara was grown, something had been lost by giving each other up a second time.

Nina leaned the broom against the wall and put a hand to her stomach at a sudden queasy rumbling. Feeling light-headed, she sat down in a kitchen chair. She'd been so busy today serving everyone else that she'd eaten only a mini quiche and a quarter of a sandwich since breakfast. She hadn't drunk more than a glass or two of wine but the alcohol on top of only a small quantity of food wasn't sitting well in her stomach. Although come to think of it, she hadn't been feeling well this morning, either. She hoped she wasn't coming down with the flu.

Nina gave up cleaning and made herself a piece of toast and a cup of tea. Then she sat down at her computer to check her e-mail. She would go back to work on Monday so she might as well get a head start on her in-box.

There was a note from her producer. Reid's interview on her talk show was confirmed. Nina propped her head in her hand and lost the battle with her tears. How was she supposed to get over him if he kept popping into her life? It wasn't just the interview. For the rest of their lives, Amy and Beebee would bind them without actually bringing them together.

THE NEXT MORNING, REID TOOK orange juice, toast and aspirin upstairs. Tara was lying in bed staring at the ceiling when he knocked and gently pushed the door open.

"How are you feeling?" he asked, coming into the room. He set the tray on her desk.

"Like a moron." She couldn't look him in the eye. Then without warning, her face crumpled. "I'm sorry, Dad."

Reid sat on the bed and pulled her into his embrace, smoothing her hair off her heated cheeks. "You learned one lesson, at least—not to drink too much. Don't forget that the next time you go to a party with your friends."

"Do Amy and Ian know what happened?" Tara asked. "I didn't even think about whether anyone else was in the house when I started raving at you and Nina."

"You didn't think, period." Reid waited until she propped herself up on pillows before handing her the glass of juice. "Don't worry about them. They were walking on the beach."

Tara took a cautious sip, then drank the rest. "They must wonder why I went to bed so early."

"I told them you were worn out from the party and wanted an early night." He paused while she took a piece of toast. "I feel like a moron, too."

Tara screwed up her mouth in a self-deprecating grimace. "Because you raised one for a daughter?"

Reid shook his head. "Because I ignored the warning signs of a daughter in trouble."

"So it's all your fault." She smiled tentatively.

"Seriously, Tara," he said. "We need to talk about your resentment toward Nina."

Tara looked down at her half-eaten piece of toast as if she'd suddenly lost her taste for it. "You *said* you weren't serious about her. But the way you acted was totally opposite. And then I heard you talking about the future and marriage and…and…" Her voice began to waver and then she fell silent.

"I should have been more honest with you about my feelings for her but for a long time I wasn't even being honest with myself. Would it be so terrible if she and I were to get married?" Reid asked. He held his breath, knowing her answer was critical to how he proceeded with Nina—*if* he proceeded—although not to was unthinkable.

"If you marry Nina you'll forget all about Mom." Tears filled Tara's eyes. "It'll be like she never existed."

"Surely you don't think that!" Reid said, horrified. Tara's fears brought home to him how out of touch he'd gotten with his daughter. Partly, he admitted guiltily to himself, because of Nina.

Tara was quiet, waiting for him to say more.

"I will *never* forget your mother," he told her with quiet emphasis, making sure she believed him. "I will *always* love her. As for forgetting she existed, how could I possibly when I've got you to remind me of her?" Smiling, he touched Tara's cheek, his fingertips brushing the soft skin tenderly. "I look at you and I see *her.* Her quiet charm, her loving ways are with me every single day. I think of her all the time and I will until the day I die."

Tara was quiet, absorbing his words.

"I love you, too, even if I don't always show it," Reid went on. "I know I've been taken up with Amy and Beebee and yes, Nina, lately but soon we'll be on our own again and I'll make it up to you. I promise."

"What about Nina?"

"Nina's gone home," Reid said. "She has to go back to work."

"Will you be seeing her?"

"Not in the immediate future."

"So you're not going to marry her?" Tara asked, traces of fear and reluctance still in her voice.

"I love her, Tara," he said gently. "If you care about my happiness then you'll accept that. Yes, I want to marry Nina." He paused. "I just don't know how she feels about that anymore. She told me she was going to be very busy in the next while." Had that been a clue for the clueless that she was dumping him? "And I— I have to finish my book."

It was the story of his life.

NINA SAT ON HER SHADY front porch and waited for Amy to arrive. She, Ian and Beebee had been sightseeing in Victoria and Vancouver Island for the past week with Jim and Elaine. Amy had called and asked to see Nina before they flew back to Halifax tomorrow morning. Nina had eagerly agreed and, although she dearly loved Beebee and Ian, she was glad Amy was coming alone so they could talk.

A cool breeze was blowing off the water this morning and the rosebushes on either side of the wide steps rustled, casting off withered petals. Summer was coming to an end. Nina wrapped her cardigan around her shoulders and pressed a hand to her stomach. Since Beebee's birthday party not a day had gone by that she didn't feel queasy in the morning and often at night. She couldn't blame lack of food and excess alcohol, nor did she have other symptoms of the flu. She wanted to wait a few more days to take the test but she was almost certain she was pregnant.

The bus rumbled around the corner and wheezed to a halt. Amy got off, saw Nina and waved. Her loose skirt flowed about her tanned legs and her long blond hair lifted with a soft gust of wind.

Nina rose, slung her large bag over her shoulder and

held her arms out. "I'm glad you could come. I thought we could take a walk along the seawall."

"Great idea," Amy replied. "Tomorrow we'll be cooped up on the airplane for hours."

"So you persuaded Ian to accept Jim's offer to buy you all tickets?" Nina asked as they walked up the block to the traffic lights where they could cross the street to the park that bordered the seawall.

Amy smiled. "He came around pretty quickly after I described the three-day bus ride across the country with a squirming toddler."

"How was your trip to Vancouver Island?" Nina asked.

"Good," Amy said. "I had a chance to talk to Mom and Dad about my adoption. We got a lot of things out in the open about how Mom never felt wanted by her adoptive parents. She decided the best way to make me feel completely loved was for me to think I was their own child."

"You can't fault her motives," Nina said. "Although it's too bad she didn't tell you when you were old enough to understand."

"She regrets that now." Amy sighed. "Trust is still an issue. I can't help wonder what else didn't they tell me. She swears there's nothing. At least we've made up."

"I'm glad." Up ahead, the light turned green and the walk signal came on. Nina quickened her pace. "Let's cross the street."

A few minutes later, they'd walked through the park

and were strolling along the seawall. Freighters were anchored offshore and brightly colored kites flew on the grassy point of land on the opposite side of English Bay.

The smell of the ocean reminded Nina of her time spent at Reid's house on the beach. She hadn't heard from him nor had she called. Their love seemed forever doomed to be just a summer romance.

"When are you moving to Ontario?" Nina asked.

"We'll stay in Halifax just long enough to pack our things then we'll rent a U-Haul and take off," Amy said. "I'm going to go to college part-time and take acting and filmmaking classes, maybe even screen-writing. I'll take general arts courses, too, just to keep my options open."

"That's wise. It's a tough business," Nina said. "How are Ian and Beebee?"

"They're good. I don't know if I ever thanked you properly for taking care of Beebee for me—"

"Don't even mention it," Nina said, smiling. "I loved every minute of it. But you've got to tell me one thing. Why do you call her Beebee if her name is Bonnie?"

Amy laughed. "It's silly. Ian used to call her his Bonnie baby. She tried to copy him, got it muddled and it came out Beebee."

Cyclists and joggers wove past; a mother pushing a stroller called to her preschooler running ahead to slow down. Finally Nina couldn't avoid asking the question uppermost in her mind. "Have you seen Reid?" she asked, keeping her voice light. "How is he?"

"He's fine, preoccupied with Tara and his book," Amy said. "It's too bad you couldn't have made it to dinner at his parents' house."

"Uh…something came up," Nina said. Like a bad case of cold feet at seeing Reid so soon after they'd parted ways.

"He and Tara are coming into town tonight to meet us all for dinner," Amy said. "Why don't you join us?"

"I have to go to a charity dinner at the Children's Hospital," Nina said. "I'm giving a speech."

"You're involved in so many good causes," Amy said as they walked past the saltwater pool at Second Beach. "I really admire that."

Nina was silent. She believed in the charities she supported but lately she'd been clinging to them. The hours they ate up were a way of taking her mind off her own life, which seemed emptier than ever now that she was on her own again. Not on her own, she chided herself. She still visited her parents once a week plus her other friends….

Face it. Soon Amy and Beebee would be gone. And Reid had disappeared from her horizon as quickly as he'd come into view a short month ago. She even missed Tara.

"Are you and Reid going to get together again?" Amy asked, divining her thoughts. "You two seem pretty hot on each other."

"No, that's not going to happen after all," Nina said.

"The day of Beebee's party, I told him we couldn't see each other again." Nina told Amy about Tara feeling threatened and Reid's need to mend his relationship with his daughter.

"That's too bad," Amy said. "You two are totally suited to each other. It would be cool if you finally got married."

"I don't know," Nina said. "We're completely different types of people."

"Being suited doesn't mean having the same personality," Amy said. "Look at Ian and I. He's so solid and practical and I've got my head in the clouds. You and Reid complement each other. Besides, I'd feel better about causing everyone back home so much grief if my running away had at least one good consequence—to bring you two back together."

Nina put her arm around Amy's waist as they walked along. "You and Beebee came into my life. That's benefit enough."

Amy met her gaze and smiled. "That's true. I wanted to meet you and I'm so glad I did."

"While you've got me face-to-face, was there anything else you wanted to ask about our family?" Nina said. "Or me, just anything at all?"

"There was one thing...." Amy hesitated, her fingers twining around a long strand of hair. "I don't want to put you on the spot. You've been so welcoming to me, I don't want you to think I'm not happy with how things have turned out."

Nina touched her cheek, encouraging Amy to look at her. Gently, she said, "What is it?"

"I understand that you didn't think you could care for me properly when I was born but if you *could* have kept me…" Amy swallowed. "Would you…I mean… did you want me at all?"

"Oh, my God, Amy." Nina put her arms around her daughter and held on tightly. Her eyes squeezed shut against the tears that sprang up instantly. "*Yes.* Of course I did. Don't ever think otherwise."

"You were young and carefree. I…I wondered if maybe you were just as glad not to have the burden of a child," Amy said, her voice thick. "I wouldn't have blamed you."

"Not a day has gone by in the past nineteen years that I haven't regretted giving you up." Nina's muffled voice broke in a sob. "My dear sweetpea. I'm so sorry you felt that way."

"I tried not to," Amy said. "Mom and Dad never let me feel unloved. But some small part of me always wondered…."

Nina drew back and wiped her eyes. She reached into the capacious bag slung over her shoulder and removed a bundle of thick envelopes tied together with lavender-colored ribbon. Handing them to Amy felt like giving away a part of herself, which in a way it was. "These are for you."

Amy took the hefty stack. "What are they?"

"Birthday cards." Nina blinked, still struggling with her tears. "One for every year of your life. With each

I enclosed a letter telling you about my life at that time and how much I missed you. Oh, and fifty dollars as a birthday gift. That might help you get started in Ontario. I didn't know when, if ever, I'd be able to give them to you but it helped, just a little, thinking that someday I might."

Amy gazed at her in wonder and her eyes filled with fresh tears. "Letters! If you knew what this means to me."

Nina smiled. "I can guess. I know what it would have meant to me to hear from you." She placed her palm against Amy's tearstained face. "Can you forgive me?"

"Of course." Amy hugged her and when she drew back she said, "I love you."

"I love you, too," Nina said. She tried to clear her voice of the neediness in her heart. "Do you think you'll ever come back out west?"

Amy's clear blue eyes searched hers. "I want to. Someday I will."

"Maybe you'll get another part in a movie being filmed here," Nina said.

"That's too long to wait," Amy exclaimed. "You have to come to the wedding. Ian and I are getting married in Halifax next month, before we leave for Ontario. We'll send you an invitation."

"I'll be there, don't worry," Nina said.

"And then there's Christmas."

"Christmas," Nina repeated. "There's so much to look forward to." She tried not to think about the time in between.

Nina drove Amy back to the hotel where she was staying then went home. Her apartment seemed so empty and quiet that she flipped on the TV, something she ordinarily never did during the day. Oh, good. The light was blinking on her answering machine. There were five messages. Maybe there would be a call from Reid—

No, she thought, pushing the play button with more force than necessary. It was ridiculous to let herself hope when every day she was disappointed. Today would be no exception. After all, she'd told him not to call.

Yet as she listened to the messages playing back, she was aware that her heart rate had increased and her fingers gripped the edge of the hall table where the phone sat.

"Nina, call me." The message was from her producer, Adele. Short and to the point, like the woman herself.

The next message was from her friend Janice inviting her to an end-of-summer barbecue that Saturday night, followed by one from Dora wanting to know if Amy and Ian had left town yet.

Two more to go. There was still a chance he'd called to see if she was coming out with them all tonight. But no. The fourth message was from the woman organizing the charity dinner wanting to remind Nina that her talk was before dinner and would she please be prompt.

Call number five. Nina crossed her fingers, praying to hear Reid's voice.

"Ms. Kennerly, this is Dan McNally from the *Leader* newspaper, returning your call…."

Nina walked a few paces into the living room and slumped in an armchair. The TV blared in the background but the words didn't penetrate.

All these years she'd held the dream that she and Reid would someday be reunited. Then Amy had come back to her, bringing Beebee and bringing her and Reid together. For a while it had seemed as if she would have everything her heart had desired.

But life wasn't that simple, you couldn't just skip over intervening years as though they'd never existed. Amy had a life with her other family. Reid had Tara, and Tara came first. Nina, knowing how precious a parent's relationship with his child was, would never get in the way of that.

She'd had her chance with Reid and, through no fault of either of them, they'd failed to come together. She was alone and probably always would be since she couldn't imagine marrying anyone else.

Nina fumbled for the remote and switched off the TV. The room, already dim and unlit, became silent. She would just have to get used to it.

REID CLOSETED HIMSELF in his office and tried to work but found it almost impossible to concentrate. His book was due today and he still had twenty pages to write. He never missed a deadline. Ever. Now it appeared inevitable. The pressure was paralyzing.

The ending just wasn't coming together. As Reid

had feared, Maria had complicated Luke's life. While Luke and Maria had been making love, the political situation in Paris had grown more dangerous. Her contact hadn't shown and Luke now had no way to complete his mission.

Reid frowned at the blinking cursor lodged at the end of a half-finished sentence. He'd written his protagonist into a corner. Was Maria a deliberate attempt by Luke's enemies to sabotage his mission? Or was Luke getting soft? He'd lost his razor-sharp edge and his ability to act decisively under stress.

Giving up in disgust, Reid pushed back his chair and leaned on the windowsill. There wasn't a lot to see outside now that the weather had turned cooler and there were fewer people on the beach.

Nina would be bound to have some good ideas about Luke and Maria. He reached for the receiver attached to the fax machine on his desk. Then he dropped it back in its cradle. He hadn't called her before because she'd told him not to and because he wanted to get his book finished before he got embroiled in emotional issues. If he called her now, she might take it amiss that he just wanted to brainstorm his ending.

Carol had been a perfect wife in that respect; she'd been used to him being absorbed in his work and hadn't demanded much of him, either emotionally or timewise. An awful thought occurred to Reid and he dropped back to his chair with a jerk that sent him wheeling backward. Was the real reason Carol hadn't asked for much that she'd known he poured everything into his writing and had nothing left of himself to give his family?

That was an awful indictment of his life if it was true. Nineteen years ago he'd allowed Nina to push him away instead of insisting on marrying her so they could be a family. Then he'd had another chance with Nina and he'd let that slip away, too. Tara came first, he argued. Nina had said so herself. Yes, but was he using Tara as an excuse not to engage with life? With love? Was his work that important to him?

Reid got up and paced the room. He had to get his book done but he couldn't get his mind off Nina. What was she doing? Why hadn't *she* called *him?* Maybe their brief affair had allowed her to get him out of her system and now she was going on with her life. Maybe she didn't want to take on a hostile stepdaughter and an emotionally unavailable man. He could hardly blame her.

From the second story came the sound of Tara's violin. Ever since their talk, she'd gone back to practicing, although she'd veered away from classical music into contemporary. She hadn't given up on her Manga drawing but her course was over and she was back at school. He was spending more time with her but this deadline meant he had virtually no time for anyone else. Including Nina.

Giving up on solving his own problems, Reid went back to trying to sort out Luke's dilemma. He needed to leave Maria behind and get back to his mission. The problem was Luke had developed feelings for Maria and for him to just walk away would leave him looking coldhearted.

The longer Reid stared at the screen, the blanker his mind became. He'd always scoffed at writer's block. Now he was experiencing it. His publicist had called with a date for Nina's talk show two months from now. At least he'd see her then. But that interview would never happen unless he actually finished the book and it was published.

What if he never wrote another word in his life? What if he was finished, through, dried up? This was to be his breakout novel. What if it became his career epitaph instead?

CHAPTER SIXTEEN

NINA LURCHED OUT OF BED, her stomach churning, and stumbled to the bathroom. She bent over the sink knowing there was little more than burning bile to come up. Quickly she swished her mouth out with water and stared at herself in the mirror. The time had come.

Damping down any emotion, she reached under the vanity for the pregnancy test kit she'd bought yesterday and tore open the packaging. She took the test and paced the tiled floor while she waited for the results. Eyes scrunched shut, breath held, she picked up the wand and opened her eyes. She was going to have a baby.

Slowly the realization sank in. And with it, all the changes that would come about in her life. The diapers, the sleepless nights, the first step, the smiles and funny stories, the growth, the changes, someone to love and care for…

"Yes!" Nina shouted to the empty apartment. She danced out of the bathroom and down the short hall to the living room, waving her arms in the air as she pranced around in circles. "Yes, yes, yes! I'm having a baby!"

She had to call Reid. She had a good reason now. Whether he was busy with Tara or not, he needed to know they were going to have a baby. Reid loved kids. This time they would do everything right and raise it together.

Nina stopped twirling and rocked to a dizzy standstill. *Would* Reid be happy about the news? Would he want to be a father to this child or would he think of it as an unwanted complication? What if he hadn't sorted things out with Tara? Nina plus a baby would place a tremendous additional strain on his relationship with his second daughter.

She tried to remember if he'd ever said anything about wanting more kids. All she recalled him saying on the subject was that his books were like his children and he'd made some weird analogy between giving birth and writing a book. As though printed and bound paper could hurt the way popping out a baby did!

Well, there was only one way to find out what he thought and felt. She picked up the phone to punch in his number. Her fingers trembled so much she needed three tries to get it right. The phone rang and rang. She counted the rings. Ten, eleven, twelve… She was about to hang up when he answered.

"Reid, it's me," she said breathlessly. "Sorry, did I get you out of the shower or something?"

"No, no, I'm sitting here at my desk." He sounded distracted, his voice going in and out of range. "What's up?"

What's up? Not "I've missed you, Nina. I'm so glad to hear your voice." She was thrilled to hear *his*.

"I've got some big news," she said, getting excited again.

"Amy and Ian's wedding?" he said. "I know about it."

"No, it's not about their wedding. It's—" She broke off, hearing the clacking of computer keys in the background. He was typing while he talked to her? She couldn't believe it. They hadn't seen each other for three weeks after parting forever and he couldn't stay interested long enough to have a simple phone conversation?

"Are you actually listening to me?" she demanded.

"To tell you the truth, Nina, you got me at a really bad time," he said. "I was in the middle of a thought."

"A thought," she repeated, flabbergasted.

"Yes. I shouldn't have picked up but I had to in case it was Tara. I almost had the ending to my book and then the phone rang and I answered." He sounded frustrated. "As soon as I start to speak it short-circuits something in the brain. I don't know how that works but it's a real pain."

Argh! There was no point telling him about the baby now. "I'm sorry I bothered you. You just go back to your thought."

"Okay," he said, still abstracted. "Talk to…you…" He trailed away again to the frantic clicking of the computer keys.

Nina sighed. Even though she didn't think he was listening, she added, "Call me when you finish your book."

TARA WOKE IN THE MIDDLE of the night, aware that something wasn't right. A faint line of light showed beneath her door. She glanced at her bedside clock— 3:00 a.m. Why was Dad still up?

She got out of bed and crept onto the landing to peer down the stairs. Her father was pacing the living-room floor, muttering to himself. Tara felt her stomach clench. So this was finally it. Social isolation had driven him insane. What should she do? She was only a teenager and in spite of her pretensions to "edgy," she knew she couldn't cope with a deranged parent.

Ever since Nina had left, nothing had seemed quite right. It was too quiet for one thing. At first that had been a relief. Tara had always thought silence was peaceful and Dad said he needed it to think. But after hearing female laughter and conversation on a regular basis, Tara was rethinking her position on Nina. The more time passed, the worse Tara felt about the things she'd said to her. Her dad had suggested she call and apologize, tactfully adding, when she was ready.

Tara was ready now.

Nina was practical and down to earth. She would know what to do about Reid. Pining for her might be making him act this way, although Tara knew his book had a lot to do with it.

They're fictional characters, she'd screamed at him once. *They're not real.* That was the wrong thing to say to a writer, of course. He'd looked at her strangely and replied, *They're real to me.* She should have realized then there was something seriously wrong with his concept of reality.

Her dad hadn't seen Nina since she'd left and Tara felt guilty because that was at least partly due to her. He'd taken Tara to the movies and to a Manga exhibition in Vancouver, and he made a point of going for a walk on the dike with her and Daisy every day and asking her what she thought and felt about stuff.

Aside from those lucid moments, there were scary times when he seemed to go inside his shell. He often isolated himself when he was near the end of a book, but she'd never seen him quite this bad. Like for instance, today he'd said Nina had called but when Tara had asked what Nina had said, he couldn't remember. Not one word.

Tara could tell he was missing Nina even though he wouldn't admit it. He murmured her name now and then, as if he were having a conversation with her in his head. While he made dinner he played the Norah Jones CD she'd left behind and sang along in his uneven baritone. Sometimes he just stared out at the bay and sighed for no reason at all.

Right now he was pacing the floor, tearing at his hair and muttering something about Luke and Maria. At three o'clock in the morning! Luke was the hero of Reid's spy novels and, as far as Tara knew, he didn't have a love interest. This was an interesting development but it seemed to be making her dad worse, if anything.

Tara had put off calling Nina because she felt so embarrassed about the things she'd said, but she was going to bite the bullet. Tomorrow, first thing. For all she knew, the fate of the free world depended on it. And if that wasn't enough, her dad's happiness depended on it.

NINA WAS WOKEN BY THE PHONE ringing. She fumbled for the receiver beside her bed. "Hello?"

"Nina? It's Tara. I hope I didn't wake you."

"Tara!" Nina glanced at the clock—7:00 a.m. "No, I'm awake." Then she remembered the teenager never usually got up before ten, especially on the weekend. "Is something wrong?"

"I'm worried about Dad," Tara said. "He's acting really strangely." While Nina was digesting this, Tara added, "I…I'm sorry about the way I acted. I should have apologized sooner but…"

"I understand," Nina assured her. "Between Amy, Beebee and I, we monopolized your father's time. It's natural you would feel left out."

"I never did thank you for paying for my Manga course," Tara went on. "Dad told me about that."

"I was happy to do it," Nina said. "Tell me about your father's strange behavior."

"His book was due yesterday and I know for a fact he's not finished because he's been up all night and he's still locked in his office."

"What else?" Nina asked.

"He's always absentminded when he's finishing a book," Tara said. "He gets lost in his story world and doesn't come out even when he's away from the computer. But this time he's the worst he's ever been.

Not eating, not sleeping, muttering to himself, not hearing a word I say."

"I can see why you'd be worried," Nina said. "But what can I do?"

"Could you talk to him?" Tara asked hopefully.

"Oh Tara, I would but the last time I tried, his mind was clearly elsewhere," Nina said. "I don't have as much influence as you think."

"Please try," Tara begged. "He needs you."

Nina suspected that right now Tara needed her more. And that was enough to make her say, "All right."

"Cool!" Tara sounded vastly relieved. "How soon can you get here?"

"I'll be about an hour." Then she thought again. She would be seeing Reid for the first time in nearly three weeks. She needed to wash her hair and iron her blue dress. "Make that an hour and a half."

"Hurry!" Tara urged.

A little over an hour later, Tara met her at the front door, opening it before Nina had a chance to ring the bell. "Finally! Thank you for coming." She stepped back to let Nina inside. "Wow, you look fantastic!"

"Thanks." Nina hesitated, not sure how deep Tara's change of heart went where she was concerned, then decided what the hell and gave her a hug. "It's good to see you."

Tara clung for a moment then drew back, her cheeks pink with embarrassment. "It's nice to see you, too."

She turned on her heel to lead the way to the back of the house. "Dad's in his office."

Nina knocked on Reid's door.

"Go away," he said.

"It's me, Nina."

There was a pause. Then the door was flung open.

Nina had spent considerable effort on her appearance, but one look at Reid's rumpled hair, slept-in clothes and bloodshot eyes and she realized she'd wasted her time. Even if he could focus, his gaze was so inward-looking he wouldn't notice what she was wearing.

"Tara told me she called you," Reid said bluntly. "Come in."

Nina stepped into his office. He shut the door. Suddenly the twelve-by-twelve room seemed too small, too crowded with furniture, computers, bookshelves… and Reid. Now that they were face-to-face, she wanted to blurt out her news about the baby but she forced herself to wait and find out what was bothering him.

"Tara says you're having difficulty finishing your book," Nina said. "Is there any way I can help?"

Reid gestured her to his chair then plunked himself opposite in a spare computer chair. He leaned forward, elbows on knees. "I need to resolve Luke's inner conflict over Maria and still have him be sympathetic to readers."

"Luke and Maria should get married," Nina said promptly. "They obviously love each other."

"That would be too pat," Reid replied. "There needs

to be just the right degree of uncertainty in order to create tension over the outcome of their relationship."

Nina sat back and eyed Reid narrowly. "By 'resolving his conflict' what you really mean is he keeps her on a string while refusing to commit."

Reid winced. "That's a bit harsh. His line of work is too dangerous for him to become emotionally involved. He's like James Bond—he gives so much to his country he has nothing left for a woman. Staying together wouldn't be fair to Maria."

"How noble of him," Nina said. "Tell me, why would she want this self-absorbed egomaniac?"

"They have a special connection," Reid said. "They have passion. They understand each other."

"That's fine then. Don't forget, Maria's a spy, too," Nina said. "She can handle herself with the dangerous stuff."

"Yes, but she's a woman," Reid argued. "She needs to nurture others and to be protected in return."

"Everyone, male and female, needs to be loved," Nina replied. "This Luke is sounding more and more like a sexist son of a—"

"No, no, he's hiding a vulnerable side," Reid said. "You know, tough guy with a soft interior." He hesitated. "The thing is, Luke was in a serious relationship once before. At first that woman was a godsend, a safe haven from the slings and arrows of international espionage."

"And from reviewers?" Nina murmured.

"Pardon?" Reid said.

"Go on," Nina said. "This is getting good."

"Where was I?" he said, frowning. "Oh, yeah. After a while he realized that, although she facilitated his life as a spy, their marriage was empty. But he was bound to her because…well, for a good reason."

Nina sat up straighter. "I've never heard this bit of backstory before."

"It was in the first Luke Mann book," Reid explained. "It was when she left him that he started taking on really dangerous missions."

"I see. But he loves Maria, doesn't he? She's yin to his yang. Pop to his crackle. Why does he want to extricate himself?"

"He doesn't want to but…" Reid's eyebrows came together, a deep furrow forming between them. "She's a wild card. Sometimes she's of invaluable assistance, like when she got him out of the clutches of the General. Other times she demands too much of his attention—"

"Demands?" Nina repeated, fixing him with a look.

"Not demands, per se," Reid struggled to explain. "He's obsessed with her. Because of her, his world is sharper, brighter, more colorful. But he loses perspective. He missed the rendezvous with his contact, for example. His work suffers—"

"Oh, it's his work that's suffering, is it? In my opinion Luke needs to come back from whatever planet he's on and realize it's *love* that matters." Nina couldn't believe her ears. Reid was giving her some half-baked reason why he couldn't love her and pretending he was talking about his character. Fuming, she stood up, ready to walk out. "You want tension? How's this for uncertainty? Will Maria knock some sense into that dough-brain Luke or will she find herself a…a Hungarian prince with a yacht anchored in the Mediterranean?"

"Nina?" Reid stared at her. "Are you feeling all right?"

"Luke needs Maria just as much as she needs him." Nina shook her fist at him from the doorway. "I'll tell you something else, Reid Robertson. I'm having this baby and this time I'm keeping it whether you want it or not."

"Baby?" Reid repeated stupidly.

"That's right," she said. "*Baby.* I'm pregnant. But don't worry. I won't disturb your precious writer's life. I know I can handle this alone. It would have been nice to be partners—"

"Partners?" Reid froze. "That's it!" He spun around to the computer and tapped the mouse to bring the screen to life. "Luke and Maria can be partners, though only in the loosest sense," he muttered to himself as he began typing. "Sometimes they work together, sometimes they're on opposing sides. But always there's the passion. Neither hostile governments nor terrorists can keep them apart for long. I'll make it into a series, the continuing adventures of Luke and Maria."

"You can't focus for one minute, can you?" Nina threw up her hands. "I'm leaving. For the last time, *goodbye,* Reid."

"Wait, Nina!" Reid dragged his gaze away from the monitor. She was walking out the door. But…but this whole idea of Luke and Maria as spy partners was just starting to gel in his brain. Another minute and he'd have it nailed.

The front door slammed.

Good, he was alone at last. With the ending to the book figured out, he could finally finish this puppy and rough out an outline for the next five books in the series.

Her car started. She was backing out of the driveway.

Reid snapped out of his trance. What was he thinking? *Nina was having his baby.* And he was here, *alone.*

He leaped out of his chair and tore down the hall.

Tara jumped out of his way, flattening herself against the wall. "Go Dad!"

Out of the front door, he ran, heart pounding. Down the driveway, onto the road. *"Nina!"* he bellowed.

Her car braked sharply. He ran up to her window.

"Yes?" she said, as cool as anything.

"I get tunnel vision toward the end of a book and I can't think about anything else," he said in a rush. "That's the one drawback about being married to a writer. If you want me, and I desperately hope you do, then you'll have to accept that about me."

"The *one* drawback?" Nina said incredulously.

"Well, there might be more but that's the worst," Reid said. *"Will* you marry me?"

"What was all that stuff about Luke trying to dump Maria?" she said. "You were really talking about us, weren't you?"

"No!" Reid exclaimed. "My characters become like real people to me but I do know the difference between fiction and reality."

"I'm glad to hear it," Nina said dryly. "For Tara's sake, if nothing else. And speaking of Tara, what would she say if she knew you were out here proposing to me?"

"She called you, didn't she?" Reid said. "I told her ages ago I loved you and didn't want to live without you—"

"Did you?" Nina started to soften then frowned. "What about the baby? Babies are noisy and time consuming. Could you handle that on a continuous basis, especially if you're starting a series? Or did you want life to imitate art and for us to be parenting partners without being married? I've got to say I don't like the idea of my child's mom and dad living separately."

"Me, either," Reid said. "I want all my family under one roof. I've been a visiting father before and I never want that again. I'll make time for you and the baby, I promise."

An SUV drove toward them in the other lane and Reid squished up against Nina's car until it went past. He bent down to the window again. "This is not the most romantic setting for a proposal but I'll ask again. Will you marry me?"

"Are you absolutely sure?" Nina asked. "Maybe you need another Carol, someone who's equally lost in her own little world, who won't demand your attention but will let you get on with writing your books. I'd only distract you."

"A little distraction can be a good thing," Reid said. "You've become the inspiration and driving force behind my work. Why do you think I've been so torn while you've been here? Even as I'm longing to take you in my arms, you say something that sparks my imagination and I have to write the idea down. I've done my best work this summer since you've been here."

"Oh, so you just want me for a muse, is that it?" Nina said but at least now there was a smile playing around her lips.

"Enough talking." Reid reached inside the car and turned off the engine. "Will you, or won't you?"

"I will." Nina raised her lips to his and through the open car window he took her mouth in a searingly sweet kiss that was a promise of good things to come.

THE NEXT MORNING, Reid returned to his computer. He'd missed his deadline by one day but it had been worth it. The conclusion to Luke's story was all there in his head. His fingers flew and it wasn't long before he was typing the last few paragraphs.

Mist swirled around the street lamps of the Rue de Bologne. Maria's slim figure was silhouetted by the yellow glow as Luke strode toward her.

"'Ow did it go?" she said in that husky accent that drove him wild.

"The documents are in Beauchamp's hands and the General and his cronies are behind bars," he told her.

"Then it's over." Her voice was soft with regret.

"I'll have another assignment when the elections are held in Chechnya next month." He paused. "Would you care to come along?"

"Chechnya. So cold," she said, making a face. Then with a Gallic shrug she appeared to reconsider. "No doubt my government would send me if I volunteer. We could…" she came closer and ran a finger down his jaw "…cooperate."

Luke felt his blood heat in anticipation. "Until then I know a villa in Tuscany where we could relax and…"

"Luke." She smiled. "You're my kind of man."

Luke linked his arm with hers. He didn't trust her an inch but he would cross the world and fight all comers to be with her. "I have a bottle of cognac in my hotel," he said as they strolled together down the misty Parisian street. "We'll toast the beginning of a beautiful partnership."

The End

Reid saved his file and shut down the computer with a feeling of deepest satisfaction. He rose and stretched, then turned out the light in his office and shut the door behind him. Nina was waiting for him upstairs, asleep in his bed. His thoughts were full of her and the baby. They'd told Tara the night before and she'd immediately got on the phone to Libby, thrilled at the prospect of having another brother or sister.

In the darkened family room, Reid stood before the uncurtained windows and took a moment to drink in the sight of the new moon, a sliver of curving light in the dark sky over the bay. He'd just typed *The End* but really, it was only the beginning.

* * * * *

"OH, NO!"

The reaction slipped out before Emma Valentine could stop it, for there stood the very man she most wanted to avoid seeing again.

He didn't look any happier to see her.

"Well, come on, get on board," he said gruffly. "I won't bite." One eyebrow rose. "Though I might nibble a little," he added, mostly to amuse himself.

But she wasn't paying any attention to what he was saying. She was staring at him, taking in the royal blue uniform he was wearing, with gold braid and glistening badges decorating the sleeves, epaulets and an upright collar. Ribbons and medals covered the breast of the short, fitted jacket. A gold-encrusted sabre hung at his side. And suddenly it was clear to her who this man really was.

She gulped wordlessly. Reaching out, he took her elbow and pulled her aboard. The doors slid closed. And finally she found her tongue.

"You…you're the prince."

He nodded, barely glancing at her. "Yes. Of course."

She raised a hand and covered her mouth for a moment. "I should have known."

"Of course you should have. I don't know why you didn't." He punched the ground-floor button to get the elevator moving again, then turned to look down at her. "A relatively bright five-year-old child would have tumbled to the truth right away."

Her shock faded as her indignation at his tone asserted itself. He might be the prince, but he was still just as annoying as he had been earlier that day.

"A relatively bright five-year-old child without a bump on the head from a badly thrown water polo ball, maybe," she said defensively. She wasn't feeling woozy any longer and she wasn't about to let him bully her, no matter how royal he was. "I was unconscious half the time."

"And just clueless the other half, I guess," he said, looking bemused.

The arrogance of the man was really galling.

"I suppose you think your 'royalness' is so obvious it sort of shimmers around you for all to see?" she challenged. "Or better yet, oozes from your pores like… like sweat on a hot day?"

"Something like that," he acknowledged calmly. "Most people tumble to it pretty quickly. In fact, it's hard to hide even when I want to avoid dealing with it."

"Poor baby," she said, still resenting his manner. "I guess that works better with injured people who are half asleep." Looking at him, she felt a strange emotion she couldn't identify. It was as though she wanted to prove something to him, but she wasn't sure what. "And anyway, you know you did your best to fool me," she added.

His brows knit together as though he really didn't know what she was talking about. "I didn't do a thing."

"You told me your name was Monty."

"It is." He shrugged. "I have a lot of names. Some of them are too rude to be spoken to my face, I'm sure." He glanced at her sideways, his hand on the hilt of his sabre. "Perhaps you're contemplating one of those right now."

You bet I am.

That was what she would like to say. But it suddenly occurred to her that she was supposed to be working for this man. If she wanted to keep the job of corona-tion chef, maybe she'd better keep her opinions to herself. So she clamped her mouth shut, took a deep breath and looked away, trying hard to calm down.

The elevator ground to a halt and the doors slid open laboriously. She moved to step forward, hoping to make her escape, but his hand shot out again and caught her elbow.

"Wait a minute. *You're* a woman," he said, as though that thought had just presented itself to him.

"That's a rare ability for insight you have there, Your Highness," she snapped before she could stop herself. And then she winced. She was going to have to do better than that if she was going to keep this re-lationship on an even keel.

But he was ignoring her dig. Nodding, he stared at her with a speculative gleam in his golden eyes. "I've been looking for a woman, but you'll do."

She blanched, stiffening. "I'll do for what?"

He made a head gesture in a direction she knew was opposite of where she was going and his grip tightened on her elbow.

"Come with me," he said abruptly, making it an order.

She dug in her heels, thinking fast. She didn't much like orders. "Wait! I can't. I have to get to the kitchen."

"Not yet. I need you."

"You what?" Her breathless gasp of surprise was soft, but she knew he'd heard it.

"I need you," he said firmly. "Oh, don't look so shocked. I'm not planning to throw you into the hay and have my way with you. I need you for something a bit more mundane than that."

She felt color rushing into her cheeks and she silently begged it to stop. Here she was, formless and stodgy in her chef's whites. No makeup, no stiletto heels. Hardly the picture of the femmes fatales he was undoubtedly used to. The likelihood that he would have any carnal interest in her was remote at best. To have him think she was hysterically defending her virtue was humiliating.

"Well, what if I don't want to go with you?" she said in hopes of deflecting his attention from her blush.

"Too bad."

"What?"

Amusement sparkled in his eyes. He was certainly enjoying this. And that only made her more determined to resist him.

"I'm the prince, remember? And we're in the castle. My orders take precedence. It's that old pesky divine rights thing."

Her jaw jutted out. Despite her embarrassment, she couldn't let that pass.

"Over my free will? Never!"

Exasperation filled his face.

"Hey, call out the historians. Someone will write a book about you and your courageous principles." His eyes glittered sardonically. "But in the meantime, Emma Valentine, you're coming with me."

SAVE UP TO $30! SIGN UP TODAY!

INSIDE *Romance*

The complete guide to your favorite
Harlequin®, Silhouette® and Love Inspired® books.

✓ Newsletter ABSOLUTELY FREE! No purchase necessary.

✓ Valuable coupons for future purchases of Harlequin,
  Silhouette and Love Inspired books in every issue!

✓ Special excerpts & previews in each issue. Learn about all
  the hottest titles before they arrive in stores.

✓ No hassle—mailed directly to your door!

✓ Comes complete with a handy shopping checklist
  so you won't miss out on any titles.

- -

SIGN ME UP TO RECEIVE INSIDE ROMANCE ABSOLUTELY FREE

(Please print clearly)

Name

Address

| City/Town | State/Province | Zip/Postal Code |

(098 KKM EJL9)

Please mail this form to:
In the U.S.A.: Inside Romance, P.O. Box 9057, Buffalo, NY 14269-9057
In Canada: Inside Romance, P.O. Box 622, Fort Erie, ON L2A 5X3
OR visit http://www.eHarlequin.com/insideromance

IRNBPA06R   ® and ™ are trademarks owned and used by the trademark owner and/or its licensee.

ANGELS OF THE BIG SKY
by Roz Denny Fox

(#1368)

Widow Marlee Stein returns to Montana with her
young daughter, ready to help out with Cloud Chasers,
the flying service owned by her brother. When Marlee
takes over piloting duties, she finds herself in conflict
with a client, ranger Wylie Ames. Too bad Marlee's
attracted to a man she doesn't even want to like!

On sale September 2006!

THE CLOUD CHASERS—
Life is looking up.

Watch for the second story in Roz Denny Fox's two-
book series THE CLOUD CHASERS, available in
December 2006.

*Available wherever books are sold, including most
bookstores, supermarkets, discount stores and drugstores.*

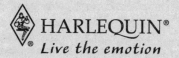

Live the emotion

COMING NEXT MONTH

#1368 ANGELS OF THE BIG SKY • Roz Denny Fox
The Cloud Chasers
Widow Marlee Stein returns to Montana with her young daughter, ready to help
out with Cloud Chasers, the flying service owned by her twin brother, Mick Callen.
Because of Mick's surgery, Marlee takes over piloting duties, including mercy
flights—and immediately finds herself in conflict with one of his clients, ranger
Wylie Ames. Too bad Marlee's so attracted to a man she doesn't even want to *like!*

#1369 MAN FROM MONTANA • Brenda Mott
Single Father
Kara never would've dreamed she'd be a widow so young—or that she could find
room in her heart for anyone besides her husband. And then Derrick moved in across
the street....

#1370 THE RETURN OF DAVID McKAY • Ann Evans
Heart of the Rockies
David McKay thought he'd seen the last of Broken Yoke when he left for
Hollywood—until a pilgrimage into the mountains to scatter his grandfather's
ashes forced him to return and face his first love, Adriana D'Angelo. That's when
he realized the price he'd paid for his ambition. And how much a second chance at
happiness would change his life...

#1371 SMALL-TOWN SECRETS • Margaret Watson
Hometown U.S.A.
It took Gabe Townsend seven years to return to Sturgeon Falls after the fateful car
accident. He would never have come back if he hadn't had to. Because he still loved
Kendall, and she was his best friend's wife.

#1372 MAKE-BELIEVE COWBOY • Terry McLaughlin
Bright Lights, Big Sky
A widow with a kid and a mountain of debt. A good-looking man everyone *thought*
they knew. Meeting for the first time under the wide-open skies of Montana!

#1373 MR. IMPERFECT • Karina Bliss
Going Back
The last will and testament of Kezia's beloved grandmother is the only thing that
could drag bad boy Christian Kelly back to the hometown that had brought him only
misery....